Retribution

Oaken, Volume 2

R.P. Wollbaum

Published by R.P. Wollbaum, 2025.

This is a work of fiction. Similarities to real people, places, or events are entirely coincidental.

RETRIBUTION

First edition. April 5, 2025.

ISBN: 978-1989210222

Written by R.P. Wollbaum.

Retribution

Chapter One

The just under three hour flight from the training base to the palace complex was uneventful. The troopers in the back were quietly talking among them selves. A few were sleeping. Most of the young troopers were from the Capital or neighbouring districts and had never been to the step lands the Clans inhabited. Of the Clans people, few had even seen the Palace complex, let alone been in it.

Sergeant Hassman looked over at Adler. He seemed bored, not like the other officers in front of them who were speculating on what the step and the palace was like.

"Not curious about the palace?" Hassman asked.

"Barracks are barracks," William said. "It's not like we are going to be invited for diner in the palace anytime soon."

Hassman chuckled.

"Not been in the complex itself," Hassman said. "Was barracked in the town just down the road for three months. Not going to be like anything you are used to though sir. No clubs, fancy restaurants or shops. There are a couple of bars and decent restaurants. Nothing to write home about."

"OK by me," William said. "I've never been a party animal. Probably be busy for a while getting things sorted out anyway."

"You guys will be alright," Hassman said. "You are all just out of training and used to all the chicken shit. Might be a little more of it, being the palace and all. But not much."

"One thing for sure sir. You do not ever, want to be on the Senior Sergeants shit list sir. Her bite is for sure harder than her bark sir. Plus, she and the royal family are tight sir."

"Oh," William said. "She's one of those then. Probably never seen a day in the field."

"No sir, the exact opposite," Hassman said. "Not only was she one of the One Hundred. She was one of the Ten sir. She has definitely been there and done that sir."

"She can't be all that great," William said. "She's still just a sergeant. All the other One Hundred and especially the Ten, are all high ranking flag officers."

William cut off any further conversation, by tilting his seat back and closing his eyes.

God damn rookie officers, Hassman thought. *This kid is in for a world of hurt.*

A series of thumps was heard and the engines changed pitch, signalling it was about to land. Adler was the first one up and grabbing his duffle from the overhead bin, Hassman right behind him. Both of them were standing in front of the rear hatch, before it started to open and were the first ones off the transport.

"Form the troops Sergeant," Adler said.

He walked one hundred yards from the rear of the transport, dropped his duffle on the ground and assumed the parade rest position, both his arms clenched in the small of his back. He was facing the fence bordering the landing strip looking at the open prairie beyond.

Hassman was yelling at the troopers to form up. The sound of feet hitting the concrete was heard. More yelling from Hassman and other voices. Then, each platoon began counting off. Reports made to Hassman, the sound of feet marching toward William ending with a foot stomp.

William pivoted around and came to attention as the Sergeant made his hand salute and returned it just as smartly as it was given.

"Compnay all present and accounted for, Sar!" Hassman said.

"Very well Sergeant," William said. "Have the troopers at ease Sergeant."

"Sar!" Hassman said. Spun around and marched back to the line of troopers and put them at ease.

While he was doing that, William was looking around for who he should report to. Ground crew and the transport crew were scampering around the transport doing whatever they did. The Queen and her entourage were gathered around some vehicles. She was giving instructions to an officer with aide de camp markings on his uniform. The man came to attention, saluted and bowed. The Queen slapped him gently on the shoulder and flicked her wrist in the direction of the lined up troopers. Some comments were made followed by a lot of laughter. As the officer marched toward them, he briefly put his right hand behind his back, which caused the queen and her group to laugh even more.

As he marched toward them, he was joined by a tall woman. Coming nearer, William saw the man was a captain, the woman, a Senior Sergeant. Once they reached five yards from him, William called his company to attention and saluted. The captain returned his salute.

"Sir!" William barked. "Company H, all present and accounted for sir!"

"Company H? I don't have no damned company H in my god damned battalion!" The Senior Sergeant belted out.

She marched right up to William, her nose almost touching his.

"Who the hell told you, you were company H *Leftenant?* Never mind, I don't want to know! Captain, clue this clueless fuck in!"

"Sorry ma-am," William blurted out.

The Senior Sergeant was just walking forward when he had said that. She spun around and was once again nose to nose with him.

"Do I look like a god damned officer *Lefteant?* Where the hell were you when they were passing out brains?"

She moved around the still at attention William headed for the company.

"That better not be a smirk on your face Hassman!" She yelled.

"No Senior Sergeant!" Hassman said. "Was a fly on my nose Senior Sergeant!"

"At ease Lieutenant," the Captain said. "At the moment, there are only three companies in the battalion. So you are company C, not H as would be normal for a new company. Once the Senior Sergeant has finished her inspection, those Master Corporals over there will show your people their barracks and I will show your officers to theirs. Good?"

"Yes sir," William said.

The Captain smiled and pointed behind William.

"Making her mark already," he said.

William turned around. Two lieutenants and five troopers were doing pushups.

The Senior Sergeant waited until the pushups were done and the offenders back in line. Then she jerked her head at Hassman and the both of them walked toward the Captain and William.

"Not bad for bunch of green as grass rookies Cap," she said. "Keep an eye on those two Louies. Early days yet, but they could be problems. Got my eye on you too *Leftenant.* Mommy will not be pleased if you fuck it up."

She pointed her left hand at the gathering of master corporals, raised her right hand above her head, made a fist and dropped the arm to her side. The master corporals jogged over to the lined up troopers and began to issue orders.

"I'll leave you at it Cap," she said. "Come on Hassman, I'll buy the first round."

"Somebody told she me she is a real softy at heart," the Captain said. "Haven't seen it myself, but that's the rumour anyway. Ok, let's grab your guys. They will all bunk in together for now. You will be sharing my officers barracks for now. Things will probably change soon."

Margarete walked toward where her horse was waiting. Her Brother-in-Law Al, was mounted on his, holding the reins to her horse. He was wearing his full uniform today, as was Margarete and the ever present, when she or Demetri were about, ten man guard squad.

She waved her hand at her forehead as a return salute, mounted, then hugged Al.

"I take it they are not back in yet then?" She said.

Al shrugged his shoulders.

"You know what it's like out in the bush," Al said. "Probably lost track of the day. If they're not back by lunch tomorrow, I'll send somebody to get them."

As they came nearer to the Palace complex, Margarete sighed as she saw the number of uniformed and un-uniformed people ranged in front of the administration building.

"Better you than me," Al said. "I did it for you this last week. What a pain. I see Janet clued poor Will into reality."

"He has to do it on his own Al," Margarete said. "Just like we did."

Both of them dismounted and handed the reins to their horses to waiting groomsmen, also in full uniform.

Margarete returned the saluted of the uniformed people and held her right hand up as the clamouring began.

"I have just spent the last four hours cooped up in that transport," she said. "I had a week of boring BS I had to put up with before that. I am hungry, thirsty, tired and cranky. If you feel what you have to say is of utmost importance. That the world will come to an end if you don't report it. Make your day. If I think otherwise, I will have one of my guards arrest you, at a minimum. No? Good. Tomorrow morning then. Come General, we have important business to attend to."

Margarete and Al marched into the Building and right through to the attached residence portion of it. They were undoing tunic buttons, loosing ties and opening shirt collars as they walked.

A waiting servant took her tunic and cap from her as Margarete took them off, another the same for Al. Another was waiting with a large pitcher at the dining table and quickly filled the mugs waiting there as the two officers sat down.

"Thanks Mildred," Margarete said. "Just leave the pitcher. We are not cripples."

"Welcome home Majesty," Mildred said. "Lunch will arrive shortly ma-am. His Royal Highness, Her Royal Highness and the Duchess, have not arrived yet ma-am."

Margarete nodded her head.

"Will the Prince be joining for lunch ma-am?" Mildred asked.

"No Mildred," Margarete said. "Janet just finished chewing his ass off. He'll be with his troops now. Not us.

"Please have someone ask Alex and Janet to join us at their convenience Mildred?"

"As you wish Majesty. By your leave ma-am," Mildred did a fast curtsy and hurried off.

The words were barely out of her mouth, when Janet walked into the room. She had already removed her tunic, tie and cap. The end of the tie could be seen poking out of a tunic pocket. She tossed her beret on the table, draped the tunic over the chair back, sat down and poured herself a helping from the pitcher.

The three of them lifted the goblets.

"Absent comrades," they all said and took the first mouthful.

"How'd it go Mags?" Janet asked.

"Not bad I guess, You know me," Margarete said. "I don't need nor require all the BS, but..."

"Ya, appearances have to be kept Mags." Janet said. "I dunno about you, but if my old man ain't back here by noon tomorrow, I'm gonna kill him."

"Already on in Jan," Margarete said. "Al, being Al, probably likes it when Grets is not around."

"Oh," Al said. "I'm just as pissed as you are. I just hide it better."

The three of them chuckled just as Alex walked in. He was dressed in a work uniform, only his generals insignia and his eagle on it.

"Hey Mags," Alex said. "Welcome back. I sent a scout air transport out to tell your wayward spouses to get the hell back here."

He poured himself a mug, raised it, gave the salutation and drained it.

Mildred, with another servant arrived. Both had two larger pitchers in hand. These were plunked down on the table and they both hurried back to the kitchen.

"Alex, I gave Steve the new company," Margarete said. "He's wasted being my aide. I want him promoted to Major. We'll be rounding up the numbers in the battalion soon, so it is warranted. Make Will a brevet First Lieutenant. His instructor commander said he should have been first in class. Keep an eye on him though. No special favours."

"Ya," Alex said. "I heard Janet clued him in already."

"Just doing my job Alex," Janet said. "Keep them on their toes. Still pretty wild out there on the steps."

The four old friends had lunch and reminisced on past days. They were just starting to get a glow on. They heard a commotion at the door to the housing apartments and a Master Corporal in a wrinkled uniform barged in, came to attention and rammed his right foot into the floor.

"Report Master Corporal," Alex ordered.

"Ma-am. They are not there ma-am. It looks like an ambush ma-am. Blaster marks on the ground ma-am. Blood stains as well ma-am. Looks like a big fight ma-am!"

Margarete dumped her chair on its back on the floor in her rush. She was running for the door, Janet on her heels, both women without tunics on.

"Get me there now!" Margarete yelled over her shoulder. The Master Corporal chased after them.

Alex and Al were chasing after them, arriving just as the scout transport took off at a high rate of speed.

"Her Majesty needs her guards! Now!" He yelled. "Get me a damned air car! Move it move it!"

An air transport arrived, the ten supposedly honour guard troopers pilled in. All of them had swords across backs, bows in hand and a quiver full of arrows on a hip. The hatch had not even closed and the transport was pealing away, accelerating to full speed.

Two more arrived. All with ten troopers in each, fully armed and in combat uniforms. Alex and Al piled into one. They too were speeding off. Unordered, troopers were sprinting to barracks and reappearing shortly after armed to the teeth.

"Fuck!" Steve said, seeing the organized confusion happening all over camp. "Get your troops armed and ready to fight Adler. Now!"

Will took a look around at what was going on all through the complex. To his credit, he didn't ask any questions. He grabbed his sword and was draping it across his back as he ran to the C company barracks.

The sergeants, had also seen what was going on and saw him running toward them.

"Stand To! Stand To!" All of the sergeants were yelling as they ran into their platoon barracks.

The veterans that had been placed in the platoons were already arranging the new troopers. The veterans were in the line, some with no shirts on, all with swords across their backs. The rookies still had their full uniforms on. Buttons were being buttoned up, all had swords either across backs already or just being placed there.

The new lieutenants arrived the same way.

"Half of your fire teams, return to barracks and get into combat uniform!" Will ordered. "When they get back, the others do the same! Move it move it!"

The Captain trotted up, properly kitted out.

"Get kitted up Alder, I'll take over here," Steve said.

Hassman marched over and raised his eyebrows. Steve shrugged his shoulders. Both were veterans. Both knew the army and its ways.

After a half hour cramped ride with six people in an air car designed for four, the vehicle came to a fast stop. The wheels barely touching the ground and Margarete was out of it and scanning the area. The four troopers formed a small perimeter, weapons drawn. The guard transport was there seconds later, the guard troop adding to the perimeter, two of them shadowing Margarete, one with an arrow knocked on his bow, the other his sword drawn.

As the next two transports landed and troopers poured out, Margarete and Janet were walking a circle in opposite directions around the camp site. Keeping as much of the scene undisturbed as possible.

The camp was totally destroyed. Tents in shreds, equipment strewn around. Evidence of blasters were everywhere. On the ground, burn marks on tents and equipment. Some were large and deep. Dried blood stains were all over the ground. Many large. The ground was torn up by horse and boots, many boots.

"Space transport landed over here!" A trooper further out yelled. "Hoof prints leading into it!"

Now Margarete and Janet started moving inward toward where the ruined camp was. Both were veterans of many fights. Both knew what they were looking at.

Receiving reports, Alex walked up to them.

"What have we got Alex," Margarete asked quietly.

"Looks like a combat insertion ma-am," Alex said. "Hoof prints leading to and from the transports mam. Drag marks, lots of them, leading to the transports. All them with blood trails ma-am, they didn't get away unscathed ma-am. They made them pay for it ma-am."

"Right," Margarete said. "This happened a couple of days ago. Leave a platoon here and see what they can see near by. Have the troops stand down back at base. Tell them it was just a training drill or whatever. Everyone that was here, everyone, camps out here, understand. Nobody, on pain of death says anything about what they saw here. Understood? Have my flag officers waiting for me when I return to base. Carry on. Janet, with me."

Margaret turned to one of her now ten guards.

"Two of you with us," she ordered. "The other eight stay here. Once we are on base, get their full combat kit and return. Rations etc for a week. Nobody says anything, got it? Just a training mission, clear?"

"Ma-am" both guards said.

Janet jumped behind the pilots position in the scout vehicle, Margarete the passengers seat, the two guards piled in the back and they were off.

Both of them marched into the filled to capacity board room, Margrete sat at the head of the large board table, Janet standing at ease behind her chair.

"Some time, it looks like a couple of days ago, His Royal Highness and party were attacked. It was a combat insertion by a space transport. It looks like it was a hard fought battle. I want all, no matter how small, ship landings anywhere on Oaken analyzed. Pinpoint the one that landed at His Royal Highness's location and back track it to where it came from.

"Have the Queens Guard mobilized. Full combat kit and loads. Plan on at least a week in the field, two days from now! That new company needs horses and they need them now! Full battalion combat training mission is all they need to know.

"Nobody, especially the civilian officials, out side of this room is to know what was just said here! We will handle this our selves! I am pissed people! Very pissed! Dismissed!"

The room emptied. Margarete walked to the door shut it and bolted it. Both women hugged each other and let the tears flow.

Chapter Two

Walker was slowly loosing the battle to stay awake. They had been on the road for almost four hours now. The only thing keeping him awake was the rough road they were traveling on. If calling two ruts in the ground made from farm tractors a road.

He was a captain in the Airial Army and a member of a combat battalion. Two weeks ago, he had been on standby after training for a month on some secret combat insertion mission. He had been abruptly told he had been replaced. His Major had thought Walker had done something wrong to deserve being replaced and given Walker every dirty job he could find ever since. This was one of them.

Some farmers had reported witnessing a bright light and loud noises coming from one of their fields the night before and Walker had been dispatched to check it out. The farmers had most likely been drunk out of their minds and saw a comet or something. Hardly something that even needed an officer to attend to, let alone a captain. So here he and three troopers were, bouncing around in an uncomfortable small scout vehicle.

They followed the little trail past the trees bordering the field and the driver jammed on the brakes.

"What the fu..." Walker started to say as he looked out the wind screen.

There was an armed space craft parked in the middle of the field. Arial markings on the fuselage. They pulled to with in two meters of the space craft and stopped. Everyone got out of the vehicle and began looking around. The rear hatch was open on the craft and it looked abandoned.

Walker went inside. Blood stains, many and large blood stains, were on the floor of the cargo bay. Other than that, the craft was empty. Walking back out, Walker parted the beaten down crops and saw hoof prints. He followed them with his eyes to the tree line where they were leading and he yelled.

"Back to the truck! Back to the truck!"

Walker began to run to the truck, his men, confused, looked on as he dove inside and came out with a long blaster. Then the thrumming of the air could be heard and men were screaming as arrows hit them. Not just one, but multiple arrows sprouting from each mans back.

Walker didn't need to see what had happened, or what was about to happen now. But he looked anyway. Two horsemen, a large man and tall woman were at the gallop headed toward he and his men, swords up raised. As he watched, the swords came down and killed his men, Walker felt the arrow that hit his right calf, followed by the one in his right bicep, causing him to fall to the ground and loose the blaster as his hand went numb. He was frantically trying to shift the blaster to his other hand and rise enough to get a shot off when feet hit the ground and a sword was at his throat.

"Hey Walker," a rough male voice said. "Long time no see."

Walker looked up and saw the tall broad man towering above him and knew he was doomed.

Another pair of boots arrived to his left, one kicked the blaster out of his reach then moved to the vehicle coming back a short time later. The first aide kit from the vehicle landed on the ground beside him and a females hands opened it.

"This is definitely going to hurt you more than me Walker," the woman said. "If we wanted you dead Walker, you would be, you know that. Now be a good boy and let me do my job. Take that damn sword off his neck Bubba."

The sword came off his neck as the man chucked. Then Walker gasped as the arrow in his leg was broken off just below the fletchings. The woman cut his trousers leg open and pulled the arrow out by grasping just below the arrow head and pulling the shaft out. She quickly spayed some medical spray on the wound, padded it with a bandage and quickly wrapped it. She did the same with his arm.

"Good boy Walker," she said. "Now, you wait until we get in the bush, then you report in eh? Tell your bosses. The Eagles are pissed and we are coming Walker. We are coming and it's not going to be pleasant Walker. See ya when I see ya kid."

She mounted her horse after helping him stand, and trotted to the tree line. Following her with his eyes, Walker saw the big man known as Bubba beside two more riders and eight more horses. Both riders had rain slickers with the hoods up so he could not see the faces. Three of the unsaddled horses had blaster burns on sides, bare skin showing. Both Bubba and the woman who had treated his wound also had them.

Then they disappeared into the trees.

"It was a scout troop sir," Walker said from his hospital bed the next day. "Their scouts work in troops of four sir. There will most likely be others around sir. We won't see them unless they want to be seen sir. The ones that attacked me sir? The two I saw I knew. Both of them highly experienced veterans sir. The woman is a flag officer sir.

"And sir, they told me to say this. 'The Eagles are pissed and we are coming.' That's all I know sir."

"No reason given?" His colonel asked.

"No sir," Walker said.

"Shit," the colonel said.

"Colonel, I have served along side these people sir," Walker said. "They just don't go around starting wars for no reason sir. And sir, if they come, there is little we can do to stop them."

"What have you got for me Colonel," Margarete asked.

Once again the board room was filled. Everyone in full uniform but her, Janet, Alex and Al, who were in combat uniform.

"The transport came from Arial ma-am," the colonel said. "Like you presumed, two days before you discovered it ma-am. An hour after it landed, it took off again and headed to our cache location here ma-am. Two hours after that it left orbit headed toward Arial ma-am."

"Right," Margarete said. "Generals, full call up if you please Bears, Eagles, full support. Arrange transport for two full battalions. Tell Oaken it's just a training exercise. That's all they need to know. Place the reserve troops on standby.

"Have the Queens Own ready to deploy once I arrive, no later than tomorrow morning. Dismissed."

"Janet, our horses by first light."

"What's going on luv?" The colonels wife asked.

Her husband was throwing his full uniform off and donning his combat uniform. He grabbed his always ready field pack, threw his sword across one shoulder and gave her a kiss and hug.

"Full call up," he said. "Big training mission. Space transport the whole bit. Reserve is on standby."

His wife saw the determined look on his face and the way he was acting. She was an Eagle Major in the reserves. *This is not a training mission,* she thought and as her husband left the house, she too was flinging off clothing and dawning combat dress.

William was at his position to the right of the lead troop of Company C. They were the first troop in the battalion column. The scouts had left an hour before daybreak, the rest of the company, just as the horizon was beginning to brighten. It was the second trot interval. After half an hour, they would dismount and walk for ten minutes. He would take off his tunic then. Now he, and the other troopers, were riding with all but the bottom two buttons undone. It was getting warm now.

The colonel had arrived just after dark with all the other battalion flag officers and his and their staffs. It was a full battalion call up. Well, half a battalion anyway, they were a battalion in name only at this point.

William heard a thundering of hooves coming from his right and looked over. Twenty five troopers were coming at the canter, three split off, headed for the main column as they came near. One had a furled and encased standard with him.

"Your fucking flankers are sleeping *leftenant!*" Janet yelled, as the now twenty riders cantered by them. "And you is now all dead, dead, dead!"

She and the woman riding beside her laughed, then spurred to a gallop, changing horses on the fly. That's when every one saw they were riding bare back and who the riders were.

"Get a move on *Leftenant!*" the Queen yelled over her shoulder. "If my goddamn lunch isn't waiting for me ten minutes after I stop, the Senior Sergeant is going to kick your ass so hard you won't sit down for a month."

William gave the order to gallop and they were soon chasing the Queen and her party.

"Send a rider out to both flanks," William ordered Hassman. "And tell that god damned right flank they just embarrassed us!" He rammed his fist into his pommel and cursed under his breath.

No matter how hard they tried, they could not get closer than a hundred yards from the Queen's party. He slowed down, they slowed down, he sped up, they sped up,

"No sense sir," Hassman said. "If she wanted us closer, we would be sir."

The Queen and her people were just dismounting, when Williams troop arrived at noon. Without dismounting, William ordered a permitter to be set up. Then watched as his troop, then the rest of the company came into camp, dismounted and while half looked after horses, the other half began lunch preparations.

Only after seeing everyone settled in and receiving reports from the other Lieutenants, did William dismount. He handed the reins of his horse to a trooper and marched over to the now Major.

He came to attention and saluted.

"All present and accounted for sir!" William said after the Major returned his salute. "A perimeter guard has been established sir!"

"Very well Lieutenant," Steve said. "And Lieutenant, we don't salute in the field."

"Sorry sir!" William said. "With the Majors permission. I have a duty to perform sir!"

"Carry on," Steve said.

William stomped his right foot into the ground, spun around and marched to his platoon.

"Sergeant, a moment of your time?" William said and he walked a couple of meters away.

Nobody could hear what was being said, but they way the sergeant was standing suggested the Lieutenant was not happy about something. The Sergeant stomped his right foot into the ground pivoted and headed back to the resting platoon.

"Right flankers, front and centre!" Hassman yelled out.

The two troopers rushed up, came to attention and saluted.

"You fucking idiots! We do not salute in the field idiots!" Hassman yelled. Both troopers quickly dropped their arms.

"Were you two idiots sleeping out there!" He yelled, he was nose to nose with first one then the other. "How could you miss twenty three troopers and sixty some horses at the gallop idiots? For fucks sake! The Queen and the Senior Sergeant for fuck sake! You have killed us all idiots! The lieutenant is embarrassed and pissed off! Me, I am just pissed off! Drop and give me twenty! Now dumb asses!"

Hassman felt more than saw William come beside him as the two troopers finished their push ups and came to attention.

"Have the platoon form up if you please sergeant," William said in a normal voice. He waited until they were lined up in their sections and fireteams and began to walk up and down the line. Talking loud enough so all could hear, no matter which end of the line they were on.

"We are the point platoon," he began. "Our job is to spot the enemy before they spot us, give warning to the main column and hold the enemy as long as we can until help arrives.

"Your jobs as lead and flank scouts are to secure our front and sides. To spot the enemy before they spot you and report back to us. That is why there are two of you. One rides back, the other goes to ground and watches. Or dies.

"It will not be just you that dies on scout. This whole platoon and company will die. Maybe the whole battalion. Yes, this is a training mission. We train so that when it is for real, we already know what to do.

"Carry on sergeant."

William turned away and walked to where his horses were and began looking them over.

"Sergeant Hassman?" It was a trooper from the Queens guard. "The Senior Sergeant requests a word Sergeant."

Hassman nodded his head, gave a dirty look to the two flankers and headed over to where the Queens group were. Janet came nose to nose with him, she was smiling though. Both of them were at ridged attention, Hassman with his eyes above Janets head.

"They weren't sleeping Hassman," Janet said. "They just saw who we were and that we were no threat. Still.. Good suggestion you gave the rookie Hassman."

"Not me Janet," Hassman said. "He chewed my ass out good he did."

"That little chat his idea or yours Hassman?" Margarete said from her position squatted on the ground, her back to him.

"That was all him General," Hassman said. "Got a good head on him ma-am. Make a good officer one day ma-am."

"If he lives Bob, if he lives," Margarete said. "Always the brightest and the best eh? OK, you can head back now Bob."

All the while, Janet had been making like she was chewing him out. Now she stopped and took two steps back. Hassman rammed his right foot into the ground, spun around and angrily marched back to the lounging troopers. Seeing how he was, they all formed up and came to attention.

"You fucking Idiots!" He yelled. "I just got my ass chewed out by the Senior Sergeant because of you idiots! Drop and Give me twenty! All of you idiots! Now!"

They could hear a lot of laughter coming from the Queens group as they did the pushups.

"Do you hear them!" Hassman yelled. "They are laughing at me idiots! I am going to hop over to those trees there and slit my throat I am so embarrassed!"

They finished doing their pushups, came to attention, only to see the sergeant walking toward the trees. The Lieutenant rushed up to the sergeant and put his hand on his shoulder and spoke to him. The sergeant nodded his head then returned walking to the trees his head hanging down.

"Dismissed," William said as he came up to the troop.

He continued walking until he was at the perimeter of the Queens group. He addressed the guard stationed there.

"If you could ask the Señor Sergeant for a moment of her time trooper?" He asked.

Seconds later, Janet was standing at attention in front of him and slamming her right foot into the ground.

"It was not the sergeants fault Senior Sergeant," he began. "I had not informed my troopers of the importance of their duties Senior Sergeant. The fault is all mine Senior Sergeant. Sergeant Hassman is a good Sergeant, Senior Sergeant. He does not deserve to be ridiculed for this Senior Sergeant."

"Oh, we weren't laughing at him son," Margarete said, still sitting on the ground her back toward him. "We were laughing at you dumb ass rookies and he knows it. Get your people with the program son. Today, we go easy on you. Tomorrow? Not so much."

"Back to your gang sonny," Janet said. "Before mommy has to come over and yank your ear."

William was fuming as he walked back to his platoon, but didn't let them see it. It didn't help that all the Queens group were laughing as he walked back.

"Scouts out," he said. "Keep your eyes open."

The scouts jumped on horses and galloped to the front and sides. The rest began to gather themselves up and head to the horses. A trooper brought William his, another the sergeants. Everyone was mounted and waiting when the Queens group mounted and took off, the lead platoon on their heels, the rest of the company and battalion right after them.

The lead scouts had the Queens fire going when they arrived just as the sun was going down. Men were quickly looking after horses and setting up the camp for the night. William made his report to the major, then moved to his horses and began to groom and inspect them.

Only then, did he move to where his tent was set up. Hassman came rushing up and made to come to attention. William waved a hand at him.

"We are in the field Sergeant," he said. "I know who you are, you know who I am, no need for all the foot stomping BS.

"I will also be joining the platoon at meals times Hassman. Easier all around eh?"

William grabbed his eating gear and headed to where the platoon was sitting around the camp fire. He told them to stay put as he came up and spooned a plateful of goo into his tin plate, tasted it, made a grimace, looked around and found a spot to plunk down on.

"Fucking Army and their fucking field rations," he said before shoving another mouth full in. "Wonder if the yahoos who came up with this shit ever eat it."

Some of the troopers chuckled and Hassman, with a coffee pot to hand made a gesture. William held his cup out and it was filled. Hassman sat beside him after retiring the pot to the fire.

"Right," William said after he saw everyone had finished eating. "I have apologized to the Senior Sergeant for our behaviour today and expressed my displeasure of her and her bunch laughing at our Sergeant. It was not his fault. It was mine. I did not properly instruct my troopers properly as to the importance of their task. She informed me in no uncertain terms that they were not laughing at Sergeant Hassman. They were laughing at our dumb asses."

William looked into the fire for a second.

"One nice thing about being the point platoon," William continued. "We don't have to post perimeter guards. Tonight. Tomorrow we do.

"The Senior Sergeant informed me they would go easy on us today. Tomorrow?

"All of us are Eagles. We know what happens to rookies. Tomorrow, we are going to be in for a world of hurt. Be ready."

"One more thing," Hassman said. "The Senior Sergeant and the Queen? They are veterans of the Ten. The Queens guards are all very experienced veterans that have been there and done that, more than once. I should know, I was with some of them when it happened. They won't kill or injure you. Too badly anyway. But they are going to do their very best to beat the crap out of us tomorrow.

"Your Lieutenant? He should have been number one in all of his classes, basic, advanced and officer training. He kept fucking up his exams. On purpose. He ain't told me why. All of you. You were all at the top of your classes all the way through. That is why you are members of the Queens Guard. You are the best. You, we, are being groomed for when the battalion is fully formed. You will be the sergeants and corporals soon. If, you don't fuck this mission up....and don't get yourselves killed before.

"We are not a show and parade battalion. We are a combat battalion. We will be sent on the hardest and worse missions because of who we are. Remember that tomorrow, you are the fucking best! You are Fucking One Platoon, Company C! The best fucking scout platoon in this god damned army!"

The platoon erupted in a great roar, yelling for all they were worth.

"Our work here is done sir," Hassman said to William, he nodded and they both went to their tents, the troopers yells in their ears.

"Me thinks tomorrow we will have our work cut out for us sister," Janet said to Margarete as the rookie camp erupted into a great yell. "That kid of yours and Hassman has them all ramped up."

"They better be Janet," Margarete said. "Or soon, very soon, many of them and our other brothers and sisters are going to die."

Chapter Three

The Queens group was gone before the first platoon woke up. They had just quietly disappeared in the night. All of them knew what that meant. They would be ambushed at some point, from some direction, today.

Nothing happened until an hour after the lunch break. It was a very warm day, almost hot. It was easy for a trooper to doze off in the heat and the rhythm of the horse walking. One of the front scouts came galloping to the formation.

William gave the order to halt.

"Ambush about two klicks up LT," the scout said. "I have the area mapped out sir. Harry is keeping an eye on them."

"Right," William said. "Sergeant, riders to both flanks. Might be they will try a fast one on us. Then the riders rejoin us."

William dismounted and pointed at the ground.

"Draw it out for me trooper," he said.

The scout dismounted, withdrew his knife from its scabbard and began sketching out the ambush on the ground. Hassman, finished dispatching the rider, came to the ground and squatted down beside them.

After the trooper was finished his sketch, both men studied it for a moment.

"I think we should do this...." William said. "Sergeant?"

"Ya, should work," Hassman said. "May I suggest sir....Just in case?"

"Sounds good Sarge," William said. "Pick two riders to head back to the main column. Tell them to split apart. Just in case. But not until after we leave eh?"

Margarete and her guards were deployed in an L shaped ambush, just on the other side of a dry creek bed the coming platoon would have to cross. They had left a plain enough trail for them to follow.

The platoon was a little late in arriving, only to be expected of rookies. But soon the ambushers could feel the vibration from the approaching horses hooves on the ground. They gathered weapons and made ready to spring the trap. Rising to a half crouch, they saw and heard the unexpected. Only five riders were coming and they came to a gallop lances pointing straight ahead and level with horses heads and they yelled!

Arrows began hitting the ground around many of the ambushers, another four horses were coming from their rear, lances also levelled. Now the ambushers let loose their own stream of arrows pulled swords from where they had been placed on the ground and rose to meet the attackers.

Now the ground was truly shaking as the rest of C company came on in line, lances out at the gallop.

"You is all dead, dead dead!" William yelled over all the noise.

The twenty looked around and saw they were totally encircled by all of C company.

"Well shit!" Janet said. She picked up a rock and flung it into some surrounding bushes hard.

"Hey! What the fuck!" A trooper, bow in hand stood from behind the bush Janet had thrown the rock at.

"Just gets fucking better and better!" Janet said, thrusting her sword back in to her scabbard across her back. "And by fucking rookies!"

"Who are we!" William yelled out. He yelled it again punching his lance in the air.

"First scout troop!" Most of his troopers yelled back.

"I can't fucking hear you!" William yelled back.

Now his troopers bellowed it out at the top of their lungs.

"And don't you old timers forget it! " William said. "Where's my fucking coffee?"

"Guess they showed us eh?" Margarete said. "Ok, have everyone stand down. Enough fun for the day. Camp is just up there. Tell first platoon to join us eh?"

The ground was vibrating, the air thundering, as the rest of the battalion came near. The ambushers walked toward where the camp for the night was to be.

"Flag officers to me at their convenience if you please," she said.

Janet was pouring herself and Margarete a coffee when the battalion colonel and majors arrived. She heard their reports and then had them stay standing as Williams platoon arrived. They spread out in a line and came to attention. William moved three paces in front of them, came to attention and rammed his right foot into the ground.

"First Scout Platoon, Company C all present and accounted for General!" He yelled out.

"Have your people at ease Lieutenant," Margarete said.

William gave the order and twenty boots went to shoulder width apart, twenty arms placed behind backs.

"You did well today, First Platoon," Margarete said loud enough so everyone at their small camp could hear. "You spotted the ambush, made a plan, warned the rest of the battalion and advanced to contact. Exactly as it should be done. As you said, the ambushers would all be dead. But so would many of you.

"That is your jobs as scouts. See, not be seen, report and hold the enemy in place. It was done and done well. My people and I are far from being new at this. Again, well done Lieutenant Adler. Well done."

She turned to the officers standing behind her.

"This is what we expect of all of you," she said. "If these rookies can do this, your veterans should be better. They are going to have to be and soon. Or many of you and them are going to die. Everybody but First Scout Platoon dismissed."

"We lost," Margarete said. "We cook. Take a load off."

Soon the old timers were sitting beside the rookies and the stories began. Soon the little camp was buzzing with laughter and talking. Except for Margarete and Janet. They stayed to themselves. They were talking and chuckling, but with many pauses and looks into the distance.

"Where the fuck are we going?" William heard one of his troopers say as they trotted along a barley discernible trail.

"Well," William said. "If rookies needed to know what the fuck they were doing and where they were going, I am sure the Senior Sergeant would let the Sergeant know, who would let me know. As it is..."

"Ya shut up and carry on," the same trooper said. "Same shit, different place."

A lot of the troopers started to laugh, then some one started a racy song and soon every one, male and female had joined in.

Margarete and her guards were now traveling behind them and heard First Platoon break into song and the song they were singing.

"Didn't take him long," Janet said. "Just like his dad."

"Ya," Margarete said. "But if anything, more intense than his dad."

Then she joined in on the song. Soon the whole battalion was singing it.

After that evening meal, William called the next days scouts to him and Hassman.

"I think we are headed to this location," he had the map spread out on the ground in front of him. "We are here. It's a cache location. We will most likely resupply there, stay a couple of days then head back home. If the Queen and her gang are still with us in the morning, take off and head for the cache. Scope it out, then one of you come back here. Good?"

"Who told you about the cache?" Hassman asked. "Your not from around here."

William shrugged his shoulders.

"Must have been something in one of my text books," he said.

As William had predicted, one of his forward scouts came galloping back from the cachet site an hour before lunch.

"Sir, it's right where you said it would be'" the scout said. "And LT? It looks like someone broke into it. There's stuff scattered all around and looks like some stuff was burned as well."

William pulled his note book out from his shirt, hurriedly wrote on a page, pulled the page from it and handed it to the trooper riding beside him.

"Give this to Her Majesty," he said. "Then chase after us.

"First Platoon! Advance to contact!"

He spurred his horse to a gallop followed by the rest of the platoon.

By the time Margarete and her guards arrived, the perimeter was set up and William and Hassman were surveying the area around the entrance to the Cache.

"Cache has been broken into and looted ma-am," William reported to Margarete. "Looks like a bunch of stuff was burned ma-am. Mostly cloth it looks like. Landing craft of some sort landed just beyond ma-am. Looks like around twenty horses entered it."

"Thank you Lieutenant, carry on," Margarete said. "Have some body inventory the cache," she told the nearest guard. "When the rest of the battalion shows up, have someone get the head herdsman to check the nearest herd for missing horses.

"Major Steve, deploy your people into expanding search circles for a couple of kilometres and see what they can find."

With Janet and ten of her guards around her, Margarete made her way to the landing site and looked around. She noted a number of drag marks in the dirt heading off into the distance and told a guard to check it out. He had not gone far when a rider came at a gallop from that direction.

"Burned bodies ma-am," he reported. "Looks to be twenty, thirty of them."

"Thank you corporal,: Margarete said. "Make your report to the Colonel and have him report to me please."

"All right Colonel," Margarete said later. "The evidence is this. An attack from Arial was conducted on His Majesty and his party. Right now, it looks like His Majesty and party have survived. How many and how badly they are injured??? They disposed of the bodies just over that rise there. Patched themselves up, gathered supplies and a large number of horses and took off to Arial.

"He is doing what he, and they, have been trained to do. He is gathering intel for us and starting to make them pay. I want those transports here in two days Colonel. Full mobilization. Only the Clans troopers. No one else is to know but us.

"Full battalion formation after the evening meal Colonel. Dismissed."

"They are alive Mags," Janet said. "If they had been badly hurt, they would have come home."

After the evening meal, the battalion was formed up on three sides of a hollow square. The fourth side was where the Queen, her guards and the Head Quarters staff and officers were standing. The unfurled colours at their head, the Queen beside the colour.

Margarete strode to the middle of the hollow square and began to speak, so every one could hear.

"Two days before I arrived back home," she began. "His Majesty, the Princess Royal, Duchess Greta and Senior Sergeant Halstrom, were attacked. It was a combat insertion by space transport. The attack came from Arial, this has been verified. All evidence supports that His Majesty and the whole party with him survived. They came here, disposed of the dead enemy, patched themselves up and resupplied them selves. Then, they loaded that same transport and headed to Arial. This is also verified.

"What their injuries are, or how bad the injuries are, is unknown at this time.

"You see, His Majesty and his party are doing what Eagles do. He is gathering information for us. In two days time, we will be loading into transports and heading to Arial to kick some asses! We, the Queens Guard, will be the first to land. We will be on our own. But we are Eagles and we are Bears and we are the Queens Guard! And we are at war with Arial!

"Dismissed!"

Trailed by Janet, Margarete headed to where her camp was set up.

It was silence in the still formed square as the information was absorbed. A single voice began to sing. Others quickly joined in. The whole battalion was singing, at first slow and soft. Like a horse walking through the forrest. The tempo came faster and faster, the voices rising as they sped up. At the end, their song was being screamed, the pace, that of a horse at the gallop. Then it stopped and the chanting began.

"Queens Guard, Queens Guard!"

The Bears and Eagles were going to war. With a vengeance.

Chapter Four

A communications Captain came to attention in front of Margarete after he had been allowed entrance to her tent. She had just come back in and sat down after doing a fast tour of the camp. The Captain handed her a message, he had an apprehensive look on his face.

Margarete quickly read the message and tossed it to the far end of her small desk.

"Thank you Captain," Margaete said. "Keep up the good work. Next time, have a corporal bring it over. I am sure you have much better things to do."

The Captain bowed his head and left the tent. He was not far away when he heard a very un-lady like curse emanate from the tent.

"Son of a Bitch!" Margarete yelled. "Janet! Get your ass in here and send somebody for the bloody Colonel!"

"Ut-Oh," Janet said.

She pointed at one of Margarete's ever present guards.

"Run over to the Colonels tent," she said. "Tell him to get his butt over here ASAP and that Her Majesty is major pissed."

Janet made sure her uniform was in order, took a deep breath and marched into the tent. Coming to attention and bowing her head.

"Senior Sergeant Olynick, reporting Your Royal Highness!" She belted out.

"A week!" Magarete exclaimed. "A God Damned week! Maybe ten days! Then they will give us one transport. Two more in twelve days! Shit!"

Margarete looked up at Janet. Her face was neutral, but she could see Janets hands had curled into tight fists. Her head, was even higher than normal looking over Margaret's head.

"At ease Janet," Margarete said quietly.

Before anything else could be said, the colonel was ushered into the tent. What he saw was Janet at a ridged parade rest. The hands jammed into her back clenched so hard they were turning white. Margarete held her hand up to him. She was accessing her comm unit.

"What the hell do you mean a week to ten days for one transport!" She yelled into the unit as soon as it was answered. "I don't want any excuses! You are to have two transports on hand, on standby at all times for just this reason! You tell that god damned pilot, if he is not at my position five days from now, I will have him arrested and kicked out of the Army! Tell your god damned commanding officer, I am going to bust him down to a supply private if I don't hear from him in the next hour!"

Margarete flung the communicator unit out the entrance to the tent, crossed her arms across her chest and began pacing around the tent. The colonel was still standing at attention, waiting to be addressed and Alex came into the tent, her discarded communicator in his hand. Almost immediately, it began to beep, signalling a message.

Margarete grabbed the comm unit from Alex's hand and hit a few buttons. As it began to transmit, it was clear that she had put it on speaker mode so everyone could hear the conversation.

"Why are My transports not available?" She began before the other person could make any comment. "There are supposed to be a minimum of two on standby at all times!"

"There were ma-am," a male voice replied. "There were three. One went down for repairs. Three of our regular transports were requisitioned by the Oaken Transport Authority. Two of those were to be on standby duty ma-am. The two that will be coming, are returning from deploying troops requested by the Federation ma-am. The order requisitioning the three transports came right from the Emir's office ma-am. Highest priority ma-am."

"How soon, can the one under repairs be back in service?" Margarete asked. She was beginning to calm down, albeit slowly.

"If we forgo the upgrades we wanted to install, by the end of the week ma-am. If we push it," was the answer.

"Very well general," Margarete said. "Don't take short cuts. Those ships are going to be busy, very busy. Good day general."

Margarete disconnected that call and initiated another.

"Scotty," she said. "Get ahold of Our ambassador to the Oaken council. Tell him I am major pissed."

"At ease," she said to Alex and the Colonel. "Everybody sit the fuck down."

"Helga!" Margarete yelled. "We need some vodka in here!"

She tossed her comm unit on her small desk and resumed her pacing.

Helga, now dressed in her captains uniform, instead of her normal house servants get up arrived, two bottles in hand. She was followed by a sergeant, also one of the house servants. This one was carrying a tray with four mugs on it.

"Grab another two mugs and come back sergeant," Margarete said. "Sit Helga, you need to hear this as well."

Helga handed a bottle to Alex, then sat, poured herself a mug full and handed the bottle to a now seated Janet. Who was still upset, but beginning to calm down. As Margarete's comm unit began to beep again, the sergeant rushed in, two mugs in hand. Margarete hooked her chair with a toe from behind her desk and shoved it toward the sergeant.

"Mr. Ambassador," Margarete began. Again cutting off any attempt at pleasantries.

"Find out who the hell in the Emire's office felt they could over ride My authority and requisition two of My transports? Now, Mr. Ambassador. No, tomorrow will not do! I said NOW!!! Or do I have to make the call myself and have you replaced?"

She cut off the communication, once again tossing the comm unit on the desk. She held out her hand, the sergeant placed a mug in it. Margarete raised it in salute and took a deep draft. Then she placed one of her butt cheeks on the desk corner, some what relaxing.

"Right," she said. "We will have one transport by the end of the week. Find out if we can jam in our half battalion into it. It's only three days to Arial. We can tough it out for that long. I want as many arrows as we can carry. Issue full armour to the troops, for horses as well. Then get them practicing with it. Good?"

Her comm unit beeped again. This time with a different tone.

"Bashire, what the fuck are you doing taking two of my necessary transports? They are to be on full time standby for emergency use only!"

"I don't really give a shit!" She said after listening for less than ten seconds. "It doesn't matter that this is only a drill! We train like it is real! All the time! Or when some real bad shit happens we are up the creek without a paddle!"

"No, you cannot come to where I am! You are not required! My location is a secret and you have no need to know! Get your shit together Bashir, or I will place the whole Transportation Department under Clan authority!"

Once again, Margarete shut down her comm unit. This time she laid it on her desk, instead of tossing it.

"Well," she said. "If they weren't shitting their pants before, they are now."

Alex chuckled. He knew Margarete well and knew she had calmed down now.

"Anything else Boss?" Alex asked.

"Naw," she replied. "Get, especially the new kids, up to speed and fast Colonel. Helga? Are you and your people going to be ready? It's been a while since you've been in the field."

"Ya," Helga said. "My ass and thighs are hurting just thinking about it. The Sarge and I will have the gang, especially the new ones as up to speed as fast as we can Mags."

Margaret nodded her head.

"Alright," she said. "Everybody but Janet, get the hell out of here. Leave the bottles."

Margarete waited until everyone had left, then pulled the zippers to both entrances shut. She walked to Janet and pulled her to stand from her chair, then as she hugged her, felt the tears begin to flow.

"Our men will be fine Jan," Margrete whispered into Janets ear. "They and Grets will make sure Willy is ok."

"Not worried about them Mags," Janet blustered out. "A lot of those rookie kids are gonna die Mags!"

Janet really broke down then. Margarete let her at it. Gently rubbing her back as they hugged. As Margarete felt the rambling and sobbing subside, she spoke once again, this time in a normal voice.

"When we join and put these uniforms on, we are dead people walking Jan." she said. "You know it, I know it and in their hearts, they know it. They are Eagles and now is the time they earn them. For real."

Janet hugged Margarete hard, then kissed her right cheek and pushed her from her.

"Fuck it!" Janet said. "Who wants to live forever anyway?"

Both women laughed, sat down and began to kill the bottles.

Chapter Five

"This is a complete waste of my and your time Colonel!" The general in charge of the Arial district said. "These are nothing but common criminals!"

"Captain Walker has experience working with these people General," the Colonel said. "He spent three tours operating with them sir.

"Captain, can you please outline how these people operate and what you feel we can expect from them?"

Walker was still in hospital. He could walk around without to much effort, but his arm was not fully functional yet.

"Their scouts operate in groups of four sir," he began. "For a deep recon like I assume this is sir, they will have at least four other teams doing the same work. Their job is to probe our positions, find our strengths and weak areas. They will report back to their battalion their findings and the battalion will make their plan of attack based on those reports sir."

"Bah!" The major who was second in command and Walker's direct superior said. "Our air and ground patrols will have them spotted and eliminated very soon."

"I agree," the general said. "Come Major, you and I have other important things to do."

As the two men left the room, the colonel looked over at Walker, who just shrugged his shoulders.

"They won't be spotted unless we are real lucky," Walker said. "Or, if they want us to see them"

"Why would they want to let us see them?" The colonel asked.

"To ambush and kill us sir," Walker said. "Also part of how they operate. Have they been doing that sir?"

"No, just raids," the colonel said. "Not much left behind when they leave. Burn everything to the ground. They haven't killed any civilians, yet."

"Anyway you can show me where they have been operating sir?" Walker asked.

The colonel accessed his comm unit and brought a map of the area up on it, marked with the locations of the raids.

"Nothing for the last three days then?" Walker said, more to himself than the colonel.

He continued looking at the map and zoomed it out as much as he could.

"I would need a bigger map sir," Walker said. "I believe they have already figured out where to hit us sir. See how they were first operating in a circle? Then changed to a straight line?"

The colonel took his time looking at the map then nodded his head.

"I believe they are out of communications with their base sir," Walker said. "They are making a map sir. Where ever that straight line stops sir? That's where they want their people to land sir."

"Are you sure Walker?" The colonel asked.

"That's what I would do sir." Walker said.

"I'll have a closer look on the big map in my office," the colonel said. "The doc said you are out of here at the end of the day. I'm giving you another company. You answer only to me, got it? Train and equip your people to do battle with these people Walker. I also know what they are capable of."

The command group was all gathered in the communications tent. A large map of a section of Aerial was on the wall. There were circles drawn on it in many places. The colonel in charge of the communications department started hitting the circles one at a time with a pointer.

He followed along a circle first, then a straight line that ended.

"He wants us to land there ma-am," the colonel said. "It's a plateau ma-am. Big enough to land and deploy on ma-am. The only approach is up hill from the plain below ma-am. Perfect spot for a battle."

"Islanove?" Margarete asked her transport services commanding officer.

Islanove was busy accessing his own comm unit and stayed silent for a few moments.

"Yes ma-am," Ilanove said. "No problem ma-am."

"Plan to be taking all the full time Queens Guards here on site," Margarete said. "Our horses, rations for two weeks and as many arrows as we can load. That is your first task. The next, take out the Arial Space Transport Facility. Any Transports on it when you arrive. Then, fuel and refuelling stations. Finally, communications sites, in the port and if you have the time and resources, in the Capital itself.

"Make sure to have enough fuel to do a high speed return flight and a fast turn around for our reinforcements. Coordinate with Alex. He will be coming in on the second wave."

Ilanove nodded his head, then was busy banging away on his comm unit.

"The rest of you," Margarete continued. "Keep at it with the training and train hard. We are on our own for at least six days after we land. Many of Arial's troops have worked with us. Don't think this will be easy people, we are vastly out numbered, especially for the first week until the Reserve Troopers join us.

"General, Colonel, Senior Sergeant, stay put, the rest of you, get at it!"

The room quickly emptied, leaving the four of them alone at the table.

"Colonel, have your officers let you know what deficiencies their commands have as far as equipment goes. The same with you Senior Sergeant. Rotate among your troop sergeants. We all know, many times officers will under or over report their readiness and equipment requirements. The Sergeants, for the most part, are veteran lifers. They will not compromise their troopers. They know to much is at stake.

"General, you are going to be very, very busy, the next little while. If you do not delegate, you are going to burn out. I can't have that General, not this time. When you arrive with the Reservists, you may be landing in a hot zone. The element of surprise will be gone.

"All three of you. If you cannot trust those under you in your chain of command, get rid of them now! All of our lives depend on it people! If we are not at our best when the shit hits the fan, we are done for!

"Dismissed!"

"Helga!" Margarete yelled as the three hurriedly left to their various tasks.

"Mags," Helga said as she came in. She knew if Margarete was going to be formal, she would have used her rank, not her name.

"Could you ask Al, to come by please?" Margarete said.

"Sure boss," Helga said. "Business or?"

"A little of both," Margarete said. "Mostly personal."

"No problem boss," Helga said.

The veterans were reverting to how they acted in the field. When alone anyway.

Margarete was busy working on her comm unit when Helga escorted Al in, a half hour later.

"Hey Sis-in law," Al said by way of greeting.

Margarete smiled and stood. Both hugged and kissed each others cheeks.

"Vodka, or?" Margarete asked.

"Beer would be fine," Al said. "It's a little early for vodka."

"Got it boss," Helga said, heading for her part of the tent.

Margarete pointed to the map on the wall and Al walked over and took a look at it.

"Well," Al said. "Some of them are alive any way. A blind man could figure that diagram out."

"Ya well..." Margarete said. "The Arial generals are hardly blind men I am sure."

"What they pay us for kid," Al said.

Al was five years older than Margarete. Both of them, especially Al, were originals. Both had been in more than their fair share of battles.

"Ya, I know," Margarete said. "It's one thing fighting ourselves. We all know we are going to live forever. But these kids. Especially one, it's hard you know. We are by ourselves for at least a week Al."

"Shouldn't be to bad," Al said. "It will probably take them a while to figure out what to do Marg. And, my kids are active duty too. So ya, I know."

Al's son, the eldest, was like his father, a heavy cavalry Bear. His daughter was in the medical corps and an Eagle.

"I am reserving one of the second wave transports for your people Al," Margaret said. "Two in the third. By then, all of Oaken will know what is going on. So we should have more transport capability after that."

"If it isn't over by then," Al said.

"I know for a fact,' Margarete said. "They have one experienced veteran company that will give us a hand full. I trained their captain my self. He is very, very good and very motivated. He knows how we operate and, in fact, he was operating almost the same way we were. His men are all full time soldiers. If he trains up a full battalion, we are going to need you Bears. Badly."

Greta, like the others, had just finished grooming, watering and staking down her four horses. They had found an open clearing with a clear running stream and small pool in the forrest. Today, they had raided two small settlements, then moved south 25 kilometres from the point of the arrow they had made for a map.

It had been a fifty mile trip today, leaving and hitting the first settlement in the pre dawn grey light, the other, four hours later. Horses and people, were tired and sore. It had been a long and hard week. The worst day had been the first day. The day of the attack from space. All of them had been wounded, Demetri the worst. Greta had done what she could with the limited time and resources they had at the time and each night since. All of them would bear the burn scars though.

They had a few hours until full dark. Greta would try and make some more magic on the blaster burns, thorn and branch gashes and other various wounds they had all picked up along the way. The plan was to stay here as long as possible and rest. They had enough food for two weeks. After that...

Greta knew better than to bother Demetri right now. He was rubbing medical salve on Barney, who was wounded almost as badly as Demetri had been. Charles had just finished digging the fire pit and he and Willa had gathered stones to ring it with. Willy, as they called her, was gathering up small branches and breaking them to start a fire.

Once the fire was going, Greta made Charles pullout his shirt and she rubbed some balm on his burns and checked his minor wounds. Now, he did the same for her. While that was going on, Willy had gone to the little stream, removed her shirt and given herself a fast rinse in the cold stream water.

She came back to Charles, wrapping a bandage around Greta's belly, to recover a deep knife wound she had on her back. Willy sat on the ground beside the fire with crossed legs, put her shirt back on and began to gather her hair to try and do something with it. She only had hair on the right side. The left had been shaved by Greta to keep the blaster burn she had received there clear.

As she worked, she looked at the others, then to where her father and Barney were. Her hands went to her lap, she stared into the fire and, no matter how hard she tried, the tears began to flow.

Greta came and began her nightly routine inspecting Willy's wounds. Willy rarely made any sounds while Greta did this, suffering, as they all did, in her pain in silence. Today was no different. It wasn't until Greta started to braid Willy's hair that a small whimper came out and she shuddered.

Greta looked at her niece then and saw the tears. They had all been waiting for this. Willy had never cried, ever, after the attack. The rest of them had, they had killed a lot of people that day. But not Willy.

"You survived Willy," Greta said softly. "We all did. It is never easy, killing. I won't lie about that. Nor will the memories ever go away. We learn to live with them, but they never go away."

"I feel so useless!" Willy blurted out. "All I do is watch! I can't even protect myself let alone help you guys! The day of the attack, I just stood there frozen!"

"No child, you did not," Greta said softly. "You were shooting arrows as fast as you could until you ran out of them. Then your dad went down...."

Greta looked away. Her hands still on the braid she had been making, but now still.

Charles came and squatted down beside her.

"You grabbed your hunting knife from your belt and the hatchet we used to split kindling with," Charles said. "You killed the two men that had put your dad down, then fended off the others until Barney came to help."

Willy was looking at her feet and saw a pair of dusty boots appear in front of her and a pair of gentle hands take her under her jaw and lift her head to see her dad's face.

"You...save...my life..." he barley squeaked out. The first words he had spoken all week. "And...Barney's...You...are not useless.. you are my daughter....and I love you."

Then, a pair of copper brown hoofed legs appeared, a big head lay on her shoulder and Barney rumbled.

Willy saw the tears running down her fathers face. She made to hug him, but saw him wince, so turned and hugged her aunt instead. Now she did break down.

The two men and Barney, moved off.

"Well," Charles said as they reached the pack saddles. "One potential problem solved. She's not a physco."

Demetri pulled a jar of beer out of a pack saddle uncorked it and took a deep draft. He handed it to Charles, who did the same.

"She went berserk Bubba," Demetri said softly, just over a whisper. "It's probably what saved us. All instinct. Just like you, at the end of that day long ago."

"I was doing my job, right up until my last two team mates went down," Charles said. "Then..."

"She has no training," Demetri said. "And we have no time to train her right now. Greta knows. She will try to explain. I can't talk well enough yet."

The evening meal was quiet. Nobody was talking. All of them deep in thought.

"Aunty," Willy said finally. "Why don't I remember what I did?"

"It's called fight or flight response," Greta said. "Just like the Bison. A lone Bison will try to run, cornered, it turns and fights. We have the same instincts. Some like me, your dad, Charles and others, learn to first, spot trouble and avoid it, then to get away, then to fight and fight hard. Others, freeze. That also is a survival trait. Many predators react to movement.

"Your instincts told you to fight. Then, you used what you knew, that you had seen others do. The body took over and blocked the mind. We call it going Beserk and those that do it, berserkers. They are fearsome fighters, don't feel any pain and are hard to kill. But, when they get that way, they will kill anything around them, even friends, until they calm down."

"Oh," Willy said. Her head sank down.

Greta patted her on the shoulder.

"It's nothing a little training can't fix Willy." Greta said. "Your dad fixed your mom."

They heard Demitre snort.

"Thought that's who she got it from," he croaked out. "I'm always killing people in a civilized manner. Asking permission and what not."

"Oh but of course," Charles said sticking his nose high in the air. "Excuse me govnor, would you mind terribly should I cut your head off?"

"Ya ya," Greta said. She tossed a clump of dirt at Demetri.

"Do you think help will be coming?" Willy asked.

"Oh yes," Greta said. "Your mom and Janet are going to be some pissed. The only thing worse than having your dad pissed at you, is your mom and Janet. If things are not happening and fast, heads are seriously gonna get chopped off."

Chapter Six

I f they were not training, they were cleaning armour, weapons and gear. Grooming horses, repairing tack, sleeping, only to find more of the same the next day.

A large amount of time was spent on full, coordinated unit attacks, not the scouting and harassment training they were used to. The armour was confining, hot and heavy. They were often in a line, almost shoulder to shoulder with the horse next to them. Arrow charges, lance charges, sword charges. Then all three. Over and over again.

During their breaks, they saw constant movement of staff officers rushing to and fro. Each morning full briefings were held. Sometimes an upset female voice could be heard yelling and something, generally a comm unit, flying out of the command tent door.

Finally, what they had been waiting for. A full battalion officers meeting. After everyone was at ease, the Queen began to address them.

"An hour after dawn," she began. "A transport will land. You will load by company. Horses first, then your selves. It will be cramped, all of us are going on the same transport. In three days, we land on Arial and begin to kick some serious ass!

"They attacked our people, on our own planet. Without warning, or provocation. Four, basically unarmed people, one of them a teen age girl. This is personal people! They tried to kill our leader, they disrespected not only Federation law, but our people. His Majesty is, right now, this very minute, making them pay. He has devastated ten settlements and killed a large number of soldiers. Now it is our turn!

"They will soon learn what many others have. Don't ever fuck with the Eagles of the Queens Guard! Dismissed!"

As the rookies, Williams half company had been loaded last. The four births they had been given, were far from optimal. They had been converted from a cargo hold, the bunks, three high and barely enough room to walk sideways between the bunks.

It was on the lowest level of the transport. Above the engine and mechanical spaces and beside the horse births. As such, it was noisy, cramped and smelly.

They had also been assigned the last meal times. That meant, their food was cool and the next meal for the first shift was already being set out on the buffet. Such was life in the army and they all knew it. Veterans were always given preference over rookies.

The engine changed pitch three days later. Thumps and bangs were heard from the under side, and bang, they were on the ground. More thunks and bangs as hatchways were opened, letting in cool fresh air. Now they gathered their gear and weapons and like always, waited.

Again, they were the last. Even their horses had been unloaded before they were. More hurry up and wait, as officers received instruction on where to set up camp, guard rotations, where the various supply areas were.

Company C was assigned an area to set up, far from the centre and on the left. As far as camp sights went, it was not to bad. Fairly level, dry and not to rocky. Every one was soon setting up tents, horse lines, cook fires, or collecting wood for fires. The same was happening all over the camp.

One nice thing about being on the edge of the camp, they had first choice on the fire wood. William set up his horse and camp guards and waited for further instructions taking in the sights of the surrounding area.

As had been predicted by the mission planners, the camp was located on a large plateau. The plateau could easily handle a camp three times the size of theirs. Behind the plateau were thick woods and rising terrain. On three sides, was ground that sloped up from the plain below. A stream cut the left corner of the plateau, giving them access to fresh water. This stream went down the hill on that side to join a broad river on the edge of the lower plain.

A vehicle came out of the woods at the end and across from the river. That is when William realized how deceptive the view was. The plateau was two hundred feet higher than the plain below. An enemy would, first, have to cross the river, form up and assault their position walking uphill all the way. In the open, under fire from arrows the whole time.

Four soldiers exited the vehicle and began scanning the Eagles position with binoculars. After a few minutes, one soldier went back to the vehicle, pulling a hand held microphone out and while watching the Eagles, made his report.

A few minutes later, Hassman arrived with two mugs of coffee. He handed one to William.

"Horse lines and camp set up. Horses all groomed and watered. One guard posted for fire and camp, two are setting up a listening post just inside the tree line LT," Hassman said.

"Thanks Sarge," William said.

Two more vehicles showed up below. One larger and with more arials on it than the smaller ones. Now William pulled his binoculars out from their pouch on his belt, scanned the vehicles and handed the binoculars to Hassman.

"Big shots have arrived," William said. "Was I them, I'd bring up two, maybe three battalions and hit us all along our lines. But what do I know? Just a jumped up looie, fresh out of training and promoted above his abilities. All book knowledge, no experience."

"Well," Hassman said after a low chuckle, "At least you was paying attention in class. A colonel, two majors and a captain down there. I recognize the captain. He was deployed with us a couple of times. Good man, him, and his men. Could make things interesting for us."

Hassman handed the binoculars back to William, who put them back in the pouch on his belt.

"I had better report in," William said. "Not much going to happen today any way. Thanks for the coffee."

William handed the now empty mug to Hassman and casually walked to where the captain had set up his tent. He arrived just as the captain was reaming out another lieutenant from A Company for not reporting properly. That's when William noticed that the captain had been promoted to major.

"First platoon, all present and accounted for Major," William said. He did not salute or stomp his foot into the ground. He was standing straight, though not at attention.

"Horses have been groomed inspected and watered. Camp is set up. One guard for the horse line and one for the camp sir. Two men established in a listening post just inside the tree line sir. Two scout vehicles and a command vehicle have arrived sir. A captain, two majors and a colonel, as well as ten troops are observing our lines sir. My Master Sergeant says the Captain and his men have served with us in the past sir. He says the captain and his men were very good and life might be interesting for us when they attack sir."

"Well lieutenant," Steve said to the not yet dismissed A Company lieutenant who was standing rigidly at attention. "A green as grass, just out of training academy luey, just made a better report than you did. I'll bet you have not even posted guards yet, let alone observed the enemy. You should be reporting to your captain, not me and your captain should be reporting to me. Adler here, is in charge of half a company, so, he has to report to me. Dissmissed!

"Nice job Adler," Steve said. "I haven't had time to look around yet. But, that's what I have you for eh? Back to it Adler, troopers, especially rookies, go all to shit when their officer is not around."

William nodded his head and started walking back to his camp. He didn't notice Steve was smiling as he went. But he did hear him blast the next captain that came to report for not noticing the enemy scouting the lines.

Steve wandered over to the command tent and was ushered right in. He came to attention, stomped his right foot on the ground and bowed his head.

"A and C companies all present and accounted for Your Majesty," Steve said. He normally would have made his report to the colonel, but Margarete out ranked the colonel and was present.

"First Platoon C Company, not only has set up a listening post inside their tree line, but, they have spotted the enemy surveying our lines ma-am. A colonel, two majors and a captain. His Master Sergeant recognized Walker was the captain ma-am. After my report, I will verify ma-am."

"Very well Major," Margarete said. "I believe we should all have a look no?"

She grabbed her binoculars from the table, plunked her beret on her head and followed by Steve, the colonel and Janet, breezed out of the tent toward Williams area of the camp. Janet was the only one armed, her ever present sword draped across her back.

"Stand to! Stand to! Flag officers approaching!" The camp guard yelled out.

Troopers not on guard duty rushed around getting in line, dressing it and placing swords across backs. All were in order and at attention when Margarete and her party arrived.

William stood straight and nodded his head.

"First Platoon, C Company, all present or accounted for Your Majesty," he said. His voice was in a normal tone, not the usual loud reporting.

Margarete gave his men a quick look over.

"Very well LT," she said. "Your troopers have done a good job here LT, you may dismiss them. I take it we have some visitors observing our camp?"

"Yes ma-am," William said. "A company of troops have arrived ma-am. I was just about to send one of my lieutenants to report it ma-am. This way ma-am."

William led the way to the crest of the hill. All of the officers and Janet had binoculars out and were scanning the enemy. The newly arrived company were setting up camp and had a skirmish line established, two hundred yards in front.

"Ya, that's Walker and his gang," Margarete said.

She continued scanning the whole area.

"You sure you have a listening post set up LT?" She asked. "You're not fibbing me now eh?"

"Ten yards up from the stream and five inside the tree line ma-am." William said.

"I've got em Mags," Janet said. "They've dug in and placed branches over the slit trench. Hard to spot them, even knowing where they are. Those yahoos down there will never spot them."

Margarete nodded her head. She didn't look over that way, nor did anyone else.

"Right," Margarete said.

She turned and started walking back over the hill.

"Have ten Eagles from B Company, set up a skirmish line in front of my camp in full view at all times to the enemy below. Hoist my banners in front of my tent, you yours in front of yours. All except the LT here. Good job LT, keep it up." She finished.

"Ah for fucks sake," Janet heard William say as the command group walked away.

Janet stopped, turned and headed for Williams camp. She arrived just as William tossed his binoculars inside his tent, none to gently, and followed them in.

"Sit on the edge of the camp! Don't set up your flags! Don't be spotted! You lying to me? Shit!" Janet heard William blurt out. She barged her way into his tent.

"When the general gives an order a lieutenant says, yes ma-am and carries on *Leftenant!*" Janet bellowed. "Not whine and snivel like a little baby."

She yelled it loud enough, every one in the camp could hear it.

William was standing with his back to the tent opening and stood ramrod straight, as Janet expected rookie lieutenants to do.

"Sir," William said softly. "When a non commissioned officer addresses a commissioned officer, you will address the officer accordingly Senior Sergeant."

William turned around and looked at Janet. She knew that look. It was all Demetri when he was not pleased. She smiled at him.

"Wipe that fucking smile off your face Senior Sergeant!" William said. "I don't give a fuck who you are! You give an officer the respect they deserve! And Senior Sergeant, you can go fuck yourself! And the Queen thinking she can protect me by placing me out here, has another thing coming! I am a commissioned officer in charge of twenty troopers, all Eagles, all the top graduates in their class and need I remind you? We kicked your asses good! So, ya, you can go fuck yourself, and the Queen can shove all this protect the rookies crap up her ass!"

"Understood Lieutenant Bekenbaum," Janet said. She was at attention now, her eyes above Williams head. "Won't happen again Your Highness,"

"Get the fuck back to where you belong Senior Sergeant," William said. "Dismissed."

Janet stomped her right foot into the ground and bowed her head.

"Yes sir!" She said. "*Leftenant* sir." She was smiling.

"Ah, get outta here Jan, it ain't your fault my mom is over protective." William said.

Janet chuckled and ducking her head walked out of the tent. She looked over at the troopers gawking in her direction.

"What the fuck are you assholes looking at!" She yelled out. "Clean up this pig stye of a camp! Hassman, get your ass over here!"

"Kids just like his mom," Janet said when Hassman arrived. She had her back to the camp so the troopers could not see the ear to ear grin on her face.

"Told me to go fuck myself he did. Got some balls on him anyway. Also told me to tell his mom to shove all this protect the kiddies shit up her ass."

"They don't know Jan," Hassman said. "Just like us in the day. All gung-ho, rah rah, kick the enemies butt shit. I trained most of this lot Jan. They are real good Jan."

"Ya, I know," Janet said. "We're gonna loose a bunch of them Hassman. Always the brightest and the best. I just hope the kid ain't one of them."

"I'll do my best Jan," Hassman said. "But when the shit hits the fan??"

"You clue that stupid fuck LT in Hassman!" Janet bellowed. "Go fuck myself indeed! I'd be surprised if the stupid shit isn't sent back home on the next transport, if he survives the battle! Go fuck myself! Why I never!"

Having accomplished her purpose, Janet stomped her way back to the command part of the camp. Yelling her displeasure at any trooper that came near her as she went.

"Ah..LT?" Hassman said. "A moment of your time sir?"

"Ya, come on in," William said. "Take a load off."

William motioned to his one camp chair. William sat on the edge of his portable camp cot.

"You ok sir?" Hassman asked.

"Ya, all good," William said. "I just got pissed off and the Senior Sergeant came in here all high and mighty and I took it out on her. I'll apologize later."

"Well," Hassman said. "She does have her reasons LT. And ya, she tends to forget to address officers correctly sir. Most look the other way sir."

"Like I said," William continued. "I was pissed off at all the shit that has been going on with us the last few weeks and her coming in here being her just set me off."

"Understood sir," Hassman said. "Look sir, the general wants us to stay out of site for a reason sir. We are under manned out here on the flank. She wants the enemy to hit our main strength. Once the battle is joined, then we line up on the hill and wait. We watch, and we wait and hit them hard in the flank when the time comes sir. Not to protect us, sir, to protect her sir."

"Oh," William said. "Still lots to learn I guess."

"Your doing ok LT," Hassman said. "Your mom expects you to do your best boss. Just like every other Eagle. Is she concerned. Ya, every mom is concerned when her kid goes into battle. But you are in the position you are in on merit, not on who you are. The Major wanted to make you a captain. She agreed you should be, but....Appearances for one. I"m not the only one who knows who you are. Second, we don't have enough troopers yet to warrant a captain. Last, you don't have the time, or real combat experience yet.

"Like I said sir, we are out here because of who we are, not because we are rookies. Your mom knows it, the colonel knows it, the major knows it and Janet does. Not only are we the only scout company here, we are probably one of the best units here. But we are still untested sir. No one knows how they will react in a fight for the first time sir. All we can do is our best sir."

William nodded his head, then stood.

"Thanks for the talk Sarge," he said. "I don't know about you, but I am starving."

William grabbed his beret, slammed it on his head, so it was leaned to the back on the crown of his head, and followed by Hassman, walked out of the tent and toward the nearest cook fire.

"I'm turning into a skeleton here!" He blurted out. "One of you yahoos better have some food cooked!"

One of the troopers gathered around the fire filled a plate and handed it to William as he sat down. Another did the same for Hassman.

"You really tell the Senior Sergeant to go fuck herself LT?" One of his female troopers asked.

"I did so, Marshack," William said. "She came into my tent without so much as a by your leave, then started yapping about how shitty our camp was. I mean really? We are not back at barracks, we are in the field for Christ sake. Then she said some other disprtespective shit of you guys and I kind of lost it. Sorry guys. I"ll go apologize after supper. She'll probably make me run around the camp for half an hour or some shit."

As expected, the last comment got a lot of laughs.

"He said what??" Margarete asked.

"He told me to go fuck myself," Janet said. "After he told me the proper way for an enlisted person to address an officer. Oh, it gets better. I quote. '*And you can tell my mother to shove all this protect the rookies crap up her ass,*' end quote."

It was deadly quiet in the tent. None of the officers present dared say a word. Margarete had just taken a sip of her vodka laced coffee, which she promptly spat out. And she started to laugh and laugh hard. She stood, put a stern look on her face and her hands on her hips.

"You will address a commissioned officer in the proper manor!" She said. "Tell my mom to shove it up her ass and you can go fuck yourself Senior Sergeant!"

Janet came to ridged exaggerated attention, belly out knees shivering.

"Yes sir! Sorry sir! Won't happen again sir!" Janet said.

She started laughing, now the whole command group started to laugh.

"Ok, ok, enough already," Margarete said after a while. "Janet and I will go and chastise that mouthy LT of mine. What happened will be all over the camp soon anyway. And we have been a little hard on and over protective of them. But, they wear the uniform, are Eagles and probably the best class that has come out of the academy for a long time. We were all young and dumb at one point and we all have to learn the hard way."

"Stand to! Stand to!" The sentry yelled out as Margarete and Janet came into view.

Unlike he had reported earlier that day, William came to attention, stomped his right foot into the ground and saluted with his right hand to his forehead.

"Lieutenant Adler, First Platoon, C Company, all present or accounted for Your Majesty" He reported, his eyes above Margaretes head.

Margarete returned his salute with a wave of her right hand to her forehead.

"The Lieutenant apologizes for disrespecting the Senior Sergeant Your Majesty," William continued. "My troopers had no part in this Your Majesty. Any punishment should be mine alone Your Majesty."

"Good enough for you Senior Sergeant?" Margarete asked. Janet nodded her head.

"You are lucky your mother is an understanding woman *Lefteant*" Margarete said. "Most mothers would yank your ear so hard she would pull it off for telling her to shove it up her ass. Let alone telling a respected woman to go fuck herself. We expect more from our officers *Lefteant*. Master Sergeant Hassman, we put you with this platoon precisely to prevent this type of behaviour. This better not happen again."

Margarete made her way down the front of the line looking each trooper in the eye and up and down their uniforms as she did so.

"Jesus Marshack," Margarete said as she surveyed the now concerned trooper. "Your mom never looked that good in her party uniform. How are all the rest of us normal looking women going to snag any guys out here eh?"

She went back to the front of the line.

"As I am sure your more than competent listening post, Master Sergeant and Lieutenant have noticed," she said. "We now have two full battalions camped out below us and a third is assembling. They will want to engage us tomorrow, before we can disperse and start doing what Eagles do best, cause mishap and mayhem. I, we, in the centre are counting on Magies Eagles to save our sorry asses tomorrow. Stay out of sight and be ready. When we need you, we will need you fast. Be ready. Try and get a good nights sleep. I will be."

Janet dropped her voice tone as low as she could.

"You can go fuck yourself Senior Sergeant and tell my mom to go fuck her self," Janet said.

Margarete came to attention like Janet had earlier, knees knocking, belly sticking out and her hand shaking at her forehead as she saluted.

"Sorry Lieutenant Bekenbaum, won't happen again Your Highness," Margarete mimicked Janet.

Both women laughed, turned and began walking away.

"I say Mags," Janet said in upper class Standard, they had been talking Oaken earlier. "Did you see that trooper in the middle. I wouldn't kick him out of my bed for eating crackers."

"Ah, like we have any chance with Marshack around Jan," Margarete said.

Both women could be heard laughing as they walked, until Janet saw a trooper from the next camp looking at them.

"What the hell are you looking at Trooper!" She yelled.

The troopers all relaxed as the two woman left. But stayed some what in line. Finally Marshack broke the silence in the camp.

"What the fuck LT," she said. "You're the Crown Prince?"

William stuck his hands in the back pockets of his trousers, looked at the ground and pushed a stone on the ground away with his right boot.

"Ya, I guess," he said softly. "You got me."

He looked up at them then.

"And my shit stinks just as bad as yours does," he said. "I put my pants on one leg at a time, unlike you Marshack. She with the uniform and bod to kill for, who never even takes a fart let alone a shit. Like you, I am an Eagle, I was fortunate enough to qualify to be an officer, or I'd be right beside you guys in the line. Just like my mother did when she was a rookie.

"I don't know about you guys, but I'm scared as shit about tomorrow. They glossed over it just now, but so are the queen and the Senior Sergeant. And they have both been there and done that more than once. If I am not at my best tomorrow, I am going to get a lot of you killed. I am going to get my mother and father killed. I am going to get the trooper on my right and ,my left in the line killed.

"Because, that who is who I am fighting for. Not my planet, or my flag or my ruler. I am fighting to keep the trooper on my left and right and all of you alive."

William turned away and walked into the darkness.

"Holy shit," a trooper in the middle of the line said. "I thought I was the only one scared out of my mind."

"I am not scared out of my mind Anderson," Hassman said. "I am...relatively concerned, about tomorrow. And that is normal."

There were a lot of Jesus's and holy shit's being expressed.

"Every one sit down," Hassman said.

"Fear is a good thing," he said after every one was seated around the fire. He began rotating around it, looking at each trooper he passed, gauging their mood.

"Fear will keep you sharp and alive," he continued. "Being scared out of your mind will just paralyze you. Just like the LT said, I fight for the trooper on my left and the trooper on my right. You see, I will live forever, but if I mess up, if I miss the enemy coming un noticed by my troop mate, they might die. That I could not live with.

"Now, the LT, his folks wanted him to get the best teachers and training. They and he, knew, that if he was known for who he really was, he would get preferential treatment. Not something, they or he wanted. I was his training sergeant all the way through and didn't figure it out until he showed me where that out of the way, hidden supply dump was. The colonel and Major Steve knew. The major was the Queens aide before this. Janet knew, well she should, she watched him grow up. Her and the Queen were the first Eagles ever trained.

"Tomorrow, do your jobs the best you can. Keep your head on a swivel, let the LT do his job, you do yours. It is going to be noisy, you are going to see horrible things, including, one of your buddies get killed or badly wounded. People are going to be screaming, in pain, calling for their mothers or god, or just because they are plain pissed off. You can't ever stop, you can't help your buddy if they fall. If they fall, close the gap and keep fighting or we all die.

"If we all do our jobs, most of us will come out of this alive. Now, pack it in and get some rest."

He watched them disperse to their tents. Some were quiet and some were making jokes. He smiled and sighed, shaking his head. That's when he noticed that William had been standing just in the shadows the whole time he had been giving his speech. Hassman walked over to where he was standing.

"They'll be ok boss," Hassman said."They are all scared, shit I'm scared, I always am. But they'll be ok."

"Important thing for you tomorrow boss, make a decision. Even if it may not be the right one, make a decision. They will be looking to you for guidance."

"How will I know?" William asked. "How will I know in all the confusion?"

"When to attack?" Hassman said. "It will feel and look different. The sound, at some point will change. Fore or against, it doesn't matter. When that happens we hit and hit hard."

William had his head down and he nodded.

"You'll do alright kid," Hassman said. He patted William on the shoulder. "Go and try to get some rest."

Hassman heard foot steps approaching out of the darkness. It was Janet. She had a bottle of clear fire in her hand. She offered the bottle to him and he took a deep pull from it.

"Come on," Hassman said. "No sense waisting this nice fire. You and me ain't gonna sleep tonight anyway."

"Boss is talking about making you Company Sergeant," Janet said.

"Ya, just what I needed," Hassman replied. "Company Sergeant to a bunch of know it all rookies."

Chapter Seven

The whole camp had eaten their breakfasts. Troopers and officers were nervously sitting around their camp fires, waiting. Waiting for something, anything to happen. It was not long in coming.

Margaret had been pacing around her tent for the last hour, when a trooper from the skirmish line came in and reported.

"Party of ten at the foot of the hill ma-am," the trooper said. "With a truce flag ma-am."

"Thank you trooper," Margarete said. "Have your skirmish line stand down and get yourselves and your horses kitted out. Helga, spread the word. Time to go to work. Janet, with me."

Ten of her fully armed body guards formed up and followed them down the hill, stopping twenty paces away from the enemy and putting an arrow to bow strings. Margarete and Janet, both unarmed, kept walking. They stopped in front of the enemy, came to attention and saluted. The officer before them was also a general.

"What the hell are you people doing on my planet!" The general demanded not bothering to return the salute. Margarete let her hand drop to her side and she and Janet assumed the position of parade rest. Feet shoulder width apart, hands tucked in the small of their backs.

"This is an unprovoked invasion and an act of war," the General continued.

"Typical," Margarete said. "You come to my home, attack my unarmed husband and daughter and two of their friends and then have the gaul to say I am here doing an unprovoked act of war. Well, your planet and my clan are at war sir. Your emperor ordered that attack. But, this is personal, not business. You have attacked and possibly killed my husband, my daughter and two of my closest friends. My planet is not at war with yours general. I and my clansmen are at war with your emperor. If your emperor apologizes and pays us reparations, we may overlook this. If not? My Eagles and I are here to make you pay. One way or another.

"Come on up general. The Queens Guard are bored. We haven't been in a fight for a while."

Margarete gave a quick salute and she and Janet began walking back up the hill. Her body guard walking back ward behind her.

"Who the hell are you!" The general demanded.

"Queen Margarete of Oaken," she said over her shoulder. "And you better hope like hell the rest of Oaken doesn't find out what is going on. Because then shit will really hit the fan."

"Every one in formation now!" The general yelled as he sprinted back to his command vehicle.

"Stand to if you please Senior Sergeant," Margarete said as she crested the hill headed for her tent.

"Stand to! Stand to!" Janet yelled. "What are you waiting for, a golden invitation? Stand to!"

Helga and her aide were already in full armour, minus helmets when Margarete entered the tent. Margaret's armour was all laid out and while she braided her hair, the two women began putting the armour on Margarete.

"To your troops Major," Margarete said once they were finished. "No spectators today. Play safe kiddies. Have fun."

Janet and Maragetes full company of body guards were mounted and armoured. Margaretes armoured horse was waiting for her.

"Colours to the front," Margarete ordered as she mounted. "Form the line."

The order was passed down the camp and those below finally saw what they would be facing. Two solid lines, one ten yards behind the other stretched almost all the way across the hill top.

All of William's platoon were armoured and mounted and in line waiting.

"Once we hear the two battle lines collide, we crest the hill. Not before." William ordered.

Then, he and Hassman, un mounted and with helmets off, went to the crest of the hill to watch.

Four riders in leather armour came pelting out of the woods to the left. Their clans flag billowing out from a make shift staff held by one large rider. The rest had an arrow knocked and three in their mouths as they galloped to the side of the nearest enemy formation. Once in range. They formed line astern and fired arrow after arrow into the enemy formation.

Men were flying from their feet in sprays of red tinted shattered ceramic armour as the arrows hit them hard. The riders were just out of range of the blasters and the few shots that were fired, were no where close to them. The four continued up the hill and stopped in front of the colour party.

"Well, look what the cat dragged in," Margarete said.

Her voice did not convey the concern she had on her face. Barney's coat was patchy in places. The hair just growing back from his burn marks. Demetri had a bandage wrapped around his neck. Her daughters head was shaved on one side and had a long burn mark up high on it. Greta's hands were burned and scarred and Charles, as always bare armed, was showing new burn scares on both arms.

"Having fun on your holiday I see," Margarete said.

"Well, I see you are all dressed up to party," Demetri croaked out. "May I have the first dance?"

"I thought you'd never ask," Margarete said.

The four joined the line. Demetri on one side of Margarete, Willy on the other. Charles to one side of Janet, Gretta the other.

"Just hang on Willy," Margarete said. "The horse knows what to do."

"Get them on the line Sergeant," William said. "They need to see this.'

He had watched the four riders join up and knew what was coming next even before the singing began.

His platoon came rushing up to the crest, William and Hassman quickly mounted and donned helmets.

"Get ready guys," William said. "Follow along the best you can. The horses have been trained for this. But we stay put at the end, understood."

William and Hassman began to sing, their horses quickly picked up on the sound and the movements all along the line, horses and troopers began to sing and move. Swords were drawn from backs and the intricate slow movements of their dance began. Hooves lifting high and slowly moving sideways, matching slow moving sword movements to left and right. The sound of the song the beat of a horse at a slow walk, just as the horses were doing.

Except for Williams line. He kept them in check on the edge of the hill.

The volume and speed of the dance and song rose higher and higher until they were moving fast and almost yelling. Almost as one, the horses all rose on rear legs and began to pivot around, fore hooves slashing out. Swords swinging to left and right at speed. Then, it all stopped.

The lines came together once again, swords were placed back behind backs. Lances or bows were drawn. Joined by the four in the leather armour, one hundred archers broke from the lines. Fifty to each side of the massed enemy formations below them. The archers flowed down each side, each archer launching an arrow as fast as they could. The enemy were dying in their hundreds now.

That's when the lancers attacked. The enemy placed their shields on the ground and braced themselves as well as they could. Blasters started firing as nervous troopers began to fire, well out of range. The ground was shaking from the massed hooves of the over one thousand horses galloping toward them. And with a crash, the horses at full stride hit the enemy, hard. Men were bowled over. Lances penetrated two men at a time and were discarded. Swords came out. The din was over powering, horses and people screaming in pain or anger, bodies flying every direction.

The horse lines had penetrated almost to the middle of the enemy formation when they could go no further. Blasters were firing, most doing little or no damage. Swords flying in great arcs of red misted strikes. All the while, arrows were flying until there were no more arrows, then the swords came out as the archers joined the fight.

William heard a shift in the sound of the battle and glanced that way. A large group of the enemy from the right flank had made their way to the rear of the Eagles, threatening to cut them off. This left that side of the enemy formation thin.

"First Platoon!" William shouted over the din. "Follow me!"

He pulled his lance out and spurred his horse to the direction of that flank. In what seemed to take forever, his lance hit the left side of a soldier killing him on the spot. Then the horse crashed into the following two men. William let the lance fall from his hand, grabbed his sword from his back and began to fight. He saw from the flashes of armour and swords, he had troopers on each side of him. But that was all. Cutting and slashing, horse pivoting, kicking to front and rear, biting anything that came near it.

The pressure in front of them lessened and men were turning and running for their lives away from them.

"Stay in line! Stay in line!" William yelled. "Kill them if you have to, but let them run! Keep the pressure on!"

They soon had no one to fight as the enemy ran. All but one formation. These were still in their square and slowly moving backward. Facing the outside of their square. They were shoulder to shoulder, shields locked together at the front two lines the rear two lines had them over head. These were not ceramic shields. They had arrows stuck all over them.

William looked around the battle field and saw they were alone. Ten trooper troops were hunting down any forms of resistance all around the battle field.

"Bows!" William ordered. He nudged his horse forward.

"At the ready and in line!" He ordered. "Nobody looses an arrow without orders!"

As he came near the enemy formation, he saw the damage it had not only received but let out. The shields were beginning to come apart at places. Chunks were torn out by sword strikes on others. Blood was spattered on shields on helmets. These were armed with hammers and long handled hand axes, not with blasters.

"Enough," William said. "Enough people have died here today. You have fought well. I have no wish to kill you all. Each of my troopers have two full quivers of ten arrows. Your shields are falling apart. You won't stop them all. Not from this range. Enough."

"You will give us a guarantee of safety if we surrender?" A voice from the formation said.

"Yes," William said. "We have no quarrel with you men. Only your ruler. I personally guarantee your safety."

He heard some discussion going on, then a shield in the centre of the front line came down and a man came forward. He proffered his battle axe to William, handle first.

"Captain Walker sir," he said. "I surrender my troopers to your care sir."

William took the axe from the man then gave it back to him.

"Have your troops stand down Captain if you please," William said. "Weapons and shields tossed to the ground in front."

"Have the troopers stand down Master Sergeant," William said over his shoulder. "These soldiers are under our care now."

Shields and weapons were tossed in front of their lines and men were sinking exhausted to their knees. Some shaking, all breathless. William heard a loud female scream, and a blood soaked, leather armoured aberration was charging the enemy formation. William spurred his horse forward to a gallop and broad sided the approaching rider, almost nocking her tired horse to the ground. The woman turned on him and swung her hand axe at him, only to have it bounce off his armour. William grabbed the arm with the axe and pulled it toward him, pulling the rider off her horse and into his arms. He wrapped her tightly with his arms around her shoulders so she could not strike him.

"Enough!" He yelled. "Enough! These men have surrendered!"

She kept fighting him, trying to break free. William looked down at her face and saw who it was.

"Enough Willy," he said softly into her ear. "Calm down. The fight is over sister. Calm down."

She looked up at his face, trying to see it through the slits in the helmet.

"Will?" She said. "Is that you Will?"

"Ya, it's me Willy," he said. "If I let you loose, you promise to behave?"

"Ya sure, why wouldn't I?" She replied.

As William let her loose, she began to look around her self. William took off his helmet and draped it on his saddle horn.

"Where's dad? What am I doing here? I was just beside him a minute ago." Willy said.

More hooves were approaching.

"Oh there you are dad," Willy said. "Look, I found Will."

"Hi son, you ok?" Demetri said. his voice was quiet and gruff. "How about Willy?"

"Ya," William said. "I'm good, I think. Looks like none of that blood on her is Willies, but we should check anyway. Captain Walker has placed himself and his troops under my care sir."

"Very well Lieutenant," Demtri said. "See to your troops and escort the Arial troops to your camp for now."

William nodded his head and moved to where his troops, still mounted, were waiting.

"Come daughter," Demetri said. "Your mother will be very concerned."

Father and daughter rode off toward the camp on the hill.

"Hassman," William said reaching his troopers. "What's the bill."

William saw two riderless horses standing in their proper positions in the line.

"Hans and Rolf are missing," Hassman said. "They were with us when we first hit the line. I lost track of them after. Probably a few nicks and bruises other wise. We'll know for sure once we get out of this armour."

"Ok," William said. "Gather up these Arial guys and take them to our camp for now. Send a runner to the Major about the prisoners. I'll catch up with you later."

As Hassman issued his orders, William rode up to the two riderless horses, gathered their reins and headed back to the battlefield. Dead, soon to be dead and wounded soldiers, mostly Arial, were strewn about the field. Some in piles two or three feet high. Medics, still in armour were working on some wounded still in place. Others were being transported back to the medical tent in the main camp in the two carts that they had transported along with them.

There were silver armour plated troops lying on the ground with the Arial troops, but not many. Like William, troop mates were looking for and collecting them. The Arial troops stayed where they had fallen.

It didn't take long to find Hans and Rolf. They had fallen not far from each other. Both had helmets that had been split. The man that had killed them lay beside them, an axe in his hand. He had an arrow stuck in a shoulder and a sword had cut him nearly in half.

It took William nearly an hour to drape both men across the saddles of their patient horses and secure the bodies. He mounted his horse and slowly rode back to camp. Willing hands rushed to help unload the bodies. Some took the three horses away, others helped as William began to remove the armour from the men.

Marshack made a comment to William about letting them do it for him. The look he gave her, told every one there to leave him be. Shortly after that, a medical team and an aide from headquarters arrived.

"You are to report to the general Lieutenant," the aide, a captain said.

William did not even look up from what he was doing.

"You run back to the general and tell her when I am finished looking after my troopers I will be there," he said.

"Lieutenant, that's an order!" The aide said.

William stood and pulled the sword from his back.

"I told you," he said. His voice cold and harsh. "I will fucking come when I am finished looking after my troopers. Now fuck off, or I will cut you down where you stand."

Hearing other swords clear their scabbards, the aide looked around and saw at least ten troopers with bared swords making an arc around him. He decided discretion was in order and beat a hasty retreat.

"Sir," one of the medical team said softly. "We can do that for you sir."

William looked over at the medic, a captain, and saw the concern on his face. He scabbarded his sword back behind his back.

"Thank you Captain," William said. "But we've got this. These are our troop mates. Please look to my other troops if you would?"

"What the fuck are you up to now Bekenbaum!" Janet yelled as she rode up, still in her armour. "When the General orders you to report you..."

The words died in her mouth as she saw what they were doing. In a flash, she was down on the ground beside William helping. Once the armour was off, she pulled her water bottle from her belt, ripped a piece of her tunic off from under her armour and wetting it down, began to wash Rolf's face.

William heard her muttering a phrase over and over again and looked at her. Tears were streaming down her cheeks.

"My poor child, my poor child," she kept repeating.

The work finally finished. William stood and looked around himself. The troopers were all gathered around, still in their bloody and some dented armour. Not a sound could be heard. Seeing Janet still on her knees beside the bodies, William bent down. He clapped her on the shoulder and spoke softly into her ear.

"Thanks Janet," William said.

Seeing that she had composed herself now, he stuck out his hand and helped her stand.

"Senior Sergeant," William said. "Form the company, if you please."

"Company C! Front and centre!" Janet bellowed as only she could.

Once the troopers were all in a proper line and at attention, Janet spun around marched up to William, stomped her right foot on the ground and snapped a perfect salute.

"Company C, all present and accounted for Sir!" She bellowed.

William returned her salute just as crisply. Then as he marched toward her, he pulled the sword from his back and laid it on his shoulder. He spun around so he too was facing the two bodies.

"Company C!" He yelled. "Prepare arms!"

Followed by clanks as swords hit armoured shoulders the troopers withdrew their swords from their backs.

"Company! Present arms!"

William and the company brought the swords in front of their faces.

"Company! Salute!" All of them slashed the swords down and to the right in salute.

"Company! Order arms! At ease!"

All the swords were replaced in the scabbards and the troopers assumed parade rest position.

William looked them over. Janet was swallowing repeatedly, keeping her emotions in check. Even the medics were in line along with the two troopers who had brought one of the carts over. William saw that Walker had his men lined up and in formation as well.

"Our brothers fought well," William began. "They died side by side. The brave man who killed them, lay with them. Eagles and Bears do not have a monopoly on bravery, courage and skill brothers and sisters. Captain Walkers company fought hard, and even though out numbered and with inferior weapons to ours, made an impact on the battle."

William came to attention faced Walker and saluted. Walker came to attention and returned the salute.

"When we fight, we fight hard and to win," William continued. "When the fight is over, it is over."

"Those troopers," William pointed at Walker, "Fought well and hard. They suffered wounded and killed comrades like we did. They did not run. They fought hard until they could fight no more. Even then, they were willing to fight, so maybe some could live. They deserve our respect brothers and sisters."

William went down on one knee, the others doing the same.

"Lord in Heaven, we ask you to bless all the fallen and wounded this day. We ask that you console their grieving families. I ask you to console my troopers, young and old, in their grief and anguish in what they had to do today. I ask, any blame to be laid at my door. It was my orders they followed and my plan."

He stayed head bowed for a moment then stood. He turned to the medical captain.

"Captain," William said. "I wonder if the Captain would indulge me and transport my fallen brothers to the medical facility sir?"

The Captain, not knowing how to respond just nodded his head.

"Master Sergeant, deploy some troopers to place our fallen brothers in the cart if you please," William said.

The order did not have to be given. Willing hands were already doing it.

"If the Senior Sergeant would form the troops as an honour guard?" William said. "We will escort our brothers from the field."

"Company C," Janet said in a normal voice. "Divide yourselves equally along each side of the cart. Master Sergeant to form at the rear of the cart."

"If I might suggest sir," Janet said to William quietly. "The medical team to look at the prisoners sir?"

"Shit," William said. "I forgot about that."

"You were a little preoccupied sir," Janet said. "Shit so was I. If I may sir?"

Without waiting, Janet marched over to the medical captain and gave the order. Then marched back.

"Anytime you're ready sir," she said.

William respond by withdrawing his sword, placing it on his shoulder and Janet beside him the same way. Marched to be in front of the horse team drawing the cart. He then began to slow march forward.

"Company A!" Walker yelled as they come abreast of them. "Attention! Present arms!"

All of Walkers men came to attention and saluted as the escorted cart came by them. Seeing what was going on, the camps all along the route lined both sides of the way. All saluting the two fallen troopers.

At the command tent, the whole staff was at attention and saluting, even Willy. Waiting medical staff gently picked the bodies up from the cart and as they moved inside, William had his company make a final salute to their comrades. He put the company at ease and as he scabbarded his sword he looked around and saw every one near, in line and at parade rest.

He looked at Janet and raised his eyebrows. Janet shrugged her shoulders then cringed as she saw the grin on his face.

"Fuck it," William said.

He punched his right fist in the air.

"Who are we!" He yelled.

He got a ragged response from his troopers. Janet dug a finger into one of her ears.

"Something wrong with my ear LT?" She yelled. "I can't hear a bloody thing!"

"Who are we!" William yelled again.

"Maggies Eagles!"

"What are we born to do?"

"Kick butts!"

"What did we just do?"

"Kicked some butts!"

William spun around so he was facing his mother and punched his fist in the air.

"Magies Eagles! Magies Eagles! Magies Eagles!"

Janet was also yelling at the top of her lungs, punching her fist in the air. Margarete was standing, her head down and face red. Even the command staff were yelling now. The whole camp was screaming now.

William clapped Janet on the shoulder.

"My work here is done," he said. "See ya when I see ya Janet."

"Come on you bums! Time to go! And one of you yahoos better have some decent booze!" William yelled.

Unlike like how they had arrived, formally marching. The company resembled a gaggle of young people coming home from a football game they had just won. Arms around shoulders, pushing and shoving, making jokes to each other.

Chapter Eight

Margarete had just returned to the command tent from a fast cleanup in the communal bath house tent. She felt somewhat like a normal human being again. A clean uniform on and washed up.

As she had expected, a harried communications tech was waiting for her, along with the medical commander and the regiments colonel.

She heard the medical report first. Five wounded, two severely, not including Demetri, Charles, Greta and Willy. Those four were having their older wounds redressed. Over one hundred enemy wounded were being treated.

The colonel reported three dead, including Williams two. Fifty wounded horses, none severely. Three thousand arrows had been expended. Stocks had been replenished and teams were out retrieving usable arrows and or heads from the battle field. Minor damage, dents and such to horse and trooper armour. Easily repairable. The one thousand lances used in the attack had been replaced from stock on hand and the same teams retrieving arrows, would retrieve lances.

Several urgent requests for communications had been received, as expected. The Emir, the Federation ambassador to Oaken, a crown official from Arial. Two more transports from Oaken would be arriving this evening with two more battalions of Eagles on board and more supplies.

"First," Margarete said. "Keep me posted on the wounded. Send some troopers to retrieve any usable vehicles from the field. Have some one bring Walker here. Have the Emir message me ASAP and patch it right to me. As far as the Arial people and the Federation, schedule a conference call for two hours from now. I will have orders for the two transport captains as soon as they are in comm range.

"If nothing else, head back to it. Colonel, inform your company commands to expect movement orders tonight."

The room had barely cleared, when Margarete's comm unit announced Bashir's call.

"Good day Emir," Margarete said. "You have questions?"

"Your Majesty," Bashir said. "What the hell is going on? The Federation is up in arms. Arial is furious and have expelled our ambassador and recalled their own. We are on the verge of war ma-am. We have been trying to contact His Majesty, but so far are unable to do so."

"I have scheduled a conference call with the Federation and Arial in two hours Bashir," Margarete said. "Ten days ago, Arial launched an assassination raid against Demetri and his party. That raid was defeated, by Demetri and party. He then used the Arial transport to return to Arial and begin recon. All this happened before we knew anything about it.

"Once we did find out, we verified where the attack had come from and began making plans for a retribution raid. Which we have now begun."

"Why that is totally unacceptable!" Bashire blurted out. "I shall convene the full council and have a declaration of war against Arial declared immediately!"

"No Bashire," Margarete said. "This is a personal matter only. By this evening, we will have three full battalions of Eagles on planet and tomorrow, we begin operations. With more transports, we can have all ten thousand Eagles from the Queens Guard and ten thousand Kings Own Regiment on planet within the week. That will be enough."

"But Marg," Bashir said. "An attack on yourselves is an attack on all of us. Please, we must declare war."

"No Bashir," Margarete said. "Under no circumstances is Oaken, as a whole, to become involved. As the heads of state, we will use our power to requisition any transport capability you have, no matter how small, for the duration of hostilities. But not as many as would restrict trade to much. Full cessation of trading with Arial would be nice. We will likely have a blockade initiated as well from us only."

"Demetri and the rest? The wounds are not severe?" Bashir asked.

"Bad enough," Margarete said. "Luckily Greta was there, but things are well in hand. The worst were Demeti, bad throat wound, he can barely talk, and Willa, who now has a shaved head on one side. But then, you know those Bekenbaum's and Charles. They could be half dead and nobody would notice."

"I will discuss your orders with the council at the meeting." Bashir said. "But, if Arial declares war on Oaken, we will be all in. Your Majesty."

"Very well Emir, have a good rest of the day," Margarete said and signed off.

At that point, Demetri, Greta and Willa arrived. All freshly cleaned up and in new uniforms. Margarete, first rushed Willa. Gave her a long hug then put her at arms length and surveyed the damage. Finally drawing her close once again and kissing the wound on the shaved head.

Next was Greta who got the hug and a kiss on the cheek. Demetri got a shake of a finger for his troubles. He grinned.

"I suppose Janet and Charles have disappeared?" Margarete asked.

Greta laughed, Demitri tried, but ended up coughing and Willa looked confused.

"Right," Margarete said. "Conference call with the Federation, the Arial palace and us in an hour and a half. Can you take the call Dem, or should I handle it?"

"You had better," Dimitri croaked out.

"I have Walker coming," Margarete said. "His gang did well. I will give them the option of joining us or not."

Demitri nodded his head.

"Got any decent booze around here?" Greta asked. "All we have been swilling is that awful Arial junk."

Margarete opened her mouth to yell for Helga, who appeared with a tray. Two bottles and several mugs were on it. She had removed her armour, but was still wearing the uniform she had worn under it.

"Well, well," Helga said. "Back from holiday, all prim and proper and clambering for booze. While the rest of us, slave like dogs."

"You can leave us be Helga," Margarete said. "Go get cleaned up."

"Nah Mags," Helga said. "Let the troopers finish first eh?"

"Took you guys long enough to get here," Greta said as Helga left.

"First, we didn't find out you guys were missing until Will came back," Margarete said. "Then we had to figure out what had happened and where you were. It wasn't until we discovered what you had done at the cache that we even knew you were alive. A little heads up would have been nice."

"No...time...comms dark," Dimitri managed to get out. "Worked..no?"

Margarete nodded her head. She was having trouble keeping herself in check, but knew she had to.

"Then, some idiot in the Emir's transportation department grabbed all of our armed transports for trade. Three were on their way back, we grabbed the first one. But it took time to convert it to carry the whole Queens Guard. The other two should be here this evening. Your man should be with them Grets.

"Bashir wanted to declare war. I told him no, this is personal. But requisitioned any transports he could give us without damaging trade. I also placed an embargo on trade with Arial and will have one of the incoming transports enforce a blockade. After they take out some more infrastructure that is.

"By the end of the week, all of the Queens Guard and most of the Kings Own should be on the ground. More info later."

Maragetes comm unit beeped and the comms officer said the conference call would be beginning shortly and that he would beam it to the big screen in her command tent.

First the Federation Ambassador appeared on one side of the split screen, followed almost immediately by the Arial official. The Arial official was furious and started right in.

"What is the meaning of this unprovoked attack on Arial!" He demanded. "We demand you depart immediately! We demand the Federation sanction Oaken and put Peace Keepers in place immediately!"

"Unless Your Majesties can provided just cause," the Federation ambassador said calmly, although he looked anything but calm. "We of course will have no choice but to impose severe sanctions on Oaken."

"What is being broad casted to both of you now, is the trajectory of armed transport serial number 865924 from Arial to a location on Oaken. It stayed at that location for roughly two hours. It then moved to the next location on Oaken. Once again, staying in place for roughly two hours. It then returned back to a remote location on Arial."

Margarete let the two men observe the telemetry diagram for a moment.

"At the first location," Margarete continued. "His Majesty Dimitri, Her Royal Highness Princess Willa, Her Highness Grand Duchess Greta and family friend, Baron Charles of the Prairie Clans were on holiday. Unarmed, but for some hunting knives and camp axes.

"Upon our investigation a week later, we found evidence of a battle that had occurred at the first location, including blood stains and drag marks made by bodies. At the second location, we found the graves of the dead. All twelve of the assault force and all eight transport crew had been killed.

"I believe we have shown enough evidence Mr Ambassador, that Oaken did not precipitate this action. Rather, Arial did."

Again, Margarete gave the two officials a few moments to digest the attached photos of the two scenes. The Federation Ambassador made to speak, Margarete put up her hand to stop him.

"Other evidence is being sent to the Federation Security Council that shows, the orders came directly from the Emperors court. It was planned and trained for well in advance," Margarete said.

"As far as the People of Oaken and the Planet of Oaken are concerned, this is a personal matter between two rulers. The people and planet of Oaken will not take part.

"Now, Mr. Minister of Defence. Three Eagles and one untrained teenaged girl, defeated your well trained and equipped assault force. With nothing but hunting knives and camp axes. Yesterday, our one armed transport, rendered your military transport facility useless. Today my under strength Queens Guard Battalion completely wiped out three of your battalions.

"Tomorrow, two more of the Queens Guard battalions will arrive. Only the house hold personal troops of the Kings Own Regiment and the Queens Guard regiment, will be employed. You have the rest of today and all of tomorrow Mr. Defence Minister.

"We require a full, personal apology from the Emperor and reparations of costs incurred by then. If not, we begin armed operations all through this part of Arial.

"Take a good look at His Majesty, Her Royal Highness and Her Highness standing behind me. This is what you have done to the Royal family of Oaken. You can expect no less from us. Good day."

Maragrete, killed the transmission at that point and took a deep breath. Then she was in Dimitris' arms. Greta grabbed Willa by the arm and took her outside.

"Come on Willy," Greta said. "Let's go find your brother and get some peace and quiet eh?"

"Gather around every one," William said.

He had just come back from the company commanders meeting and things for he, and Company C were changing. He waited untill everyone was settled in and began his briefing.

"The Colonel is extremely happy with our performance today," William began. "He has put us in for a unit citation, and in any case, the unit has been mentioned in a battalion and royal dispatch. He didn't tell me who, but several individual mention in dispatches were also included. Don't thank me, I was to damn busy trying to stay alive to see anything, just like you guys. But somebody noticed.

"That's the good news.

"We have the rest of today to celebrate. At some point this evening or night, two battalions of reserve Queens Guard will be arriving. They are short of people that do what we do. As a result, three sections of you will be split from us to join three of their sections. They are all active reserve troopers, so it shouldn't be to bad for you guys.

"By scrounging available bodies, regiment was able to come up with a section of qualified inactive reservists. They will be slotted in with my section. We are still two troopers short of a full compliment, the colonel assures me replacements will be here before we deploy.

"I was not informed on where, or who with, you will be sent to. Nor where our deployment areas will be. Just to be ready to commence operations day after tomorrow.

"Enjoy the night. It will most likely be the last time off for a while."

Everyone but Hassman, split away into their sections and fire teams. Hassman stayed with William and proffered a tin mug. The coffee in it was heavily laced with vodka.

"Inactive reservists eh?" Hassman said. "That is going to be fun. Not."

William grimaced as he took a draft of the coffee. He was still getting used to booze. He shrugged his shoulders.

"They cut it or they don't," William said. "I, we, don't have time to play pissy seniority BS games. Colonel says I am Company CO and you are Company Sergeant. They don't like it? Tough shit. They all are Eagles."

"Who are you pissing off now Nephew?" Greta said as she and Willa walked up. "I hear you got shit and had to apologize for telling Janet off."

Hassman jumped to his feet, came to attention, clicked his heels and bowed his head.

"Your Royal Highness, Your Highness," Hassman said to Willa and Greta in order of ranking.

"Get off the high horse Hassman," Greta said. "We've known each other for twenty years. Willy here is not even a probie yet. Candidate yes. I have the price of admission."

Greta held up a bottle of clear fluid.

"Guess the reservists are short of Recon troops," Hassman said. "Splitting us up. Three sections to the Reservists. They are giving us a section of Inactive Reservists."

"That should be fun," Greta said filling up her tin mug. "Bunch of out of practice, overage and grumpy old timers. Who's the boss?"

"LT is the company CO Grets, I'm company sergeant." Hassman said.

"You do know telling the Senior Sergeant, any Senior Sergeant to go fuck them selves is not a career enhancing move," Greta said.

"Ya well," William said. "She was out of line and issued me orders. It's all straightened out."

"She was worried about Charles and us and you," Greta said. "She doesn't have any kids of her own. You and Willy are like her own children. All of you young troopers are."

"Ya," William said looking at the ground. "She took my two KIA real hard."

"Tough fight for a first one," Greta said.

She too was looking at the ground. Then she glanced over at Willy, who was looking all around her at the camp and the troopers, not much older than she with awe.

"Hassman," Greta said. "Why don't you introduce Willy to your section? Just no Your Royal Highness shit eh? She is after all, barely a Candidate."

Greta stood and opened her arms.

"Come give your old aunt a hug eh nephew?" She said quietly.

"You ok hun?" She whispered.

"Dunno yet," William said, releasing her from the hard hug. "Happened to damn fast. I heard the change in tone of the battle, saw what was going on and yelled follow me. After that? Just trying to stay alive."

"Sit," Greta said. "The action took just short of four hours Will. You guys saved a lot of lives today."

They both sat quietly for some seconds.

"I am going to ask you a favour," Greta said. "On Oaken, Willy killed four troopers on her own Will. She stood above your father when he went down and killed anyone who came near. All on instinct. Just like today. She emptied her quivers, almost broke her sword and was using that camping hatchet of hers at the end. It's all instinct. She has no discipline and will get herself and any team mates killed if she doesn't learn."

"Ya, I saw that," Will said. "She was charging Walkers gang by herself. I was able to stop her and calm her down. She didn't even know where she was, or what she had been doing."

"She has the heart and the instinct," Greta said. "Things that cannot be taught. You are two troopers short. I would like her to be one of the replacements. Hassman knows how to handle people like her and she listens to you."

"I dunno..." William said. "Mom might have a bird."

"Mom might have a bird about what Will?" Margarete said.

She and Dimitri were walking up and she had caught the last words.

Greta repeated what she had just said to William. Margarete's face turned ashen.

"No," she almost whispered. "No damn way!"

"Y..e..s..my..love," Dimitri said. "It..must be."

Margarete looked up at him and saw how much it was costing him to speak.

"She...save...our lives...We...owe her." He said.

Margaret looked from Dimitri to Greta and back. Then to William.

"Up to you Will," Margarete said. "Your sections area is the furthest away and far from any support."

William sat looking at the ground for a moment.

"Ok," he said. "I'll take her. As a candidate. Give her the choice though and let her know what being a candidate means."

William had to get away, he needed time to get his emotions under control. To much was happening to fast. He quickly stood and strode away.. He found a nice quiet spot away from the camp and overlooking the stream. He lost himself on his thoughts. What could he have done differently so his men would not have died. How was he going to face up to his troops, knowing they knew he had killed two of their friends.

He was so lost in his thoughts, he had not heard the arrival of the new transports. He felt a hand touch him gently on the shoulder and he startled himself back into reality. He heard his father chuckle softly and felt his rough hand ruffle through his hair on his head.

"Much wool you gather," Dimitri said. "Not so good this close to end of battle. Could be bad guy hide in bush."

His father sat beside him and the both of them looked out over the stream at the forrest beyond.

"My first time," Dimitri said. "I lost twenty. Most friends, knew all the others. Reading and studying books is one thing. Actually doing it, something else again."

"I keep wondering," William said. "What could I have done differently. Why them and not me?"

"Because it was their time Will," Dimitri said. "I had seen the same thing you had and we were heading the same way. But then, there you were, doing what needed doing. They may have turned your mothers flank Will. Walker has trained his men well. We still would have won, but paid a heavy cost for it."

The babbling of the stream had masked the approach of Greta, unnoticed until she spoke.

"They need you back at command Dem," she said.

Dimitri chuckled.

"Gave Will shit for wool gathering," Dimitri said. "Loose the ruler and an heir all in one shot."

He clapped Will on the shoulder and stood, then quickly walked back in the direction of the camp.

Greta took his place, sitting beside Will.

"I was only four, when the Holy Warriors attacked our home," she began softly. "Dem had grabbed me and carried me away into the tall crops. He pushed me down, I couldn't see anything, but I heard it. The screams, the angry below of my father, the scream of anger from my mother."

"Demetri had seen it all. Our father had killed three of them, mother one, before they themselves were killed. My older sister died, an axe in her hand charging three of them. My brother, a shovel over his head, had already laid two out when he was hit by four shots.

"Dimitri told me this on the transport to Home Wold after the Holy Warriors had found us. They almost killed him too, he was fighting so hard. I remember biting at least one."

Both aunt and nephew sat quietly for some minutes.

"Then your father found those books and computer records," she said. "And I knew right away, why we had fought so hard that day. It is because of who we are. We come from a long, long, line of warriors Will. It is on our DNA.

"I don't like to kill, but I will when I must. Your father and mother, most of us, are the same. These people here? They have no flippen idea what they have just done. Now we are extremely upset."

"Like mom said," William continued for her. "You have pissed off the Eagles and the Bears. God may have pity on you. We will have none.

"What they did to you Aunty, and Charles and Dad and especially Willy? Anybody with a weapon in front of me dies!"

William stood and held his hand out to help his Aunt stand. The both of them took one last look at the forrest beyond, then, together, walked back to their responsibilities back at camp.

Dimitri arrived back at Williams camp and walked up to Hassman, who was chatting with two troopers.

"He's blaming himself for his two KIA," Dimitri said loud enough for the two troopers to hear.

"No way!" One of the troopers blurted out. "Clark got himself cut off and Jones went in to help him. I saw it all...um..Your Majesty sir. Jones forgot our training sir. We lost two instead of one."

"Yes, I see," Dimitri said. Dimitri nodded his head and walked quietly away.

The troopers in the section gathered around as Dimitri left and the trooper clued them into what had just happened. This was the sight that greeted William and Greta when they arrived. The troopers quieted down, made a line and Hassman saluted. Greta returned it.

"Permission to speak ma-am?" Marshak asked. Greta nodded her head.

"LT, no way were you responsible for killing Clark and Jones," Marshak said. "Clark got himself cut off and Jones went in to help him. Karl saw it all LT. Shit, Clark was a dead man already, and Jones made it two. We all know, during an attack, you don't stop to help your buddy. Sir, Ma-am."

"Regardless," Greta said. "Jones and Clark did their jobs. They, and you are mentioned in dispatches and Her Majesty has recommended a unit citation for C Company."

"Shit Ma-am," Karl said. "What about the LT and Hassman Ma-am? They both deserve awards Ma-am. The LT was in the thickest fighting, Sarge was everywhere doing what he does Ma-am. I never seen the like of it Ma-am. Was both of them that gave us the courage Ma-am."

"Sergeant Hassman has been promoted to Company Sergeant," Greta said. "And has been recommended for a medal. Lieutenant Bekenbaum has been promoted to brevet Captain."

"But Ma-am?" Karl said.

"Never mind Karl," William said. "I have the wrong last name is all. Goes with the territory. Thank you for the support guys. That's all that really matters.

"So, where is our new green candidate?"

Marshak pointed to the left and William saw Willa dumping a pile of gear on the ground. Then she walked the pack horse that had brought it all to the horse lines, unsaddled it and began grooming it.

"Pay back time," William said.

He had a huge grin on his face as he walked toward where Willa was. The rest of the section started to laugh.

"Who gave this section permission to laugh and skylark?" Janet said walking up, the huge Charles by her side.

Hassman pointed over at William walking up to where Willa was. He changed his saunter to a stiff march and wiped the grin off his face. Janet was about to yell something. William beat her to it.

"Who the hell dropped all of my expensive equipment all over the ground!" William yelled.

Willa had just finished grooming the horse and started walking back to where William was now standing over her pile of gear. She smiled and came rushing over.

"This your gear candidate?" William yelled. "You think mommy is going to come running over and put it all away for you? Get that Goddamned grin off your face! Stand at attention Candidate!"

"But.." Willa began.

"If God wanted a Candidate to talk, God would not have given the Candidate an officer and a sergeant Candidate!"

Willa, having gone through cadet training knew what to do and was standing at rigid attention, her eyes above Williams head.

"Who the hell left all of Her Majesties expensive equipment laying on the ground!" Janet bellowed as she walked up. "What the hell are you teaching these people Captain! This is not how the Queens Guard treats Her Majesties equipment Captain!"

Janet was now nose to nose with William, who was looking directly in her eyes not above her head.

"The candidate is newly arrived Senior Sergeant," William said, loud but not shouting. "I was giving the candidate her instructions before you interrupted me Senior Sergeant."

"This how you treat your shit at home candidate?" Janet now gave her full attention to Willa, standing with her nose almost touching Willas.

"Well mommy and daddy are not here to wipe the little princesses nose for her! Drop and give me twenty Candidate!"

Both William and Janet watched Willa punch out her pushups and come to attention.

"Getting a little soft eh Senior Sergeant," a gruff voice said.

Charles, a major came up and gave Willa the once over.

"Goddamned rookie Candidates," Charles said. "Better you than me Captain. If the Senior Sergeant has the time. I could use your expertise."

"Yes sir!" Janet said. "At your service sir!"

"Hassman!" William yelled. "Get this damn candidate sorted out! Now!"

William, Janet and Charles turned and walked away. A stunned Willa dropped to her knees and began gathering her gear only to stand and come to attention once again as Hassman came up and started harassing her.

"A little fun is good," Janet said. "Don't go over board."

"Nah, no time," William said. "I'll put her with Marshak. She's a smart ass but has a heart of gold and tougher than nails."

"Kinda like somebody else I know," Charles grumbled and chuckled. "Yes sir, at your service sir."

"Ah shit," William said.

He had just seen the new section setting up next to his. All of them in their late thirties or early forties. All dressed in pristine uniforms, gear all shinny and spotless. Tents all in a line and clean.

"I've served with most of them," Janet said. "Good people. Give them a chance Will."

William nodded his head and walked toward his tent. Janet heard him muttering to himself.

'No time for this BS,' she heard his mutter.

"What you fucking looking at LT!" Charles growled. There was no reason for the section to have a lieutenant, nor the sergeant they had with them. Both were Eagles, but had always been staff Eagles, not combat and especially not elite scout Eagles.

Then Charles saw a major approaching and swore.

"Just gets better and better, somebody really screwed the pooch here," Charles said.

He and Janet hurried away before they would have to talk with the Major.

"Major coming up," Karl a corporal said at Williams tent flap. "He's inspecting the new guys."

"Right," William said from inside the tent. "Get the gang ready then."

William came out of his tent and placed his beret on his head. Not in the normal cocked to the back of his head, but down over his eyebrows. The rest of the section saw this and did the same. Willa still had the beat up one on her head she had arrived with, Marshak quickly whispered into her ear and Willa brought it down from the crown of her head to match the others.

"Fall them in Hassman," William said as the Major, accompanied by the new lieutenant and sergeant headed their way.

The section, was all at attention when the Major arrived. William snapped out a parade ground salute and held it. The gesture was unnoticed by the Major, who just as smartly retuned it. And just that fast, the section knew this was a rear echelon officer, with little field time.

"First Section, First Platoon, C company, all present or accounted for sir!" William barked out.

"Where is your second section Captain?" The Major asked. "Or, the rest of your company?"

"Sir," William said. "We were an undermanned company sir! My other three sections have been redeployed sir. I am awaiting the arrival of my new section sir. I have received one replacement for my section sir and am awaiting the second sir."

The Major made his way down the line of troopers and stopped in front of Willa. He had a look of disgust on his face. Then he looked over the camp and became angry.

"I'm putting you on report Captain!" the Major said. "I am going to recommend you be relieved of command and the lieutenant here put in your place. The same with your sergeant. These troopers are not in ship shape nor is this camp! I want to see these troopers in proper uniform and this camp in shape when I inspect it in the morning or more heads will roll!"

The new lieutenant had a smirk on his face as he made a sloppy salute to William.

"Attention," William said in a normal voice.

The sergeant caught the look on Williams face and came to attention. The lieutenant did not.

"We do not salute in the field *Leftenant*," William continued. "And if you had spent more than five minutes in the field you would have known that. Now, run along back to your section. I will be along shortly to do an inspection."

"Marshak!" William said addressing his section. "Get the damn candidate Bahr kitted out so she don't embarrass us any more eh? Company Sergeant with me, Master Corporal, you are in charge. Dismissed."

"Ut oh" William heard Karl say as he and Hassman walk away. "Some rear echelon fucks are gonna get their asses handed to them.

What the fuck are you smirking at candidate? Get this fucking candidate clued in Marshak!"

The lieutenant had his section in line and at attention when William and Hassman arrived. None had weapons with them.

"Did I not say I was going to inspect this section Company Sergeant?" William asked as he walked up the at attention line of troopers.

"Yes sir, you did sir," Hassman said.

"Why is my second section in line for inspection with out weapons lieutenant?" William said. "Fucking now *Leftenant!*"

Troopers broke and dashed into tents, returning, buckling swords over backs, bows in hand. They resumed their line.

One by one, William had each trooper present their sword and bow for his inspection. Once done, he, with Hassman beside him stood in front of the still at attention section.

"Pretty," William said. "Don't you think so Company Sergeant?"

"Pretty disgusting," Hassman growled.

"All your swords are good for is clubs!" William said. "Not fucking one of them is sharp! Your bow strings are worn out and unless. Now, I don't know any of you from shit, so if you wanna die, go for it! I lost two already today. Ten more is no skin off my ass! We are not on parade here people, we are at war! Those fucking kids over there? Today they fought in a major battle and survived! I don't give a shit how pretty you are or how shinny your swords are! You are all Eagles, Recon Eagles! Start acting like it or you are all going to die!

"Fucking pretend fucking soldiers! Dismissed!"

"Uh Cap?" Hassman said as they walked away. "The blond at the end of the line? She is Jones' mom."

"Fuck!" William said.

He spun around and with Hassman at his heels walked back to the now rushing back in line section.

"As you were," William said in his normal voice. "Master Corporal Jones, a moment of your time?"

He walked to the open space between the two sections camps and a little behind. Hassman was with him. The new Lieutenant accompanied Jones.

"Leftenant, your presence is not wanted and what I have to say to the Master Corporal is personal and private. So get the fuck lost!"

William turned his back and Hassman heard him take a deep breath. When he turned around, the Master Corporal saw the look of grief on his face and began to shake.

"Master Corporal Jones," William said. "I'm so sorry. I have killed your son this morning ma-am."

She took it calmly.

"And the other?" She asked.

"Trooper Clark, Master Corporal," William said.

"His father is with one of the assault companies Captain," she whispered.

"Thank you Master Corporal Jones. I will inform him ma-am. You are dismissed master corporal. And ma-am, anything you need ma-am, let myself or Hassman here know right?"

"Yes Captain, thank you sir," she said.

She slowly made her way back to her tent went inside, and they heard her shriek her anguish.

"Fuck, fuck fuck," William kept saying all the way back to his tent. "Find out where Clark's dad is for me Hassman."

William steeled himself as he came to the company command tent of the B company reserve unit. An older Major was conferring with one of his captains and saw William arrive.

"Excuse me sir," William said. "If I may have a moment of the Majors time sir?"

"Carry on Captain," the Major said to William. "I have no secrets from my officers in this company, Captain."

"Yes sir," William said. "I regret to inform you Major Clark, that this morning, I was responsible for the death of your son sir."

"That's not the way I heard it Captain Bekenbaum," Clark said. "But thank you just the same. I lost my son, but your actions saved many other sons and daughters Bekenbaum. I, we, all thank you Captain. His mother has been informed. And Captain? Keep up the good work. We are counting on you Recon guys."

When William arrived back at his camp, he saw the new replacement had arrived. He was an older trooper that should have been at least a Master Corporal, not a common trooper. Supper was being dished out and the new man, after glaring at William, made sure he sat down beside Willa, elbowing has way between her and Marshak. He kept elbowing Willa as he ate.

Hassman was about to put an end to it. William put his hand on his shoulder.

"Let it play out," he said. "She's tougher than she looks."

Not getting any response from Willa, the new man reached over, took her mug, took a deep drink, spit in it and put it back. Willa exploded. The man was soon fighting for his life as Willa had him on the ground, her right hand on his neck, her left coming down with her hunting knife to cut his throat.

William grabbed Willa's knife hand and held it high. Then he wrapped her up in a tight bear hug and pulled her feet off the ground.

"Easy Willa, Easy," he whispered into her ear. "It's all good Willa. I'm here."

Like a switch had been tripped. Willa calmed down, she looked up and saw the knife in her hand held away from her head and the confusion around her. Including the now stunned man on the ground. He was rubbing his throat with one hand and scrabbling away with the other.

"Lesson learned I hope?" William said. "The candidate here killed at least half dozen men this morning and god only knows how many when she was with His Majesty the last couple of weeks. She also killed four more, with that same knife in her hand and the hand axe she carries, saving His Majesty's life the day of the ambush. That's why she is here dummies. Maybe you can learn something. But I doubt it.

"Hassman, get that new guy and report eh?"

"You dumb fucks!" Hassman blowed out. "The only fighting we do in this section is killing the fucking enemy, not each other! You don't need to go around provoking a fight asshole! This ain't on planet in barracks! Get your ass up!"

"Sir! Reporting as ordered sir," Hassman said coming to attention and stomping his foot in the ground.

William held his hand out. Hassman gave a scabbarded sword to him. It was the new mans. William took it out. The hilt was worn, but with new padding on the handle. The blade was not shining, but very clean and the edge was very, very sharp. He put it back in the scabbard and handed it back to the man.

"If you try more of that shit," William said. "If one of my troopers don't kill you, I will. Now get the fuck out of my sight."

Hassman took the man outside and around the corner. He spun him around.

"You dumb fuck Hans!" He said. "Your fucking lucky the Cap pulled her off you. She would have killed you, no question about it. She had you by the balls man. Fuck me. What the fuck were you thinking? These kids are the best of the best of the best Hans. The best I have ever seen. They will let you live. This time Hans. Don't ever fucking try that again. The candidate is with us, one, because we need her, two, to get her so she doesn't loose it all the time when she gets like that.

"Now, fuck off and try and fit in right?"

"Sorry Cal," Hans said. "Won't happen again. That new LT and Sergeant are trouble Cal."

"Not for long Hans, not for long. They have no idea who they are fucking with."

"The candidate apologizes for her behaviour Company Sergeant," Willa said at attention in front of Hassman. "No excuses Company Sergeant."

"See Hans," Hassman said. "The candidate is apologizing. Not like you. Drop and give me ten Candidate. I should make you do a hundred Hans. Letting a dumb female candidate kick your ass. Elite Recon Eagle my ass."

"But Sarge, I is jet lagged Sarge," Hans said. "Cooped up in that damn transport for three days with all them rear echelon reserve fucks Sarge. Gimme a break Sarge. I'd apologize to the Candidate Sarge, but she is after all only a Candidate and as such.."

"To low on the totem polite to even recognize," both men said at the same time.

Both of them laughed.

"Right you guys," Hassman said. "Me and Hans go way back. He ain't much for spit and polish, but...man can he fight. The Cap just chewed his ass out good. 'Nuff said. Just don't let that shit happen again."

Hassman turned and walked back toward Williams tent. Hans reached a hand down to Willa and helped her stand.

"Sorry kid," he said shocking everyone, including Willa. "Been in garrison to long. Forgot I was coming to a line outfit. Sorry guys, won't happen again. Now fuck off like a good candidate eh? Kid."

"Cap?" Hassman said outside William's tent. He came in once William gave him permission.

"That guy going to be a problem Hassman," William asked.

"Nah," Hassman said. "Well, maybe for a bit. Till he fits in. Shouldn't take long. Your kids know their shit and now he knows it sir. I clued him in."

"Let them have the night Hassman," William said. "You stay behind when I leave for the meeting. I'll clue you in after. Everyone, including the new section, ready to leave the minute I get back. Minimum of two weeks rations. You keep an eye on the new guys until I find one of them good enough to be in charge. The sergeant and Lieutenant will not be returning from the meeting."

"Thank Christ," Hassman said. "You sure about that Cap?"

"Sometimes my last name comes in handy Hassman," William said.

Chapter Nine

William waited until the other sections lieutenant and sergeant had left for the meeting, then went over to his new section. They saw him coming and formed up. Most of them had been busy restringing bows and sharpening swords.

"Who's in charge?" William asked.

"Uh...I guess I am," Jones said. "Nobody told us Captain."

"Right, at ease you dumb fucks," William said. "We ain't on parade for all the Aunties and Grandmas's here."

"We begin operations in two days," he continued after letting them chuckle for a moment. "It's two days travel to our area of operations. That means we leave the second I return from the meeting. You going to be ok Master Corporal Jones? I can have you reassigned if you need it."

Jones came to attention and stomped her right foot into the ground.

"No sir! These fucks are about to find out that pay back is a bitch and I am the meanest bitch on this planet! Sir!" She belted out.

"Very well Master Corporal," William said. "Just don't let the Senior Sergeant hear what you just said eh?"

"Who Janet?" Jones said. "She's just a pussy. Ya you Senior Sergeant, you heard me!"

"I love you too Jones," Janet said as she walked away. "You make sure and take good care of my orphans eh? Sorry about Jimmy, Candice."

"Your in charge, Master Corporal," William said. "Two weeks rations. Coordinate with the Company Sergeant. You snooze, you loose gang. Keep up or get left behind."

"Fuck," William heard somebody say behind his back. "He's worse than his old man."

"Sir," the new Major that had chastised William said as the assembled meeting came to order. "I am putting the Captain of Company C on report for dereliction of duty and recommending he be demoted to his true rank of lieutenant and reassigned to a line company Colonel."

"Is that so," the female Colonel said. "What do you have to say for your self Captain?"

"Ma-am," William said standing. "Unfortunately, when the Major arrived for his unannounced inspection, my troopers were just reequipping after the battle ma-am. We had just received one of our replacements, a new green candidate ma-am, and she had not had time to change into uniform ma-am. I had not been informed that my new section had arrived, nor had their lieutenant reported to me as yet ma-am. The Major also informed me that my Company Sergeant was to be reassigned ma-am."

"Really," the Colonel said. "Your reasons Major?"

"The Brevet Captain was obviously promoted because of need ma-am," the Major said. "The other lieutenant is senior in time of grade ma-am, thus he should be in command ma-am. As well, the Company Sergeant obviously does not know what he is doing ma-am."

"Let me get this straight," the Colonel said. "The Captain, who graduated at the top of his class and ambushed the Queen and her guards before we deployed. Then, yesterday, personally saved the battalions ass, loosing two of his men while doing so and a veteran Company Sergeant with over twenty years of experience should be replaced with people who know nothing but how to shuffle papers, should both be removed from their positions?

"Bullshit Major! Get your ass out of this tent and take that lieutenant and sergeant with you. We will talk after the meeting! All three of you! Get!"

"Captain Bekenbaum, I have been told you have already been briefed?"

"Yes ma-am," William said. "My troopers will be ready to depart when I arrive back at my camp ma-am."

"No rush Captain," the Colonel said. "We have two days."

"With respect ma-am," William said. "I am not sure of your orders ma-am. Mine are that I am to begin operations in two days ma-am. It will take me two days to reach my area of operations ma-am. I have to leave right now."

"What??" The Colonel said. "Let me see those orders Major!"

"Shit! Captain Bekenbaum is correct! Get your people ready to deploy, right now! Someone will be along to give you your areas of operation right away. God Damn it! Have that fucking Major and his two cronies put on the transports back to Oaken, in the god damned brig!"

Officers burst out of the command tent rushing to their commands. Janet took William aside.

"You take care eh?" She said. "Look after my orphans as best you can. Your new section are good people. Rusty but good."

"Ya," William said. "You too Aunty. See ya when I see ya. If we couldn't take a joke..."

"We shouldn't have joined," Janet finished for him.

The reservists part of the camp was a beehive. Officers and sergeants yelling orders. The Regulars were in, organized fashion, getting ready. All except Williams platoon. Their camp was taken down, gear packed away in horse packs or saddle bags. All was in readiness. Both sections were grouped together.

William waved his arms to gather them around. He passed a map to Hassman and another to Jones.

"Master Corporal Jones is now section two CO," he said. "We have two days travel to our area of operations and we begin operations in two days. By that time. I want every trooper to have committed to memory those maps.

"On the way, we by pass the bad guys as much as possible. They get in our way? Well, sometimes shit happens eh? Unless a civilian shoots at us, we let them be. Hassman, give the pennant to the new guy. Maybe he'll behave then."

His briefing finished, William walked to where his four horses were waiting. Jumped on one without a saddle and waited. The troopers mounted the same as he, bare back. They lined up, their spare horses beside them. Hans had their colours, a miniature version of the battalion colours, in a small stirrup on the outside of his right stirrup that normally held their lances just before a charge. The colour was still in its leather covering.

"Colour unfurled," William ordered. "Platoon, in pairs, prepare to march! March!"

William at their head, Hans and the colour beside him, led them off. In pairs, their spare horses beside them or behind them. The platoon formed the line of march they would be using from now on.

Now Willa fit right in. Her well worn field uniform and battered beret, not that out of place from the rest of the platoons. Swords across their backs, two quivers of ten arrows on each saddle horses flanks. Saddle horses to the right of each trooper. Pack horses with four lances and ten quivers of arrows on top of panniers. The spare un saddled horse beside the pack horse.

The platoon was the first on the move and every eye in camp followed them as they walked toward the east side of the camp. A group of officers was gathered out side the main command tent.

"Company C!" William yelled as they came up to the command tent.

"Eyes Right!" He grabbed the sword from his back and slashed it to the side. Hans lowered the colours in the direction of the Queen and King.

As each row came abreast of the now at attention and saluting command group, they snapped their heads sharply to the right until they past the last officer standing in line, then snapped them right forward again.

The last trooper let out a whistle as they past the last officer.

"Who are We!" William yelled out.

"Magies Eagles!" Section one yelled back.

"Janet's Orphans, Janet's Orphan's!" William began to chant.

Soon, both sections were chanting it. William began their regimental song and brought them to a canter. The die had been cast, the example had been set. As each new Recon troop left camp, the three sections from Williams old platoon made the same chant.

"Fuck me," Janet said wiping a tear from her eye. "Those fucking kids."

They had bypassed four towns on the way and were now bedding down outside the fifth. The one they would hit in the morning. The reservists were rediscovering muscles they had forgotten they had. Thighs were not quite as sore on the second day. The first section kept their silence, for the most part. Once in a while one of them couldn't help themselves and would let a chuckle escape.

Once they saw Hans was acting like a normal person, they even made cautious fun of him as he hobbled around after dismounting. He laughed right along with them. Always finding something to get back at them with.

William motioned for Hassman to join him and they walked out of ear shot of the camp.

"What's with Hans?" William asked. "He seems to know his shit. He should be at least a sergeant, not a common trooper."

Hassman, took a deep breath and thought for a moment.

"He was my lieutenant in the big one," Hassman began. "Both of us green as grass rookies. We were doing shit like we are about to do now. And we were damn good at it. They promoted him to Major and he took me with him."

He went silent then and looked off into the distance.

"As long as he kept in active duty he was fine," Hassman continued. "Then they made him a Lieutenant Colonel and put him on staff. Things went down hill right away. He drank to much to often. Got himself in trouble more than once. Took offence to some dandy, challenged him to a duel and killed him. That was the end.

"They court marshalled him. Gave him the option, back in the line as a common trooper or busted out of the army. He stayed in. When he is in the field, he's fine Cap. Just can't handle the BS in garrison sir. I think if he retired, he'd be dead inside a year."

"Shit," William said. "I remember mom and dad talking about him. Ok, tell him I'd like to speak with him."

"Sir!" Hans said as he came up.

"I didn't know who you were trooper," William began. "Hassman just told me. My mother and father have the greatest respect for you Hans."

"Thank you Your Highness!" He said.

"No Hans, out here, I am Cap, or Captain if you must," William said. "I have a favour to ask. You can refuse. I won't hold it against you of you do."

Hans shrugged his shoulders.

"The Candidate is my sister Hans," William said. "She kind of...losses it. She's all instinct Hans. Greta asked me to take her in and try to train her. You have the experience. Can you help me do that?"

"Ya I saw that," Hans said. "She would have killed me and anyone near her had you not pulled her off me and calmed her down. Damn she's fast."

"Walker had his company in good order, well armed and in formation at the end Hans." William said. "We would have killed them all, but to what point. The battle was over by then. He was surrendering and Willa, on her own, was attacking their formation. Like with you, I was able to calm her down. She would have killed a bunch of them, no doubt about it. But some of my people might have died trying to get her out of the mess."

Hans nodded his head.

"Ya, I seen that a couple of times," He said. "Trooper dies, after a time or two. Ya, I'll help you out. If I can."

"One more thing," William said. "I think Hassman may have figured out who she is, but nobody else knows. For her and our sake, let's keep it that way. Call her Barh when you feel the time is right. And oh ya, you are now a corporal. Hassman has enough shit to do."

Both of them came back to their rough camp.

"Right," William announced. "Hans here is now section one's corporal. Candidate, you are his team mate. Everyone else, carry on the same way. Hans, at daybreak, I want you and the candidate scoping out that town. I want to hit it and be gone by ten."

Hans and Willa had taken an hour to crawl a hundred meters to a small rise they could observe the town from. If anything, Willa had been quieter than Hans as they made their way forward. They watched the town for an hour, then crawled back to their horses and back to camp.

"Not much there boss," Hans said. "No troops in place. Just a normal sleepy back woods town. Comm towers, that's about it."

"If the candidate may speak?" Willa said.

William frowned at her but nodded. Willa pulled her knife from its scabbard on her boot and began to sketch the town with it in the dirt.

"Com towers here," she said. "Looks like a warehouse of some sort over here. And a police station with four cops, that I could see, here. Post office here. Otherwise, ya, typical sleepy town."

William looked at the sketch for a minute.

"Right," he began. "Section one, the police station first, warehouse next. Section two, comm tower, then post office. Any one resists, kill them. Don't mess around. Grab what we can use from the warehouse, then torch it. Same with the cop shop. Any intel we can get from it, then torch it. In, out and gone guys. Get at it."

"A little rusty there eh corporal," William said. "Don't feel bad, I missed the post office myself. I was there last night."

"You stay right beside me all the time," Hans said to Willa once William had left. "And, believe it or not, I am a big boy and for sure know how to use this sword kid. Your job is to watch my back, not do my fighting for me. I don't need you going all bananas on me and killing a bunch of unarmed civilians. Got it?"

"Yes Corporal, the candidate understands corporal." Willa said.

The four policemen were just finishing their morning coffee, when two troopers, on horse back, burst threw the front door, swords raised. They didn't even have time to draw their blasters and they were dead.

Towns people were yelling and screaming as mounted troopers galloped threw the town. Horses brushed people to slow to get out of the way down. Twenty minutes later the comm tower, post office, warehouse and police station were ablaze and twenty heavily armed troopers were galloping out of town.

The camp had already been torn down before they had left. They gathered up their spare horses and were gone. By the end of the day, they were thirty miles to the east and out of sight among the trees.

The troopers were all giddy, laughing and chatting away. William left them be, until the evening meal was finished and everyone one was relaxing.

"Good job gang," William began. "Nobody, human or horse got hurt, we got some fresh veggies and meat. And I see some decent booze. All good. This time. We might get away with this one or two more times. Then they will be gunning for us and hard. But that's our job, what we get paid for.

"We bye pass the next town and hit the one after that. Get some rest. Soon we will not have time."

They hit four more towns the rest of the week. Like William had predicted, the first couple were easy. No resistance at all. Then it began to get tougher. Roving patrols were everywhere. Towns were emptying out as terrified residents ran closer to the capital region. Empty towns were torched, every building.

The enemy was having trouble figuring out what was going on. There did not seem to be a pattern at all to the attacks in this sector. All the other sectors had a pattern and whole districts were attacked at once. Not this one. Constant hit and run attacks. No non combatants were ever killed. Only armed soldiers or policemen. Unless the town had been abandoned, only important infrastructure was destroyed. The abandoned towns were always completely destroyed, which was becoming more and more prevalent as civilians were abandoning the district in droves. A whole battalion had been deployed to curtail these raiders. The raiders were never seen, only the aftermath of their attacks.

The next town to fall was a district hub. It had a platoon of soldiers assigned as protection, with armoured vehicles. One of the vehicles had made a hasty cry for help before it had been destroyed. A full company arrived, to see shattered armoured vehicles, dead soldiers and a burning town with towns people grabbing what ever belongings they could salvage into what ever vehicle they could grab as the town began to burn around them.

The company commander saw a group of twenty horseman, in a line watching them from the edge of the Forrest that bordered the town. He glassed them with his binoculars. None of them wore armour. The men had beards beginning to show. All the troopers had mussed uniforms. All had dull eagles on their collars.

The commander saw he was being scanned by a trooper with binoculars. The trooper pulled them down smiled, saluted and then along with the rest, turned and slowly rode into the trees and were gone.

While that company and another scrambled around trying to find these troopers. Just before the sun went down that night. Another town, ten miles away was hit, with the same results. The first time that had ever happened. The single survivor of the attack reported seeing a battle flag.

"They must have at least a full company out here," the Major of the two companies reported to his colonel. "We need more troops."

"They have to have set up a base camp somewhere," the colonel said. "But damned if I can figure out where it is."

"You have them on the run son," Dimitri said. It was the first time that week William had reported in. "Keep it up. We are rolling them up. They will not fight us. They have just called in another battalion to find you. Start hitting their patrols now. We need them concentrating on you.

"We are coming Will. It will be a week at most, but we are coming."

"Yes sir," William said. "Don't take to long eh. We are running out of booze."

"That's the spirit son," Dimitri said. "Comms dark. How's your sister?"

"Hans has taken her under his wing," William said. "A little warning about him would have been nice. Willy damn near killed him the first day."

Dimitri laughed.

"Well, he survived anyway," Dimitri said.

"I asked him to help dad," William said. "Now I think he has adopted her. They work well together and she doesn't loose it anymore."

"He's a warrior Will," Dimitri said. "Fine in the field. Useless and a head ache otherwise.

"Ok, comms dark now eh? See ya when I see ya."

William gathered the troops around him after the evening meal, like normal.

"Command tells me the enemy is deploying a second battalion to look for us," he began. "Other wise, they are abandoning the whole district."

"Woo hoo!" Marshak said. "More boy toys to play with."

"Also," William continued. "Command wants us to add hitting patrols to hitting towns now. So we will split into two sections. One hits patrols, the other towns. We also need to find a place to build a fortified position. If I was the commander of that army, I would ring this whole area and start to squeeze.

"We are good. But not that good. Twenty against two thousand is not exactly healthy."

Not even Marshak made a smart ass remark this time.

"His Majesty says the rest of the Queens Guard and a lot of the Kings Own, will be here in a week." William said. "Just one more week guys. Then off to the beach for us."

"Oh my," Master corporal Jones said. "And here I am with nothing to wear. Oh dear me."

If it wasn't Marshak being a smart ass, It was Jones.

Chapter Ten

Arial was beginning to suffer. Shortages of almost everything were beginning to be felt. Planet wide. All space transport facilities had been destroyed or heavily damaged. The damage could only be repaired by manufacturing or importing needed parts and materials. The manufacturing plants needed raw materials imported, mostly from Oaken.

Citing an unwillingness to commit Oaken's transports to deliver goods to Arial because of the ongoing hostilities, Oaken refused to send any. While nothing had been said, officially, unofficially it was clear that Oaken was supporting their monarch. It would not matter anyway. Six armed Oaken transports had been commandeered by the monarch and were in constant orbit around Arial. Transport goods from other planets were intercepted and warned off.

Even the few small independent transports that tried to evade the blockade were having problems. Some were stopped and turned around. A few had been shot down and of the few that made it threw to land somewhere. Most were boarded, the crews incarcerated and ships confiscated. Even had all the small transports made it through, the amount and type of goods they brought, were no where near enough. They barely made a dent in the shortfalls.

The district that the invaders were taking over, produced all most all the agricultural needs of the planet. This was starting to have an effect on stored stocks of food stuffs and rationing had been put in place.

At first, the official news reports had stated this was only a small group of bandits doing the damage. But as more and more refugees poured into the bordering districts, they spread the story of a large, fully armed army, not bandits, were responsible. The people were becoming restless.

The decision had been made to not defend that district. To find an area suitable for them to defend. Where their weapons and technology would be at best advantage. Right now efforts were concentrating on the furthest east sector of that district. An estimated two enemy companies were conducting raids, even attacking patrols of armed vehicles sent out to pin point their location.

A critical town with three major road hubs had been reinforced with two companies of troops, with heavy weapons. A base had been set up to house the two battalions that had made a circle and were contracting it, forcing the enemy to one area. They finally had them. They had made a mistake. Making a pattern in their attacks and the location of the enemy base of operations had been pinpointed.

The area was not very defendable and perfect for Arial to attack and destroy them. A third battalion had been dispatched. They needed a victory, no matter how small, to show the people that victory was possible. The attack would come the next day.

"Shit!" Alex said after reading the latest intercepted enemy communication.

"They spotted Will's camp. They're going to attack it in the morning, with two full battalions and another half battalion."

Alex took a pencil and marked where the attack was going to occur. It was in the centre of a ring of recent attacks Will had made.

"They must be getting tired," Margarete said. "They have fallen into making a pattern."

Dimitri took a good look at the map and took out a magnifying glass to look at the terrain more closely. He shook his head. Then he looked at the dates of the attacks. Nothing had been made for two days.

"I know he is young and inexperienced," Dimitri said. He could talk almost normally now.

"But he is not dumb. Even if he was, Hassman would have clued him in and for sure Hans would have. No they are setting them up for something."

Everyone was poring over the map now. Magnifying glasses to eyes.

"Here!" Alex said. He ruffled through some communications intercepts, found the one he was looking for and threw it on the map. He made a big circle around a town with two critical road junctions in it. One of which lead directly to the Capital region.

"He's drawing them away from this town," Alex said. "He will hit them when they attack in full force where he has led them believe his base is."

"We take that town, we have a clear shot at the capital," Margarete said. "That platoon has just won the war for us."

"If they survive," Dimitri said. "No way he will be able to conceal what he has done, where he came from, or where he is going to after that. They are out numbered and out numbered badly."

Margarete did not hesitate.

"Every mounted Eagle and Bear to deploy, now!" She said. "Ignore everything on the way! The infantry to follow at best speed!"

First platoon had made good progress on their defences. It was a perfect spot for them. To their backs was an impassable ridge higher than the longest blaster could reach them from. The spot was the only flat and dry spot. All the other sides were soft and marshy. A vehicle could, maybe, navigate it. But measures had been put in place to make that even more difficult. Large poles had been cut down and put down close enough together to prevent a vehicle from passing between them. These were well within bow shot range of their position. Efforts to dislodge the poles would be costly in dead and wounded.

Even then, things would not be easy. Six foot deep and square holes had been dug and sharpened stakes placed in the bottom of them. These quickly filled with water, masking the pits and the deadly stakes.

A six foot deep and three foot wide ditch had been dug around their position. The dirt piled up on the edge of the ditch effectively making a ten foot high wall. Sharpened stakes had been placed at an angle all along the front edge making it even harder for an attacker to assault them. Easily defendable gaps, wide enough for one body to pass through had been left between the stakes.

It was going to cost any attacker a lot of dead and wounded to assault the rampart.

All but two of the platoon were relaxing. It had been a lot of hard heavy work the last two days getting the defences set up. The two missing troopers were Hans and Willa. They were late returning from a scouting mission to get last minute information on the town they would all assault the next morning.

William was beginning to get concerned, when they both made their way around all the traps and into camp. A gap at one edge of the defences and been left clear of stakes for that purpose. That gap would be filled in once the enemy attack began.

William looked at them and smiled. The tall, gruff wily old veteran and the short teenager. Both were covered in twigs and branches, faces dirty from the mud they had smeared on them. Over the days, they had become inseparable. Two peas in a pod.

"Was starting to get concerned," William said as they dismounted. "Thought maybe you were gonna try and take them all on yourselves."

"Well," Hans said. "We is dumb, but not that dumb."

He started washing the mud and grime from himself from a bucket of water. That's when William noticed the new blood stains on both uniforms.

"Trooper Bahr come up with a good idea," Hans continued. "We come across two scout vehicles. They was all relaxed and such. Willy here says, 'Hey Corp, those guys are even sleeping. Easy pickings. Maybe we can get some intel.' So I says sure why not and start to get ready. She says, 'This is my deal Corp, you are way to big and noisy. Back me up eh?' Then wham, bam, she was gone."

Willa was also splashing herself down. She shrugged her shoulders.

"Cherist, she is damn fast!" Hans said. "Only left me one to kill she did. Gunning for my job she is."

"You snooze, you loose Corp," Willa said. Then she caught herself.

"The candidate apologizes for her behaviour Corporal," she said quickly.

Hans stood up and made a show of looking around the camp.

"Who let a candidate in here?" He asked.

He turned to Willa and hugged her. Then he took his cap badge off his beret and gave it her.

"You earned it kid," he said. "Every one! Captain! As far as I am concerned Candidate Bahr is now trooper Bahr!"

"Thanks a lot Hans!" Jones yelled out. "More competition for us normal looking females!"

She came over and gave Willa a long hug. She walked away to the far end of the camp. Tears streaming down her face.

Willa made to say something, but Hans put a gentle hand on her shoulder.

"It's not you Willy," he said softly. "It's her son."

He walked over to where Jones had sat and sat beside her. In seconds she was in his arms. They could barley make out her cries as Hans gently rubbed her back.

"So?" William asked Willa. "You get any intel?"

"Oh, ya," Willa said.

She dug into her tunic and came out with a sheet of paper in her hand. She handed the paper to William.

"Sorry sir. The Candidate apologizes Captain," she belatedly said.

"You are a trooper now Bahr," William said. "Just don't let it get to your head eh? Now go play with the rest of your gang of ruffians."

William looked at the paper and smiled.

"Got you you bastards," he said to himself, but loud enough for those near him to hear.

Hassman came over, William handed him the sheet of paper and after reading it, Hassman also smiled.

"Just like you planned Cap," Hassman said. "That third battalion is going to make it at lot harder here though."

William shrugged his shoulders. They both knew there was not much they could do about it. They were surrounded.

"You gonna warn HQ?" Hassman asked.

"Can't risk it," William replied. "Maybe once they start the assault. If I have time."

He looked over and saw Hans and Jones were making their way back to the camp. Followed by Hassman, William made his way to the big camp fire they all shared. Willa was basking in all the harassment she was receiving, knowing now she was accepted as one of them. William filled first his mug, then Hassman's from the ever present coffee pot.

He raised the cup and made a point of making eye contact with Jones.

"Absent comrades," he said and took a deep draft of the heavily rum laced coffee. He raised the cup again.

"Our newly promoted trooper, speedy mini Willy!" He said.

Everyone roared and toasted a now embarrassed Willa.

"Ok gang," William said after a couple of minutes of Willa ribbing had occurred.

"Speedy Mini and Root'em Toot'em Hans have provided us with the latest intel," William continued. "As planned, the bad guys fell for our little deception. We hit the town tomorrow. Hit hard, hit it fast and get the hell back here.

"Now. This is what we are going to do...."

Other than the two heavily armed companies of soldiers, the normal bustling town was almost deserted. All the civilians except a few die hards, had all left. Even the die hards were ready to flee at a moment's notice.

Two heavy armoured vehicles and their crews were at each of the three roads leading into town. Four more were on standby and every soldier went about armoured and armed. They were taking no chances.

One of the sentries guarding the west road noticed movement coming out of the trees and swung his binoculars to take a closer look. A line of horses was moving out of the trees.

"Hey LT," the sentry yelled. "Movement on the road!"

The Lieutenant in charge swung around to look in that direction. Horses continued to come out of the trees. They began to make two formations of thirty. One on the left and one on the right.

"Commander," the Lieutenant reported into his comm unit. "They are forming up to the west. Sixty horsemen in sight."

Seconds later a siren began to blare and every soldiers comm unit came alive, telling them to form up on the west side of the town. The commander was one of the first to arrive. He was scanning the distant horsemen with his binoculars. The riders were just standing there. He had been one of the few survivors of the initial battle and what he saw next made him turn white. The horses began their dance.

"Get ready boys! Just like we planned. Two rows of shields up front, the rest overhead! Heavy blasters, be ready as soon as they get in range. Going to make you bastards pay this time!" He said.

The commander had trained both companies in the tactics he had seen Walker use so successfully. They might loose this time too, but this time the enemy was going to feel it.

His men were formed up in two squares, one left and one right. The horsemen would have to split their forces to cover both squares. Which they began to do. They further split into two lines each holding fifteen riders. They were in no hurry. They were slowly walking toward his squares and based vehicles.

The ground began to tremble as the horses began to trot first. Then canter. Just when the commander discovered there were only two armoured riders on the approaching horses, he heard the dreaded thrumming that heralded the arrival of arrows. From his rear. Then everything turned to a shambles.

Three flights of arrows hit his rear and as his men reacted, lances and horses were impacting the rear. Men were screaming. Then the horses to the front hit his disintegrating squares at a gallop and added their bulk and hooves to the battle. The commander's last sight was of a young girl towering over him on her horse. Her visor was up and he could see the hate in her eyes as she looked at him. A sword in her right hand and a hand axe in her left. Both weapons, the front of her armour and her face dripping in blood.

"Let them run!" William yelled as the enemy troops began running away from his troopers as fast as they could. Most of them tossing weapons and shields away from them so they could run faster.

"Smash these vehicles!" William yelled. "Torch the town. Don't piss around! Ten minutes, that's all! Go! Go! Go!"

He turned a concerned look at Willa's direction then relaxed as he saw her dismount to help a wounded trooper. Hans was smashing a sledge hammer into a vehicle. Other troopers were setting fires to buildings and still others were gathering loose horses.

William rode over to where Willa was ripping leg armour off the wounded trooper now laying on the ground.

"Shit, shit, shit," Jones kept repeating. She had volunteered to be one of the two troopers with the spare horses.

"Asshole had a spiked hammer," Jones said. "Punched right through my leg armour."

"It's not to bad," Willa said. "Most likely have a nice purple bruise though."

She pulled out her hunting knife and cut a piece of cloth off of a nearby dead soldiers tunic which she quickly wrapped around the wound. Finished, she reached a hand down to help Jones up. Jones tested the leg and found she could walk. She quickly made her way over to her horse and gave it a once over, then grunted.

"She's ok," Jones said. "I'm gonna need a hand to mount though."

By the time she was mounted, the rest of the platoon was forming up, their spare horses automatically forming with them. With out orders, they galloped west out of town to their camp.

Once there, four troopers quickly filled the gap they had made so they could get in and out of it easier. Others were going over horses and them selves. More than just Jones had been wounded. None of the wounds were serious. One thing was for sure. The enemy was learning.

William, like the others had first looked to his spare horses. None of them had any damage. Then removed his armour and quickly went over himself, looking for wounds. Then checked Hassman's back while Hassman did the same with him.

The buckets of water came out and blood was being cleaned from their bodies, clothing and armour. Weapons were starting to be gone over. Nicks on swords being removed, edges sharpened. All the lances they had left, were now gone. Used up in the attack. Only used arrows had been used, leaving their dwindling supply of new ones back at camp. They had just over one thousand new arrows and five hundred usable used ones left. They would need every one of them.

William had finished working on his weapons and looked around the camp. The whole platoon was joking around. Some, even the females, only in their underwear, washing clothing. All of them were beginning to relax and joke around. The older reservists and the young rookies. All now one big happy family.

William stayed by himself and quiet. He burnished his chest plate armour so it shone brightly. Then took a stick and began to sketch a two headed eagle with wings outstretched on it in charcoal. Others saw what he was doing and began doing the same thing. Making their own family crests or animals on them. Most using the camouflaged sticks they used to camouflage their faces.

Willa's eagle was in red. She had put the same red on the bottom half of her helmet. Others were making their own designs on their helmets. William left his alone. Hans had no decorations at all on any of his armour.

"Your one of us now Hans," William said. "Draw something."

"Can't draw," Hans said and shrugged his shoulders.

"I can," Willa said. She held her hand out. "Let me Corp."

The two of them moved off and Willa was soon drawing away on first his breast plate, then his helmet. What ever she had done obviously made him happy as he hugged her once she was done. Then he covered both up so none could see the designs.

As much as they tried, nobody slept much that night. They were all to keyed up from all the adrenaline from the attack.

The sun was barely up when the first two scout vehicles arrived. By noon the area beyond was full of vehicles and soldiers. Tents were going up. Officers were constantly scanning the defences and approaches to them. Meetings were being held, plans made.

All the while, five members of the platoon sat with their legs dangling over their ramparts. Suntanning.

Chapter Eleven

Horses had been fed and breakfast had been finished. Everyone knew today would be the day of the attack. Last minute checking of swords edges and armour fittings were being conducted. Today, there was little kidding around and a lot of silence.

Bugles were heard coming from the enemy camp, waking the soldiers for the new day. The two troopers watching the enemy were doing just that. Watching. Nothing to worry about, yet.

After a couple of hours, one of the sentries whistled.

"They're gearing up Cap," she yelled down. "No rush yet."

Even so, troopers began to dawn their armour. Each was sporting their family crest on the chest plates. Helmets ran the gamut of coloured lines to animals. William was unique, he had nothing on his. The troopers had made spears by fastening lance heads to poles they had made. These were being tested as were the bows and strings. Ten quivers of ten arrows each were placed by each position. These would be the last of the used arrows.

The only one not in armour, was Hans. He was just staring off in the distance, absently rubbing a rag on his worn sword.

"They're starting to form up Cap," came from the rampart.

"Come on down and gear up," William said.

"They don't appear to be in a hurry Cap," the sentry said as she came down and starting putting on her armour.

William took a deep breath. This was hard. Many of them would die today.

"Brothers and sisters," he began calmly. "Our orders were to scout and cause mayhem. This we have done and done well. Our second task was to draw the enemy in, so our main force could attack them to our advantage. I think we may have gone a little overboard on that one."

A few chuckles could be heard from the platoon.

"We have designed our defences so they can only hit us in lines of twenty to match ours," William continued. "That gives us a chance. We just have to hold them brothers and sisters. The Queens Guard are on their way."

"Today, I am fighting to keep you alive foremost. Then I am going to make them pay.

"For Jones! For Clark! For what they did to His Majesty and Greta and Charles! And especially for what they did to my sister Willa! She should be back home getting ready for her high school graduation dance! Instead, she is here, with us about to die!"

"Not in this fucking life time brother!" Willa yelled back. "I have nineteen of the best of Magies Eagles fighting with me! For Clark! For Aunt Greta! For Charles! And, especially for Jones! I have come to love his mother as my sister!"

"Lastly, for my brother William! Who has given us not only the chance to make the bastards pay. But to live!"

She rushed up and gave William a clanking hug, which drew a lot of laughs.

"Fuck it!" William said. "Who wants to live forever anyway!"

He moved toward his position at the centre of the rampart. The others, but Hans joined him. All of them standing so just their eyes could see over the ramparts, watching the enemy form up.

That's when Hans strode to the top of the ramparts. He had their colour with him in his right hand. The big sledge hammer in his left. He rammed the colour into the rampart to fly freely, then raised the sledge hammer and pointed it at the enemy.

"Come my lovelies come!" He yelled as loud as he could. "Come if you dare! Come if you are brave enough. My Valkyrie is bored, she has nothing to do! Come my lovelies come! The Queens Guard is waiting! We are bored!"

Now he stood, feet shoulder width apart, the hammer held now on his shoulder. He looked down at them. His helmet had a black eagle on it. The black wings folded back on both sides of the glistening helmet. Outstretched talons coming down his check piece to his jaw making his eye piece look like an eagles head. He turned his back on the enemy and they saw the chest. An armoured women, sword raised above her head, blond hair flying behind her, mounted on a winged horse.

"Come brothers and sisters," he said calmly. "It is time to dance."

As one, the rest of the platoon joined him on top of the rampart. In full view, they began their sword drill singing low and slow as they began the slow movements. They could hear drones flying over head. They started the song again, this time they sang louder and moved faster. William caught movement out of the corner of his eye. He nudged Hassman standing beside him and pointed behind him with his chin. He did the same with Hans standing on the other side of him. The gesture was past down the line. Then they all turned their backs to the enemy.

Their horses were lined up doing their dance movements as well. The song went faster and louder the movements ever faster. The ground began to tremble from the eighty sets of hooves hitting the ground.

The last singing was almost at a scream. The moves of horse and trooper in perfect harmony. Now horses were screaming as well. Movements so fast at times they blurred. And then it stopped and silence once again reined over the rampart. The platoon save for Hans all went back down the other side of the rampart. He turned back to the enemy and began to swing his big hammer around his head.

"Come!" He yelled. "Come see how an Eagle dies!"

Now he nonchalantly walked back to join the others. He, like the others, crossed his legs and sat. Waiting.

They heard someone making a speech in the other side, followed by a great roar. Then a bugle blared and minutes later, whistles blew and they heard the tromping of many feet in unison. Every few steps something banged on what was most likely shields. Still they sat and waited. Next came the cries as men fell into the first of the pit traps they had made. Now William stood, placed two arrows in his mouth and a third on the draw sting. He stood and went to the top of the ramparts, the rest of the platoon followed.

Next the creak of bows as arrows were pulled back to ears. And the killing began. Flight after flight of arrows began to hit the enemy. All targeted on the first rows of soldiers. Men began to fall, the tactic of holding shields above heads failing as soldiers floundered through the slippery mud and gaps from where men had fallen into the traps.

Empty quivers were replaced by full ones and the arrows flew and men in their hundreds began to die. Now the men in addition to the mud and the traps had to clamber over the bodies of the fallen and the lines became even more ragged. A bugle sounded from the rear and whistles blew from the column and the enemy began to withdraw. And still the arrows flew, until they reached the pit traps. Then the arrows stopped coming.

The platoon went back down the rampart. Empty quivers were flung to the rear and full ones brought forward. The next attack began and the platoon waited. They waited until the new column reached the second set of pit traps and the arrows began to fly again. Again men by the hundreds began to die. Again they with drew. This time, arrows did not follow as they left.

Ten troopers quickly stripped off their armour, grabbed five empty quivers each and ran over the rampart. They began to collect arrows. Many had missed targets and stuck in the ground. These were the first choice as they were mostly undamaged. The quivers full, they dashed back to the rampart and tossed them over and more empties were tossed back. This time they were more hurried as the third column began to move. The troopers tossed the quivers over the rampart, then them selves. Section mates waiting to help them redone their armour.

This time they waited until the column was twenty yards from the rampart and began to fire as fast as they could. Not even aiming, just firing to hit the column. Now the shields were useless. At this range, the arrows went right through them to the body behind. The first three rows of the column fell into the ditch. Then, bows were tossed behind them, spears were brought forward and the real killing began.

It was when the horses began to scream their anger and frustration, that the enemy realized that not one word had been spoken by the Eagles the whole time. Spears were broken and tossed aside. Swords were now in play. The ditch was now filled with the enemy and the platoon began to take damage. Still the swords or hammers or axes rose and fell. Still the enemy died.

Still the enemy came, still the weapons rose and fell. Then a tremor could be felt in their feet and low thunder could be heard coming closer. The horses, all of them, began to whinny as loud as they could. In the distance, answering whinnies could be heard.

Still the enemy came, still they died. It was an all out effort now from them. They had committed all of their troops. Then the ground began to visibly tremble and the thunder was loud.

"Oaken! Oaken! Oaken!" Was being yelled.

A mighty crash from the enemy rear and screaming began. The fight at the rampart began to slacken.

"Kept at 'em! Keep at 'Em!" Hans roared. "This ain't over yet!"

William had no one facing him or to either side. He looked down the line in time to see Willa swing her left handed axe at a soldier swinging an axe at Hans. She first took the arm off, then crashed the axe into his skull. And their part of the fight was over.

William looked to the rear of the enemy. Leading the charge was Janet, flailing her big battle axe around her. Next to her was Charles and his even bigger one. Then his mother, father and Aunt and all of the original One Hundred were carving a big swath threw the enemy that the following Eagles made even bigger. The heavy cavalry was wrecking havoc on the other side.

The troopers on the ramparts went to their knees. Hands on hips or thighs. Gulping big gulps of air and watching the show. Even the wounded crawled back up to watch.

"Holy shit!" Willa exclaimed. "Will you look at that!"

Weapons were rising and falling, horses were kicking and stomping anything in their way. The dance at its deadliest and for real, playing out beneath them.

"Well shit," Hans said.

Willa looked at him and sprinted to his side. She pulled his heavily dented helmet from his head. He was bleeding from several places on his head. There was a big gash in his armour just below his shoulder on his side. Blood began to dribble out of his mouth.

"No! No!" Willa screamed. She made to remove his chest armour, but he put his arm on her and stopped her.

"No love," he said. "They have killed me. You can't fix this one hon."

He coughed up some blood then.

"You are the daughter I never had Willa and I love you dearly. Hey mom, you ok? How's dad?"

Willa thought he was hallucinating but a pair of armoured legs knelt beside them and a helmet hit the ground. Janet kissed Hans on the forehead.

"Yes, dad is here," she said softly. "We are both fine. Nice design on the armour. Better than the one on our crest."

"Willa drew it for me mom," Hans said.

He looked over at Willa.

"It's for the best hon," he said. "I would have just drank myself to death on civiy street. You done good kid. You earned your eagle today. You hear me William? Your sister earned her eagle today."

"Yes Major Klemple, I heard you," William said. "It has been an honour and a privilege to be allowed to fight alongside you sir."

"Aw shut up eh." Hans struggled out. "Mom, you tell uncle Demi, Will and Willy done good hear? The honour was all mine Will. You planned it, I just killed them for you is all."

One last look at them, his eyes glazed over and he died. Janet pulled him to her chest and screamed.

"Shit," Dimitri said as he came up.

"Your Majesty!" William, said coming to attention and bowing his head. "First Platoon, Company C all present. Ten wounded, one dead sir! Major Klemple was instrumental in our defence Your Majesty. Without his guidance and inspiration, we would have failed sir!"

"You get all that?" Dimitri asked his aide who was feverishly writing in his note book. The man nodded.

Dimitri looked behind him and saw the battle was over.

"Call assembly," he ordered.

The battalions of Queens Guard and Kings Own formed their lines side by side. Dimitri keyed his comm unit so all could hear.

"I ordered First Platoon, Charley Company to do a deep recon of this sector," Dimitri began. "To find a defendable position and draw the enemy to them. To hold them as long as they could for us. And held them they did.

"Twenty of them did all this. Look around you. See from how the enemy dead lie and the arrows in them and on the ground. The piles of enemy dead in front of the rampart. Twenty did this. Ten overage inactive reservists and ten green as grass just out of training kids did this.

"Let's face it people. We finished it, but First Platoon won this battle. Captain Bekenbaum credited Major Klemple for his courage, experience and providing the troopers of First Platoon the courage to fight. Just before he died from his wounds, Major Klemple said, 'heck, Captain Bekanbaum planned it all. All I did was kill the bastards for him.'

"Twenty over aged and to young Eagles against three thousand! Ten wounded and one dead.

"First Platoon, form up!"

The nine whole troopers helped the ten wounded form their line. Janet gently laid Hans on the ground and stood beside Dimitri. He withdrew the sword from his back and placed it on his shoulder. Janet did the same.

"Royal House Hold troops! Attention!" Dimitri said. "Royal House Hold troops, Salute!"

They swept the swords to their sides and back to the front of their faces. Then rescabbarded them.

"At ease!" Dimitri ordered. "Senior Sergeant Klemple, join First Platoon if you please."

Janet marched up beside William and turned around, going to parade rest like the rest of them.

"The original intention, had been for First Platoon to make up the core of an all new Company C of the Queens Guard," Dimitri continued.

"That has now changed. Senior Sergeant Klemple is promoted to Colonel of the second battalion of the Queens Guard. First Platoon, Company C is transferred to the Second Battalion. Now you are the core of a whole battalion. You even have your own nick name. Janet's Orphans!"

Margarete was the first to begin the chant punching her fist in the air. Greta and Charles right behind her. Dimitri too joined in. The air was trembling from the shouted chant.

Janet's Orphans! Janet's Orphans!

Chapter Twelve

The full Imperial Cabinet was assembled in the throne room. His Imperial Majesty the Emperor of Arial sat uncomfortably on his throne looking at those beneath him.

"Three battalions," he said. "Three battalions, just gone like that," he snapped his fingers. "Plus another battalion days earlier. How many soldiers have We left?"

"Six battalions in total, Your Imperial Majesty," the minister of defence said.

"Can we hold the Capital?" The Emporere asked.

The minister of defence looked at the General of the Army.

"In my opinion, no your Imperial Majesty," the General said. "They have two thousand Eagle light Cavalry, two thousand Bear Heavy Cavalry and four thousand Bear infantry Your Imperial Majesty. We stand absolutely no chance."

"The Federation will not help?" The Emperor asked.

"The Federation feels this is a personal matter between royal Houses your Imperial Majesty," the minister of foreign affairs said. "They offered to help negotiate a peace but that is all."

"How about you Mr. Ambassador," the emperor said. "Home World promised to support us if we started this venture for them."

"Unfortunately your Imperial Majesty," the ambassador said. "Any help we could send is three months away and would in no way be in enough numbers to effect the out come given our transportation capabilities."

"So much for that then," the emperor said. "Very well, set up a meeting to discuss a cease fire and peace negotiations with this Bekenbaum fellow then."

The emperor rose and left the throne room.

"Does he not understand that His Majesty can take over the whole damn planet?" The General asked the foreign affairs minister. "He can bloody well make the peace, not negotiate for it!"

"His Majesty has always been reasonable in my previous dealings with him," the Minister said. "To save even one of his troopers or ours, he will negotiate. But the price will be steep I am afraid."

"Anything you can do Minister," the General said. "That idiot on the throne has to go. He has ruined the planet with his schemes."

"Good morning Minister Shultz," Margarete said two days later.

The meeting was being held in a small town just taken over by the Oaken troops, three days travel from the capital of Arial.

"His Majesty has asked me to negotiate on his behalf just as the Emperor has asked you to do the same."

"Actually," Shultz said. "His Imperial Majesty has asked me to procure a cease fire and to begin negations for a time and place to begin peace negotiations Your Majesty."

"Well this will be a very short meeting then," Margaret said. "Request for a cease fire is denied. Our demands are and always will be the same. The Emperor takes full responsibility for all this nonsense and apologizes. All costs incurred by His Majesty in this business to be paid in full. And now, a new one. The Emperor is to abdicate his throne and be replaced with a system of Constitutional Monarchy, much like the one we have on Oaken.

"He can agree, or not. If not, many, many of your people are going to die. Most from starvation. Good day sir."

Margaret stood and walked out of the building.

"Form up the troops!" She yelled. "We march on the capital!"

"I warned you!" An angry General said the next day in the throne room. "I warned you this would happen! Either you agree to their terms, or I will have my soldiers remove you from office and agree to them myself on behalf of the people of Arial!"

He made the advance to contact order with his arm and a fully armed and armoured company burst into the throne room.

"Take that idiot into custody!" The general ordered. "Take his whole damn family into custody! Now!"

"Get me Her Majesty on my comm ASAP," he ordered a nearby soldier.

A few minutes later his comm unit went off. He keyed it. It was Dimitri, not Margarete.

"Morning Harold," Dimitri said. "It's a beautiful day today. Nice and sunny and warm. I am afraid Her Majesty is busy, getting her nails done or some shit. Umph! Hit the other damn shoulder next time eh? Mags says high by the way."

"Not such a nice day in this damn place Dimitri, and high back to Margarete," Harold said. "The Emperor has been forcibly removed from the throne. He and his family have been arrested. On behalf of the people of Arial, I accept your conditions and apologize for all of this unpleasantness. Please believe me your Majesty, we warned him not to do this sir."

"Good enough for me Harold," Dimitri said. "Can you enforce the coupe?"

"Ya, Iv'e got three battalions in the capital." Harold said. "Almost all the Ministers are on board. We'll sort it all out once you get here."

"Ok good," Dimitri said. "We should be there in a couple of days. Just us and our body guard. I'll have the rest stop a day out."

In the two days following the over throw of the Emperor, Harold had consolidated control of the capital and the planet wide vid system had been continuously broadcasting the change in government and that a cease fire had been put in place. That the military disaster had occurred because, against all advice, the Emperor had tried to assassinate the ruler of Oaken. The Oaken royal family had retaliated. Oaken and Arial were not and never had been at war. It was hoped that the peace agreement would be official today.

A scout team had reported two hours ago, that fourteen riders and twenty eight horses were rapidly approaching the capital. The standard they were flying was the Oaken Royal Families flag.

The cabinet was informed and officials were hurrying to and fro. Alerted that the riders had entered the city proper, all the ministers were summoned. The Federation and Home World ambassadors had also been summoned to attend.

Harold was dressed in his formal uniform, the rest in their official garments. Everyone in the throne room were nervous, except the two ambassadors. The Federation ambassador looked bored. The Home World ambassador had his normal arrogant air about him.

They heard the sound of boots approaching, a guard at the door began to demand something. The next sound was of a body hitting the door, before it was kicked open. Audible gasps were heard as the cabinet saw what was entering the throne room.

They had been expecting formal uniforms with all the shinny badges and medals with sashes. Just as they themselves were dressed. What arrived were fourteen people in dusty, dirty and sweat stained uniforms. Swords draped across backs. They marched in two lines right up the centre of the aisle and the assembled people saw the dried blood stains on the uniforms. Across backs and along arms.

They stopped and made a line in front of the General and came to attention. The tall man in the centre, with a bandage around his neck saluted and the general just as smartly returned it. Then both men smiled and shook hands.

"May I address the cabinet General," the man asked.

The General nodded.

The troopers all turned around and placed feet shoulder width apart and both arms in the pits of their backs.

"I am Dimitri, ruler of Oaken," he began. "On my right, is Her Majesty, Queen Margarete, On my left, Her Highness, Grand Duchess Greta, on her left, His Royal Highness, Prince William. To the right of the Queen, Her Royal Highness, Princess Willa. On the far left, Major Klassman, Company A, Second Battalion, Queens Guard. On the far Right, Colonel Olynk, Commander of the Second Battalion Queens Guard and Baroness of third clan, prairie clans.

"At the rear, First Platoon, Company C, Second Battalion Queens Guard. What is left of it anyway.

"Myself, Grand Duchess Greta, Princess Willa and Major Klassman were on a holiday in the back woods on Oaken. We were attacked by an armed transport from Arial and sixteen of your elite assault troops. They all died, we did not.

"Two weeks ago, First Battalion, Queens Guard, landed on Arial. The next morning, the First Battalion completely destroyed two of your battalions.

"Four days ago, Prince and Princess William and Willa and eighteen of their platoon, killed an estimated one third of the three battalions sent to attack them. We, in the Kings Own Regiment and the Queens Guard, killed the rest. First Platoon had the only casualties. Ten wounded and one killed.

"I assure you, the fourteen of us will kill everyone in this room if a weapon is even pointed in our direction.

"I apologize for our appearance. For myself, Princess Willa, Grand Duchess Greta and Major Klassman, we have been on Planet for almost two months now, the rest for close to a month. We have been sleeping in tents, if we have the time, or just on the ground.

"Like yourselves, we would like nothing more than to end this unpleasantness in the next little while and go back home to a shower, clean clothing and a good home cooked meal.

"General, my comms people have just sent you our peace proposal. Share it with your cabinet and discuss it. Ambassador Alcott, it may be appropriate for you to excuse yourself for a moment and check for updated Federation information.

"We will remove ourselves to the ante room and you can discuss all this."

As abruptly as they had arrived, the Oakens marched back out to the ante room and slammed the door behind them. The Federation Ambassador had gone with them. The Federation Ambassador went out in the hallway and checked his comm unit.

It took him five minutes to read and digest the long communication he had received. He walked back into the anti room. The fourteen troopers had found what ever they could to sit on, chairs, tables, all of First Platoon, including the Prince and Princess, were sitting on the floor, backs against the wall, sleeping.

"You people certainly don't let any moss grow under your feet," Alcott said to Dimitri. "It normally takes months if not years to get the Security Council to agree on anything."

"We have to move fast, or we die," Dimitri said. "We gave the Security Council verified intelligence. They could do with it what they wanted."

A knock was heard at the door, the sleeping troopers were instantly awake and alert. The General pocked his head around the door.

"We are ready for you Your Majesty," Harold said.

With the Federation Ambassador along, the Oakens returned to the throne room. This time staying at the rear by the door and fanning out.

"Your Majesty," the Minister for Foreign Affairs began. "Your terms are most generous, better than we had hoped for. But we are wondering, why is Oaken being so lenient? Does Oaken plan to Annex Arial?"

Dimitri laughed.

"Shit, I have enough work to do on Oaken," he said. "I don't need more hassle.

"The second that agreement is signed, our blockade will stop. Our transports, will begin returning our troops back to Oaken. Within seven days, none of the House Hold troops will be on Arial.

"Emir Bashir has agreed to send immediate assistance, food, materials and expertise, to help you begin to rebuild. You people can work out the details yourselves. The People of Oaken were not involved in this mess. Only our personal troops were involved."

Now he looked at the Home World Ambassador, who seeing the look on Dimitir's face turned white.

"Mr. Ambassador, it is no secret of the animosity between Oaken and Home World. It has been eighteen years since we severed diplomatic relations between our planets. What has happened recently has increased the tensions to a fever point of no return.

"We have sent verified intelligence regarding Home Worlds, not only involvement, but the planning and payment, for the raid conducted on my family and friends. In addition, we provided intelligence on Home World's future plans to attack and assimilate the whole Federation of Planets. Ambassador Alcott?"

"At the request of His Majesty," Alcott said. "The Security Council of the Federation of Planets convened an emergency meeting this morning. The intelligence His Majesty provided was examined and a resolution passed, in unprecedented speed I might add. As of now, all Home World diplomatic missions any where in the Federation are closed and terminated. All diplomats and citizens of Home World, Federation wide, are expelled from the Federation.

"Any Home World bound transports, will be stopped, inspected and any trade goods confiscated. Any inbound transports from Home World, will be boarded, the transports and goods confiscated, crews and passenger embarked on life boats with enough supplies to reach Home World. Any transports trying to evade, will be destroyed."

"Nice job Home World did eh?" Dimitri said. "Now you are at war with the whole Federation, not just with Oaken. Good luck with that."

"So, do we have an agreement or what?" Dimitri said to the Foreign Affairs Minister. "I am dirty, tired and getting cranky."

"Yes, yes," was the answer.

"Hey, you awake over there?" Dimitri said in his comm unit. "Tell the transports to come down and start loading us up. Send one to the outskirts to pick us up eh? I don't feel like riding for another two hours."

"Two hours?" Harold said. "You said you'd stop your troops two days out."

"I did?" Dimitri said. "Oops, must be tired."

"Hey Bashir," Dimitri said into his comm unit. "Ya, it's all good. No, wait for a bit, they haven't signed it yet."

Dimitri looked at Harold and raised his eyebrows. Harold quickly scribbled his signature on his copy. The other ministers did the same.

"Ok Bashir," Dimitri said. "Send them in. Landing pads are fine. My comms people will guide them down. See ya when I see ya."

Dimitri looked at his copy of the agreement, quickly scanned and saw no changes had been made and it had been signed by all the ministers then signed it himself. By the time he had finished, transports could be heard coming in to land at the capital cities space port.

"Gentlemen," Dimitri said. "The first four transports with aide for you have arrived. I am sure the crews could use some help unloading them.

"Your Majesty," Dimitri said to Margarete. "I believe a nice stroll to the out skirts of the city would be nice."

"Oh yes, Your Majesty," Margarete said. "It's so very lovely outside this time of year here."

"Hey!" Marshak said. "They got any good fast food joints around here? I'm famished."

"Maybe some good shops too?" Jones said. "I need a new party frock. This one is getting a little ragged."

"Jesus," Harold said. "You people." He was shaking his head and smiling.

William stopped in his tracks and turned around.

"I got Jone's son and Janet's son killed general," he said softly. "So, she and they are allowed to be a little flippant eh?"

Then he turned and hurried to join the departing group.

"Hey!" He yelled out. "Any of you bumbs got any decent hooch left. I'm dying of thirst over here."

"First Platoon broke up the advance the first day Harold," Greta said. "He lost two of his troopers then, Jones was one of them. Janet's son was on the ramparts with them. He fought right to the end and died after the battle was finished. He was in the centre along with William and Willa."

"It was Hans that was taunting us then," Harold said.

"Oh, that's not all," Greta said. "All of the original One Hundred punched the biggest hole in your lines when we hit. I was with them. You were not just fighting green rookies and show troops Harold. You were facing the best of the best. You had absolutely no chance.

"Demmy ordered Bashir to stand down. The whole planet was out raged Harold. That more than anything swayed the Security Council to decide the way they did."

"Oaken could take over the whole Federation if it wanted to," Harold said.

"Like Demmy said, who needs the hassle," Greta replied. "You do what you do, we do what we do. Live and let live. Have to go Harold.

Al will be worried a handsome foreign general is sweeping me off my feet."

"Ah shit," Harold said. "Al and his gang are here too? We were well and truly fucked."

"What was that all about Harold," the Foreign affairs Minister asked as Greta sashayed her way outside.

"The troops on planet right now?" Harold said. "The majority of them are from Dimitri's home clan. All except Company C, veterans from the war with Home World. Company C is the best of the best new graduates from their training collage. The Queens Own, were not even a full battalion when they arrived here. The ones that arrived the next day are their reserve troopers.

"Bashir, they're, what we would call Prime Minister, wanted to declare war. Dimitri forbade it. Other wise, we would have had over one hundred thousand veteran troops on Arial, with more on the way taking over every single district on the planet, not just the single one they did this week."

"Oh my God," the minister said.

"That was exactly what Home World wanted," Harold said. "For Oaken to declare war. The Federation would have been forced to intervene and a federation wide war would have broken out. Then, they would ride to the rescue and take over the whole Federation. But they forgot one thing.

"Oaken out guns all of us, and them."

"What happens now?" The minister asked.

"Oaken will go back to sleep," Harold said. "They don't want the hassle. The complete isolation of Home World will see them flounder. They import most of their materials from the Federation. I predict, within one or two generations, Home World will be just legends and tall stories told to frighten children at night."

Chapter Thirteen

Willa's initial return to the palace complex was low key. Due to her time in service and veteran status, she had been promoted to Lieutenant, instead of the more normal Second Lieutenant after her training classes were finished.

She had been given a full platoon of twenty troopers. Ten were from the class the year earlier, had served on Arial as she had and were veterans. The other ten were from her training class year and rookies.

As usual when first arriving on any post, Willa had to report to her company commander, who, as this was Company C, was her brother William. It was the normal cold, non-personal, military report.

William informed her of where she would barrack, where her platoons barracks were and who her sergeant was, then dismissed her. The sergeant was waiting for her outside with a corporal, also a veteran. They both came to attention, with the Sergeant saluting. Willa gave her parade ground salute, as she had been taught, over and over and over again, in her training class. The sergeant was smiling, but only with his eyes.

"Sergeant Nuscomb and party, Lieutenant Bekenbaum," the sergeant said.

Willa pointed at her name tag.

"Sorry ma-am," Nuscomb said. "I meant, Lieutenant Bahr ma-am."

Willa shrugged her shoulders.

"Like you guys," she said. "I don't make the rules, just follow them. You guys settled in alright?"

"Yes Ma-am," Nuscomb said. "Corporal Jackson here is your sections 2IC. I have the second section Ma-Am."

"Your gear has been sent to your barracks ma-am," Jackson said. "You have your own room ma-am, but the barracks holds eight in total ma-am. Right now, it's just you, First Platoons lieutenant and two second lieutenants ma-am. Both of those are from Third Platoon ma-am. First Platoon Lieutenant is senior ma-am."

"Corporal Jackson will escort you to your barracks ma-am," Nuscomb said. "I have to check in with my rookies ma-am."

"Very well Sergeant," Willa said. "Lead on corporal."

Jackson lead her to officers territory and to a building, that in regular civilian use, would have been a duplex with two three bedroom dwellings sharing a common wall. In this guise, the common wall had been removed, the two single washrooms replaced with an enlarged single one and a centrally located common room. Four individual rooms were located off the central area on each end, two rooms to a side, separated by a hallway.

The corporal said he would wait for her outside and Willa found her room, the last one in the front at right. It was small, but larger than the space she had when she had shared accommodations with ten other officer trainees at training camp.

The room had a bed on the outside wall, a small desk, with chair, and a slightly larger than a troopers locker, as a closet. Her duffle bag holding her clothing and the other holding her weapons, were both on the bed. The bed was unmade, but sheets, blankets and pillows were folded neatly at the head of the bed.

Willa quickly hung her uniforms and placed her weapons in the locker, then quickly made her bed. Another skill learned over and over and over again, with many pushups in-between for her failures. In fifteen minutes, she was outside.

The corporal led her to Second Platoons barracks. She put her hand on Jacksons and shook her head as he was about to announce her presence. She wanted to gage the room first. Satisfied, she nodded and Jackson yelled out.

The troopers stopped what ever they were doing and came to attention in front of their bunks. Nuscomb came to attention and saluted by stomping his foot in the ground at the doorway end of bunks on the left. Jackson assumed the same position at the right side.

Willa made her way down first the right side, then the left. Looking each trooper up and down as she went. She stopped by the door and turned around facing the room.

"Sergeant," she said in a normal voice. "This barrack had better be in much better shape than it is now, when I do my morning inspection. Or your ass is going to be so sore from my boot kicking it, you won't sit down for a week. Dismissed, carry on."

Willa turned and walked outside.

"Thanks a lot you goddamned assholes!" Willa heard Nuscomb roar. "You just got me in shit with the new LT! Everybody drop and give me twenty! Jackson, make sure these slack asses do every single push up. And the recon way, not the pussy army way!"

Nuscomb stormed his way out of the barracks and saw Willa leaning against the wall smiling. He grinned and shook his head.

"What the hell are you rookies doing!" They heard Jackson yell. "Are you that daft! You can't see the guys across from you! Now you've done made me lose my count! Start over!"

"Now get this damned barracks in shape!" He yelled, the push ups obviously complete. "If the LT comes here tomorrow and is pissed, she is gonna give the Sarge shit, who is gonna give me shit. And I can guarantee fucking tell you, if I get shit, this twenty push ups ain't gonna be nothin to what I'll give you! Get at it! Idiots!"

Jackson came out side and saw both Willa and Nuscomb leaning against the wall grinning and he couldn't help himself. He laughed.

"The room is pretty good," Willa said. "Troopers too. Tomorrow, I'll go through the lockers and find something wrong someplace. Then, we will all go on a nice two mile run. Which we would have done anyway...But..."

All three of them laughed.

"I have to go set up at the O club," Willa said. "Never been on that part of the base. Just point me in the right direction, I'll find it. I am after all, a root'em toot'em, Recon trooper. See ya in the morning guys."

"Take our guys aside Jackson," Nuscomb said as Willa leisurely strode away. "We all know who she is and, what she has done and is capable of doing. The higher ups want her under the radar. Just like her brother was at the beginning. Her name is Bahr and she is just out of the training academy. The rookies don't have a clue."

Willa wandered around the base for a while. While she had spent a lot of time at the palace complex growing up, she had never actually been on the base itself, other than the parade square on special occasions. Hearing her stomach grumble, she went to the O club, provided her ID, had her account set up and found a table toward the rear. She had the place to herself. The duty day was not over yet.

She looked at the menu, saw something she liked and ordered. As the duty day finished, a trickle of officers began to appear. First, the older senior officers, then in increasing numbers, the younger ones. The server had just taken her empty plate and beer mug away and provided her a full mug.

"Well, well, if it isn't my new rookie LT," she heard.

Looking up, she saw her brother with two lieutenants standing there. As she made to stand he shook his head.

"Definitely a rookie," William said.

He grabbed a chair and sat down. The two lieutenants also.

"Me you know already," William said. "The goof on the left is my 2IC Bekam, the goof on my right has my third platoon, Walker. This gentlemen is my newly minted LT of Second Platoon, Bahr. Hope you was paying attention Bahr, there will be an exam after."

Bekam looked at her mug of beer and frowned.

"You old enough to drink that Bahr?" He asked.

Willa didn't say anything, just looked at him, her face neutral.

William pointed at the eagle on her collar and the 'I was there' ribbons on her chest.

"If she ain't" William said. "Those say she is."

"I was there for one of those ribbons," Walker said. "Pleasure to finally meet you Lieutenant Bahr."

"Um..." Willa said.

"He was on the other side Bahr," William said. "He was also a captain at the time and a little beat up if I recall. Some gungho rookie tried to attack them all on her own."

"Oh," Willa said. "I apologize Lieutenant Walker. I am afraid I didn't recognize you."

"No problem Bahr," Walker said. "You look a might different all cleaned up yourself. If the Cap wouldn't have said anything, I wouldn't have known."

"How's your gang look?" William said.

"I haven't gone through their personnel files yet," Willas said. "The sergeant and corporal I have run into before. The vets are all good. The next week will show me a lot."

"Ya," William said. "Nuscomb and Jackson are good men. You can rely on them."

Willa quickly finished her beer and stood.

"Captain, Lieutenants, I have an early morning," Willa said. "By your leave?"

Willa walked away and didn't see the other three smile as she walked away.

"Not going to be easy for her the first couple of weeks or so," Bekam said. "Green LT just out of the academy and female."

"Nuscomb will clue her in," William said. "And them. Going to be a fun next few weeks for all of us. Lots of rookie LT's"

As Willa had predicted, she found several deficiencies to do with the troopers lockers or how their bunks were made up. With the veterans as well as with the rookies. After the mandatory reprimanding of the sergeant and the troopers twenty pushups, they ran their two miles and formed up again.

"Section one appears a bit out of shape Sergeant," Willa said walking up and down the line. "Comes from lazing around the barracks the last few months.

"Recon troops can be mobilized on short notice at any time people. That means we have to be at our best, all the time.

"I also don't like how the sections are organized sergeant. Five troopers from Section One are to be reassigned to Section Two and five from Section Two are to be assigned to Section one. You have the rest of the day to make that happen Sergeant. Carry on."

"Shit," she heard one trooper say. "Don't she know things ain't like they are at the academy? What a hard ass."

"Not your job to question orders Albertson," Nusomb said. "Your job is to follow orders."

Unlike the other platoons, their lieutenant was with them every morning for PT and the mandatory two mile runs every morning. The other platoons officers only showed up after breakfast. She also had them doing weapons training every day. She not only supervised these activities, she actively participated. She was pretty good, but some of the veterans and rookies could beat her.

This was only after she had given them shit for not treating her like any other trooper. She had to learn, to get better, just like they did and she couldn't if they were holding back on her.

The troopers soon began to respect her. She worked them hard, but never spared herself. Her criticisms were always justified and she also gave praise when it was warranted. One day the colonel and the senior sergeant came by and observed their combat drill.

Every one knew the colonel had come up from the ranks and was generally known to be a bad ass. She didn't look all that happy while she was watching them.

She called Willa over.

"Why are you trying to get my Second Platoon killed *lefteant?*" Janet asked just loud enough for the whole section to hear. "If we do not train like it is for real, in a real fight we die.

"Section One! All of you! Against the *Leftenant*, now! And if I see any of you holding back on her, I will cancel your leaves for the rest of the month. Move it! You too Nuscomb, you're looking a bit flabby."

The ten members of Section One made a rough circle around Willa. For her part, she turned sideways and began to slowly rotate around. She had her left arm pointed where she was looking, the right held her practice sword above her head. Nuscomb was the first to come at her, she easily swatted his sword away and danced aside. One by one, the other troopers came at her, with the same results.

"Oh for Fucks sake!" Janet said.

Janet grabbed a practice sword from one of the watching troopers and launched a furious attack on Willa and then anyone standing around in the circle watching.

"Get the fuck at it *Leftanant!*" Janet yelled.

A switch went off and Willa was in full attack mode. Janet was back pedalling as fast as she could, to no avail, she was the first to go down. The veterans knew they were in trouble, they attacked all out now. At times in twos and threes. Willa was in constant motion, spinning, ducking, kicking, lashing out with her free hand, grabbing an attacker and swinging them in the way of another.

Janet stood and baked away, she tossed the wooden sword to the trooper she had taken it from and went back observing. After two minutes, five troopers were on the ground, but Willa was not having it her own way, she had taken a few hits herself. Janet nodded her head at Hassman. He pulled out his whistle and blew it. The action stopped. Willa stood, still at the ready, but still.

"That people," Janet said. "Is how I expect my orphans to train. You out of practice LT? Last time I saw you, you and that bloody axe and big assed knife were all a blur. Lieutenant Bahr, a moment of your time. The rest of you, get at it. And no fucking around this time!"

Janet took Willa out of earshot, Hassman trailing them.

"You ok Willa? You took a couple of pretty good shots," Janet said quietly.

"Ya, I'll live," Willa said. "Pretty good bunch I have here."

"You had a chance to get home yet?" Janet asked.

"No time," Willa said. "Gotta get these guys working as a team."

"Keep at it," Janet said.

Now she started poking Willa on the chest and raised her voice.

"Next time I come by to watch, you better be doing it right *Leftenant*. Or I will replace you with some one who can. Now, get out of my face!"

Willa came to attention, snapped a smart salute, about faced and marched back to her watching troopers. The troopers, expecting a sever tongue lashing, formed up in a line at attention. She put them at ease.

"The colonel is correct," she began. "I have been holding back on you. I apologize for that."

"No way LT," Albertson said. "You are busting our asses harder than any other platoons LT ma-am. Wasn't fair what the colonel made you do ma-am. Besides, when are we ever going to face ten to one odds?"

Willa took a deep breath and went to one knee. She waved them to her.

"Gather around," she said. "I watched the Captain and his platoon hit a whole battalion from the side on Arial. Twenty against one thousand. He lost two troopers killed. But broke up the enemy formation and saved our asses.

"He did the same thing a couple of weeks later. This time holding three battalions long enough for the rest of the Queens Guard to come and destroy them. At the end, they had no arrows left. Five were down, five more all most out of the fight, everyone tiring and wounded some where. The war ended right then. Twenty against three thousand. It was estimated that First Platoon killed around a third of the enemy facing them. He suffered one dead and ten badly wounded."

"Ya," Albertson said. "I was there. We saw those kids and old timers fighting and fighting. Especially the big guy with the Valkyrie on his chest and the eagle on his helmet and the little girl beside him. She had a big ass knife in her left hand and a big ass hand axe in her right. She was a right demon her. Prancing and swirling and rushing down the whole line to help the others and fill the gaps. Damn! Wonder if she made it out."

Nobody had noticed that William had walked up on them. Nor had they noticed that Willa had dropped her head and was looking at the ground.

"Ya," William said startling them. "She made it out. Janet has her doing some kind of hush hush shit.

"Lieutenant Barh, a moment?"

Nobody noticed Willa quickly brush her cheeks as she stood. She and William walked out of earshot.

"What was all that about?" He asked. He saw her eyes were still moist.

"Jan came by and watched us train," Willa said. "She gave me shit for holding back on them. She was right, I am, sort of. A girl needs some secrets eh? Then she had ten of them come at me and joined in herself. I had no choice then.

"After she left, I gathered them around and we chatted. Albertson asked me when we would need to fight ten on one...."

"And you told them," William finished for her. "Rightly so. Not all our deployments are going to be like that Willa. Probably never. But we will be behind the lines alone a lot. Shit happens.

"Janet not to rough on you I hope?"

"Naw," Willa said. "She was concerned is all. I'm gonna have a sore rib for a day or so. Then we had to make it look good is all."

"Ok," William said. "I just came by to give you a heads up. Officers meeting

tomorrow morning. Keep at it sis. I have a feeling we are going to get orders tomorrow. See ya sis, take care."

They both made the required salutes and broke apart. William to the other platoons and Willa to hers.

"Alright gang," Willa said. "Gather up your gear, stow it in the barracks, check your ponies and get cleaned up. Enough work for today.

"Sergeant? A moment?"

"Captain says keep up the good work Sarge," Willa said. "Says the gang looks good. Also, officers meeting in the morning. Cap figures they are going to deploy us."

"Thanks for the heads up LT," Nuscomb said. "I'll let the guys know and check with the other platoon sergeants for any scuttlebutt."

"Carry on Sergeant," Willa said, returned his salute and walked toward her barracks.

'Shit', she thought. 'I am in no way ready for a deployment.'

As no orders had been received other wise, Willa wore her best work day uniform to the meeting. Except for the colonel, her major and the Senior Sergeant, who were all in full uniform, the rest of the officers in attendance were dressed the same way.

"Starting Monday morning," Janet began. "Company A will be deploying with First Battalion Kings Own Regiment off planet to quell an uprising someplace. They will fill you in on the details on the transport. Prepare for the worst.

"Company B, to stay in garrison.

"Company C, minus Lieutenant Bahr, to prepare for escort duty for their Majesties and retinue, and the Emir and his party. It is an official diplomatic visit. Prepare accordingly. Company C also deploys Monday.

"Every one, but, Captain Bekenbaum and *Leftenat* Bahr get at it!"

In short order, all that was left in the room was Janet, William and Willa.

"You are not in shit Willy," Janet said. "Just had to make it look that way for the rest. Officially, I am giving Will shit for not letting you take your two month leave you have accumulated. Officially, after the duty day is over, you are on two months leave Willy.

"The whole Royal family is required for this visit Willy. Will can, and is required, to continue as the commanding officer of Company C. His second in command can take over for him when he has to attend official meetings and such.

"For security reasons and others Willy, we want to keep the deception of you serving on active duty as secret and as long as we can. Hence, you going on leave. We will schedule it so that your platoon does not have escort duties around you.

"Your parents will fill you in on the details tonight when you go home. Good? Ok, get at it, I got a lot of shit to do today."

"Nuscomb will take over for you Willa," William said once they were out of the HQ building. "Pretty routine stuff for him. See ya at home tonight sis."

Second Platoon couldn't decide if they were happy or not to be in the Royal escort. They were happy they would get the chance, but not happy about their Lieutenant not going them. Willa just shrugged her shoulders.

"Follow orders guys," she said. "There will be other chances for me later. Gotta go. Got a hot date tonight."

Willa arrived at the Palace complex guard post just after six that evening. She had orders showing she had been ordered to report to the queen herself which she showed to the officer on duty. A member of the House Hold staff was waiting for her and relived her of her two duffle bags.

"I will take these to your room Your Highness," he said. "The family is waiting for you in the dining room, Ma-am."

Willa added her thanks at him and strode toward the closed dining room doors. The guard posted outside the closed door went inside, closing the door behind him. Willa quickly went over her uniform making sure everything was where it was supposed to be and in proper order.

"At Your Royal Highness's pleasure Ma-am," the guard said, holding the door open for her and bowing his head.

Willa stiffly marched into the room, her beret held firmly under her left arm. She stopped three paces from the dining table, came to attention, rammed her right foot into the floor and bowed her neck.

"First Lieutenant Bahr, Second Platoon, Company C, Second battalion, Queens Guard reporting for duty!" Willa said standing at attention her eyes pointed above those seated at the table.

"Well met Lieutenant," Dimitri said as the door closed. "Lieutenant Bahr is temporarily relieved of her duties. Now come and give your old man a hug eh?"

Formality was quickly gone and everyone was hugging everyone. Willa had not been home for over a year. Ever since before the attack in fact and not seen her parents for the three months she had been in training.

The four of them, Dimitri, Margarete, William and Willa, spent until well after the meal was finished, dishes cleared away and many glasses of beer or vodka, catching up. It was late into the evening before they headed for their respective bedrooms.

Willa walked into hers and looked at the room she had not seen for over a year. Other than her duffle bags on a chair, it was a typical teenaged girls room. Posters of the latest male heart throbs on the walls, gay colours, stuffed animals galore.

Willa grabbed her duffles and went to her over large and filled to over flowing walk in closet. She found a space to hang her uniforms and a shelf to place her weapons on. Then undressed from her uniforms and in her underwear, like she did in barracks, went to bed.

She was up at her now customary dawn, going through her clothing, looking for something to wear. She found something not to gaudy to put on. Finished dressing, she made her way down to the kitchen where breakfast was just starting to be prepared. Her nose was filled with the wondrous smells of fresh baked breads, frying ham and especially the coffee. She found a clean cup, poured it full of coffee, grabbed a still warm from the oven scone and took a seat at a handy preparation table.

She had finished her first scone and was reaching over to grab a second before she was finally noticed.

"Your Royal Highness!" A startled baker, arriving with a new batch of scones said. He quickly set down his tray of scones and bowed.

The rest of the kitchen staff, now warned, also bowed or curtsied.

"Your Royal Highness," a woman, who, by her clothing, the morning chef, said. "Had Your Royal Highness just given a call, someone would have brought you coffee and scones to your room Ma-am."

"Nonsense Chef," Willa said. She looked down at her feet counted them, then her hands counting them as well. "Yup, they are all still here. I can walk and pick things up then. Hardly an invalid. I am Willa, and you are?"

"Beatrice Your Royal Highness, breakfast Chef Ma-am," she replied.

"Good to meet'cha," Willa said sticking out her hand.

The woman took it and bending over, meant to kiss her knuckles. Willa quickly grabbed her hand away.

"Now, now, none of that eh?" Willa said. "Adults shake hands, not kiss them."

The woman gingerly grasped Willa hand then.

"I thought you were new," Willa continued. "The rest of these yahoos generally call me squirt or Willy."

A round of heavy laughter went through the others gathered around.

"So Chef," Willa said. "Yes I can ring up for coffee and scones. However, there is nothing better than fresh right out of the oven scones. As far as waiting until breakfast time? Well, I am a growing girl and hungry all the time. Just ask these guys."

"Oh yas," one of the cooks said. "When she was living here, she was always coming around and swiping whatever."

Another round of laughter, which Willa took part in, occurred.

"Not even back for a day and causing havoc in the kitchen again eh?" William said as he walked in.

"Oh give me a break brother," Willa said. "What the hell are you wearing? You have a special meeting or something?"

William shrugged his shoulders. He was dressed in an expensive designer business casual suit.

"Gotta look the part you know," he said. "It's just not done you know. Shit what the hell are you wearing? Mom's going to have a bird."

Willa was wearing a loose fitting sleeveless t shirt that left her navel exposed. And a fashionably ripped pair of blue jeans with a pair of white sneakers on her feet.

"Well," she said. "These are about the only pants that fit. And the T shirt was the only one that did fit. I've grown a bit since I was last here. Not that you noticed."

Willa plucked at the T-shirt above where her breasts were.

"My stupid Captain never gave me enough time to go shopping," Willa continued. "It was either this or one of my work uniforms. Mom can have all the birds she wants. Too bad, so sad."

"Mom can have a bird about what?" Margarete said as she walked in.

She, like they, had poured herself a cup of coffee and grabbed two scones. Unlike them, she put her scones on a handy plate. She, like William, dressed in designer business casual skirt and blouse. She looked over at Willa and wrinkled her nose.

"I suppose it will do for this morning," Margarete said. "Under no circumstances do you leave the residences looking like that. And definitely not with your belly on display eh? Not that your abs are not great, just what's on them. Come then, away we go, we have distracted these hard working people enough for this morning."

A gasp was heard as one of the younger women saw the burn scar running across Willa's belly.

"Ha," Willa said. "This is nothing, a mere scratch. You should see the one on my head or this one."

Willa made to pull down the collar of her T-shirt.

"Willa!" Margarete said, knocking Willa's hand away from the collar. "Enough!"

"Oh," Willa said. "Sorry. It's been a long time since I was in civilization."

"Sorry mom, I forgot where I was." Willa said as the three of them walked toward the dining room.

Margarete stopped her and hugged her. She pulled the T-shirt collar down and kissed the scar just below the collarbone, then her head above where the scar, now hidden by regrown hair was. Her eyes were misty.

"It's ok luv," Margarete whispered. "Just not in public right?"

"Won't happen again," Willa said. "Well, it might. Only clothing I have is my uniforms, or shit from when I was a kid. These were the only ones I could find that sort of, kind of, fit."

"Not to worry," Margarete said. "The tailors and seamstresses will be here after breakfast. I'll have someone run to town and pick you up a few casual things to get you by. Then you and I can go shopping eh?"

Chapter Fourteen

The rest of the weekend was a blur for Willa. She had been fitted for her formal wear and her full uniform. Hair had been done, nails trimmed. Makeup shades determined and applied.

Late evenings and early mornings were beginning to take their toll. As expected of her, Willa was dressed to the nines in expensive designer clothing as they arrived at the space transport hub. William, in uniform, was supervising the loading of the companies and the Royals horses. Seeing her platoon, Willa made to go and say high. She was stopped by Margarete.

"No luv," Margarete said. "Lieutenant Bahr is on holiday. Now, you are Princess Willa. They have no need to know."

They met and greeted the Emir, his family and retinue. Then Dimitri, with Margarete and Willa trailing, inspected the lined up honour guard of the Emir's guard. And in order of precedence, Willa and the emir's son, bringing up the rear, entered the transport.

Once inside the transport, the groups broke up and the Royals were escorted to their section of the transport. This transport had been specifically designed as the Royal transport and the Royals section was separate from the others.

There was still no time to relax. Crew members were scurrying about, making sure each of the Royal Family was seated securely. A guard was posted in their own take off and landing seats and belted in. A beep was heard and Dimitri listened to his comm unit for a second and told some one to carry on.

Five minutes later a klaxon went off. Noises started as the engines fired up and with some minor shaking and muted roaring, the take off happened. Once Willa felt the auto gravity kick in, she didn't wait for help, but hit the harness release button and shrugged off her safety harness.

"Well," she said as the rest of her family did the same. "That was defiantly better than the last trip I had on one of these things."

Dimitri chuckled.

"The job does have a few benefits," he said.

The guards, seeing they were not required, discreetly went out of the Royal State room. Only to be replaced by a harried looking Chief of Staff. Dimitri sighed.

"No rest for the wicked," Dimitri said. "What now?"

"The Windsors are demanding an update on our arrival Your Majesty," the Chief of Staff said.

"Like I would somehow know that," Dimitri said. "Inform the Captains staff of the demand and ask him to politely reply, when he can find some time. Demand indeed."

"Arrogant bunch," Dimitri said after they were once again alone. "This is going to be a shit show."

"Now now Dem," Margarete said. "Be nice. bureaucrats are the same everywhere. The Windsors themselves are most likely like ourselves."

"Somehow I doubt it," Dimitri said. "To much tradition and honour and the like."

"Windsors?" Willa asked. "Who are they?"

"Old Royal family from Home World, or what's left of them anyway," Margarete said. "They came out here about a hundred years after our people did. Just at the beginning of the troubles on Home World. They settled on Britannia. It's the one thousandth anniversary of their reign. Which is why we are going. Why we were invited I don't know. We have little to nothing to do with Britannia."

"Long trip for a party," Willa said.

"Ya well..." Dimitri said shrugging his shoulders.

"Well," Willa said. "I am so tired I think I'm half asleep right now. Where do I bunk in?"

"Third one on the left," Margarete said.

"Night all," Willa said.

She made her way down the hall and into the room, just falling on the bed and was instantly asleep.

It took a week to reach Britannia. While she had some free time to explore her surroundings or relax, most of Willas time was spent in elocution lessons. How to do this or that. Which utensil to use for which dish. Orders of presidency, things of that nature.

It took half an hour to get ready to depart. Everyone had to look just so and be wearing just the correct clothing. At the foot of the loading ramp were a large crowd of officials. The foremost of whom were all dressed in lavish dress military uniforms.

A line of immaculately red uniformed soldiers, with large, towering black hats were ranged on each side of a red carpet. These crashed to attention, placing their blasters in front of their faces. The second her father's foot hit the ground, the Oaken National Anthem broke out from the massed band.

Not in uniforms themselves, the Oaken Royals just came to attention. Then the introductions were made. Hands shaken. Kind words spoken. The honour guard inspected and they were split-up into groups and taken to waiting horse drawn carriages. Willa, forewarned, paid no attention to the massed news reporters taking photos and vids. She smiled and waved her hand when the woman she was with did. That's all. Then they were in their carriage along with some ladies in waiting.

"I noticed your brother was missing Your Highness," the woman she was with said. They spoke standard with a nasal and marbles in their mouth accent.

"Unfortunately, Prince William is the commanding officer of our Guard Company," Willa said. "For today, he has to provided escort for Their Majesties, Your Royal Highness."

The woman with her was, like Willa, the daughter of the king of Britannia. Only a couple of months older than Willa was.

"Such a bother all this, what?" The princess said.

She was continually looking out the window of the carriage and waving. Willa was mimicking her.

"Appearances, always bloody appearances," the princess said. "Such a bloody bore don't you think?"

"I wouldn't know Your Royal Highness," Willa said. "At least, I don't have to put up with this kind of thing. Last week Her Majesty and myself went shopping in town. If we wouldn't have had our guards around, nobody would have even noticed. Not that they did anyway."

"Really?" The princess said.

She looked at Willa when she said it. Willa thought as she was scrutinized, probably noticing her for the first time.

"Right," the princess said as the carriage slowed and stopped. "Here we are then. Everyone out eh? Your Highness first, you are the guest after all."

They all had to line up again. This time for the official photographs.

"Oh my," the princess said in a low tone. "Your horses are much different to ours. Do you ride?"

William's Platoon, still mounted, was in line across from the kings carriage. Their copper coloured horses contrasting with the blacks of the Britannic troops. As were the uniforms. The dark blue almost black uniforms of the Queens Guard, contrasting with the ornately embellished red with brass helmets and chest plates the Britannic troopers wore.

"A little," Willa said. "I don't have much time to ride lately."

"Oh," the process said. "I will have my chief of staff arrange for us to have a ride then. Well, off we go. I'll show you to your rooms Your Highness. You must be tired from the long journey."

The princess chatted away about whatever as they made their way down long hallways. Servants were rushing to and fro, carrying luggage and other things.

"Right," the princess said coming to two doors across from each other.

"You two scurry away now, shoo shoo," she said to the two ladies in waiting.

Both curtsied and hurried away. Giggling to each other. The princess sighed.

"The things I have to put up with," she said.

"That one is yours," the princess said pointing to the door on the left. "This is mine. If you want, I can show you your room and you can rest. Or...I can show you your room and you can come to mine and have a drink what?"

The princess giggled, shocking Willa. The princess flung open Willas door and dragged her by the arm inside.

"Sorry for how small it is," the princess said. "The heirs get the big rooms. The spares, that means us, get the smaller ones."

Willa took in her surroundings. The bedroom itself was twice as large as her own suite at home was. Then there was the dressing room and the sitting room and the huge walk in closet that her clothing hardly made a dent in and the large bathroom.

The furnishings and decor were opulent, also unlike her more humble room at home.

"So?" The princess said. "Meet your expectations Your Highness. We can fix anything you don't like right away."

"No, this is fine," Willa said.

"Goody," the princess said. "Now, rest or??"

"I would not say no to a small drink," Willa said. "Just one though. If it is no bother Your Highness."

"Bother? Hell no," the princess said. "Always a good time to drink I say."

She took Willa by the arm and whisked her into her own room. Which, while the same size was decorated much, much differently. More like how a rich young woman in her almost twenties would decorate.

"Whiskey or?" The princess asked.

"I'll try a whiskey," Willa said.

The princess poured a generous portion into two glasses and handed Willa one.

"Cheers," the Princess said raising her glass.

"Absent comrades," Willa said, raising hers.

She followed the princess's lead and drained her glass.

"Who, good shit this eh?" The princess said breathlessly.

"Not bad," Willa said, shocking the princess.

She had thought to see the younger woman choking on the strong liquor. Not smiling at her.

The princess poured the two glasses full again.

"You expecting to get the kid drunk then eh?" Willa said. She laughed and drained the glass again. "Good luck on that one."

"Ya, ya, Laugh it up," the princess said. "I'm hung over from last night is all.

"I am Anne." She stuck out her hand.

"Willa," was the reply and a fist bump instead of a shake.

Willa tapped the comm unit in her ear.

"I need a bottle of the good stuff. Ya right away please. All Her Highness has is some god awful watered down whiskey. Ya Her Highness's room."

Minutes later a nock at the door before it was opened. A young trooper in dark blue was standing there. He had a bottle of clear fire in his hand.

"Thanks Kurt," Willa said taking the bottle from him and closing the door.

She grabbed two new glasses, filled both and handed one to Anne. Then she drained her glass.

"Holy shit!" Anne struggled to get out. "You drink this? Good shit."

"Take it easy Anne," Willa said. "Goes down easy, kicks you in the ass right after. Ninety nine proof."

Willa filled their glasses again, this time only a quarter full. She took a sip from hers and sat down on one of the chairs. Anne sat across from her tucking her feet under her as she did.

"I must say," Anne said. "You are not at all what I was expecting. A little quiet and reserved, still."

Willa shrugged her shoulders.

"I am who I am," Willa said. "Nice hunk. Your guy?"

"No," Anne said looking at the picture Willa was pointing to. "My younger brother."

"Nice," Willa said. "I wouldn't throw him out of bed for eating crackers. Only once though."

Anne choked on the sip of vodka she had just taken.

"What?" Willa said. "A girl has to have options no?"

"Well," the Queen asked Anne before diner later. "What's she like? Boring and stuffy like we thought?"

"I don't know, yet." Anne said.

"Well her parents are...well...more like commoners," the Queen said. "Only to be expected from Colonials from the back and beyond."

Anne swallowed her reply. She knew it would go over her mothers head. She and Willa had a good time at diner. They were seated together.

"We have nothing on for tomorrow," Anne said as they walked back to their rooms.

"We can relax, sleep in or go for a ride if you wish."

"Sure, I'd like that. The ride I mean," Willa said.

"Good, so would I," Anne said. "Tenish then? After breakfast? You have riding clothing? I can have some sent over. We are about the same size."

"No. I'm good. See you then." Willa said.

Willa had been briefed and arrived at Annes knock on her door, properly dressed and ready to go. Anne chatted gaily the whole way to the stables about what ever. Willa discreetly took in her surroundings as she walked. They arrived at the stables and were helped to mount the thoughobred horses waiting for them.

Of course there were half a dozen accompanying riders with them. They started off at a walk, which was good, because Willa needed to get a feel for the horse and unfamiliar tack. The stirrups were much shorter than she was used to. As all horses do, hers tested her and quickly found out she knew what she was doing.

Anne led them into a very large tree lined field and they began to trot. Anne and the rest doing the elegant posting riding. Willa doing what she did. Then the canter for a short while, back to the trot and then a walk again.

'She obviously rides seldom,' Willa over heard one the hangers on say behind her. Willa smiled to herself.

"Oh look," Anne said. "My little brother and his bunch are practicing. Come, you must see this Your Highness."

Anne broke into a trot toward a line of men with long bows in their hands and targets in the distance.

"Well sister, you are up early today," her brother said.

"Oh poo," Anne said. "Her Highness and I wanted to go for a ride this morning. And here you are, making all kinds of noise and ruining my ride."

Anne jumped off her horse and gave her brother a hug. Anne was breathing heavy from the trotting. Willa, more sedately, dismounted and approached them.

"Your Highness," Anne said. "My younger brother, His Royal Highness Prince James. James, Her Highness, Princess Willa of Oaken."

"Your Royal Highness," Willa said bobbing a shallow curtsy.

James bowed to her in return.

"Nice bow," Willa said. "Do you mind?"

James handed her his bow and Willa looked it over.

"Do you shoot?" James asked.

"A little," Willa answered. "Our bows are not as long though."

"These are British long bows," James said. "No better bows anywhere. Deadly to a hundred yards."

He took an arrow from a quiver at his hip, placed it on the string brought the bow up, pulled the arrow back to his ear and let it fly. It hit the target, just outside the bulls eye.

"Care to try?" James asked handing the bow to her. "Careful now, it is quit a draw weight."

Willa took the bow and the offered arrow. Looking at the arrow she saw it had a rounded practice point on it. She took the arrow, placed it on the string and in one smooth and fast motion, aimed and let it fly. It hit the target a little low and to the right. She held her hand out for another. This one hit the bulls eye a little to the left.

"Not bad, good bow," she said handing it back to James. "Like you said, a little to heavy of a draw for me though. My arms are going to be sore for a week."

"I'll bet," James said. "Good shooting."

Willa shrugged her shoulders.

"Don't ask me to do it again though," she said. "The arrow wouldn't make it to the target."

"Shit," she heard one of James friends say as she walked back to her horse. "Two shots with a bow she has never seen before. Both on target and one bull. Shoots once in a while my ass."

Unlike Anne, Willa didn't wait for a hand up to remount. She just mounted and was waiting for Anne while she mounted.

"We using the same road to go back?" Willa asked.

Anne nodded. Willa kicked her horse and was off at a gallop.

"See ya slowpokes!" She yelled over her shoulder.

"Jesus!" Anne said. She spurred her horse and galloped after a disappearing Willa. The laughter of her brother in her ears.

Willa had dismounted already and was handing the reins to a waiting groomsman as Anne came crashing into the yard and slid to a stop.

"Shit!" Anne said breathlessly sliding off the horse. "You ride like you are part of the horse. You are not even winded!"

Willa shrugged her shoulders.

"You said you only ride a little!" Anne said as they walked back to the estate.

"No, I said I haven't ridden much, lately," Willa said. "There is a difference you know."

Willa laughed.

"Ive been riding horses since I was born," Willa continued. "I was riding my own horse right after I could walk. A real horse, not a pony. It's a cultural thing."

"And the bow?" Anne asked.

Willa shrugged her shoulders again.

"National sport," Willa said. "Another cultural thing. I think my boobs are going to be sore for a month. Your bows are much harder to pull than ours are."

"You drink like a fish, ride a horse like you are one and shoot the damn bow better than my brother, the planet champion," Anne said. "What the hell else can you do?"

"Not much," Willa said. "A little of this and a little of that."

She was prancing and swirling around as she said it.

"Pretty boring actually. Not allowed to be like the other kids you know. Such a pain in the ass."

"I hear you there," Anne said. "At least my brothers get a little more freedom. They are both in the army. I, as a female, am not allowed."

"What are you allowed to do then?" Willa asked.

"Not much, officially," Anne said. "I have my charities. They take up a lot of my time. I am still allowed to compete in some horse shows. But no polo. Just not done. Hunting? Playing with weapons, oh no, it's just not done. Bull shit I say.

"I hear you allow women in your army?"

"Some do," Willa said. "It's mandatory for the men."

"We allow women to serve," Anne said. "Just as auxiliaries though. Much the same as you I am sure. I have an auxiliary officers commission. In the communications divisions, as a bloody staff officer."

"We have women serving in all branches of the military," Willa said. "Combat arms, whatever they are qualified for. Like yourself, it's kind of expected that I do my bit. I'll see after we get home. I am always interested in learning new things. What is this horse showing you are speaking of?"

"It has two main elements," Anne said. "Designed to test the skill of the horse and rider. The first, is a series of tests in agility. The second, is jumping fences. I can arrange a demonstration for you if you wish."

"Oh yes," one of the ladies in waiting said. "Her Highness is quite good. She wins many meets."

"And this polo thing?" Willa asked.

"The men charge up and down a field whacking a ball with mallets, on horse back," Anne said said. "I'll have my brother arrange a match for you."

The rest of the month went like that. Anne and Willa would do something by themselves, mostly, during the day. News people always followed them wherever they went. In the evenings, some gala or ball or something. Some, not many, were fun.

She was getting tired of the over indulged children of the high aristocracy. How they put down those lower in station to themselves. Especially to the common people. Anne was better than most, but even she was condescending to her servants.

She was also getting tired of the veiled and unveiled, put downs the aristocracy made about her, her parents and her planet. Calling them Colonials. The worst was at the official banquet for the anniversary. She, and Anne, were seated with an over bearing older sister of Annes father, who let Willa know in no uncertain terms, where Willa and her family stood as far as she was concerned.

Once all the official after diner speeches were finished, the King stood and addressed the assembled dignitaries. He started off by thanking everyone in attendance for their attendance and kind wishes.

"I would especially like to thank His Majesty, King Dimitri of Oaken for accepting our invitation. He has travelled a long way to be here. In the past, our two families were quite linked together. Until we were all banished out here that is.

"It is my hope, that once again, the people of Oaken and the people of Britannia, join hands. To once again, become close and prosper together."

A round of clapping and here here's from the assembly interrupted the king.

"His Majesty, King Dimitri has agreed to have his famous Eagles perform one of their training drills for us. All of us have heard of the skill of his Eagles.

"On Thursday, the day before they once again return home to Oaken. The Eagles will perform their drill on the archery training area. All in attendance here today are invited to witness this once in a life time event."

Chapter Fifteen

Willa had asked and been given permission to ride her own horse. She, and they were becoming restless. Anne accompanied her every morning. Anne was a good rider and could now keep up with Willa for the most part.

Willa slowed to a walk, allowing Anne to catch up. They were far from the riding path going across country to places Anne had never seen.

"I have to say," Anne said. "You took my aunt very well last night. She is such a bitch. I gave her shit for acting like that after. Not that she ever gives a shit. And now you are going to shrug your shoulders again."

Willa did and they both laughed.

"You and that bloody horse of yours," Anne continued. "Both of you, not breathing hard or sweating. Shit. My horse and myself, are breathing hard and sweating. And don't you dare bloody shrug your shoulders."

Willa laughed instead.

"You breed for looks and short term speed," Willa said. "Our horses can go like this and much harder and longer, all day, every day."

"You have two with you, correct?" Anne asked.

"I have four," Willa said. "But was only allowed to bring two. Buster here is my main pony. Cody is my second."

"Only two? My goodness, what a hardship," Anne said. "I only have two horses."

"The guards have four, each," Willa said. "But, as I am not a guard..."

Anne laughed.

"Look Willa, my father really wants to have closer ties," she said. "We hear all the good things you people are doing, how you are prospering."

"And there you have it Anne," Willa said. "You people. Do you know how much that phrase pisses me off?"

Willa stopped her horse in his tracks.

"Just who the fuck do you think you are?" Willa was starting to get more than a little worked up now.

"My father will ask the Prime Minister to look into it. If the people of Oaken and parliament agree, we might do something. Depends on what's in it for us. From where I am sitting. You need us more than we need you."

Willa turned Buster around and took off. As hard as she tried, Anne could not catch her.

Anne did not see Willa again, until the demonstration on Thursday. Willa was once again seated beside her.

"Willa, I apologize," Anne said before Willa could say anything. "Honestly, I didn't think I was being patronizing. That is a phrase we use all the time here. I am truly sorry Willa. I have come to think of you as my friend and I don't have many, or any come to think of it, any real friends."

"Ya, my mom gave me shit for loosing it," Willa said. "That I apologize for. Look Anne, we are very similar in some ways, not so much in others. Unlike you here, we on Oaken leave the governing to the people. If we are asked, we will give our opinions and if needed, take control, as we did on Arial. Usually we ask, that time we just acted."

"What happened to you and your father was horrible," Anne said. "Was it bad?"

Willa gave her shoulder shrug.

"Bad enough I guess," she said. "But what the hell do I know?"

"If it can be arranged," Anne said. "Would it be possible for me to visit you one day on Oaken? Nothing official. All low key. I need to get away from all this for a while."

"Feel like slumming it eh?" Willa said.

Seeing the look on Annes face she laughed.

"Sure why not," Willa said. "You can share my room on the way back. It's nothing fancy like you are used to though."

"You can do that?" Anne said.

"Sure, you're my bud and mom said I can bring a buddy along anytime," Willa said. "Go easy on the clothing though eh? I only have so much room in my little cabin."

Anne hugged Willa.

"Thank you, thank you Willa" she said. "I won't be a bother. I will just bring enough cloths for the trip, a week yes?"

"Ya a whole week crammed in that sardine can," Willa said. "Ah shit, is that your aunt? Who's that pompous looking ass with her."

The portly man walking with the aunt was dressed in a gaudy generals military uniform. Complete with all the shining buttons, gold lace and banging medals.

"My Uncle, her husband, commanding general of the mounted horse guards," Anne said. "Try and keep your cool eh? It's only for the next little while."

"No promises," Willa said. "I'll try."

"Uncle, Aunty!" Anne said. "So glad you could make it!"

She air kissed her aunt and uncle as was the norm in upper class Britannic culture.

"Bah," the uncle said. "Waist of time. What can a bunch of colonials do that my Guards can't do better."

Willa's Platoon had been chosen to do the demonstration.

"Bah," the general said after the first few drills were done. "My men would have blasted them out of their saddles by the time they finished the first drill in a real battle."

Willa stood.

"If you will excuse me?" She said. "Must have been something I ate."

She walked away. Anne could tell she was upset.

"What the hell is wrong with you two!" Anne said and hurried after Willa.

"Get my fucking horses and gear ready!" She heard Willa say. "You heard me. Right the fuck now! They want a fucking demonstration? I'll give them a fucking demonstration!"

Anne stopped in her tracks.

Willa looked back at her, hate in her eyes.

"You fucking people have no fucking idea who you are fucking with!" She said and marched off.

Anne ran to where her mother and father and Willa's were seated.

"Excuse me Your Majesties," Anne said.

"Anne, join us, plenty of room," her father said a smile on his face. "Willa is with you?"

"Um.. no father. Aunty and Uncle did something to upset her." Anne said. "She took off, I couldn't stop her."

"Oh shit," an older woman in a colonels uniform next to Annes mother said. She pointed.

At the far end of the training field stood two horses. A rider, bare back, was on one of them. She, and the unridden horse were fully encased in shiny full armour. The riders helmet was decorated with a large red eagle, wings outstretched on both sides of the helmet, the talons outstretched to below the riders cheek peace. A depiction of a woman, sword raised, riding a winged horse on the riders breast plate.

They barely heard the song that began. A woman was singing in an unfamiliar language. It was slow, in the rhythm of a walking horse. The women with drew the sword she had behind her back and as she sang, she began to move and the horses, both of them, moved with her. A slow rhythmic dance, horses and rider in perfect harmony. The movements slow and graceful.

The king, queen and every uniformed Oaken stood and began singing as well. The Prime Minister and his wife standing and singing the same song. Anne recognized the horse the rider was on. It was Willa.

The song became faster, the rider and the horses movements did the same. Now the platoon of troops on the field joined the song and removed their swords placing them on their shoulders. The horses wanted to move. The troopers held them in check.

The song came faster and faster. Horse and riders movements faster and faster. The movements now fast and violent. Right at the end, rider and horses were screaming. Then they charged!

At full speed, Willa changed horses, drew three arrows and her bow, placed two arrows in her mouth and one on the draw string. She pivoted and at two hundred yards, let her first arrow fly. The arrow and the three after it went right threw the targets in the bulls eye. She dropped her bow and drew not a sword, but a large and wicked looking hand axe with a spike on top and the end of it. She went down the line of practice dummies and decapitated each of them with one blow. The ones she didn't strike, the horses did.

The rider put her axe back in its scabbard on her belt and withdrawing the sword she had placed back in its scabbard behind her back as she had changed horses, put the sword on her shoulder and walked toward the review stand.

"Christ ain't that the LT's horse sarge," she heard as she approached her troop. "You don't think sarge??"

"First platoon!" Nuscomb yelled. "Prepare to salute!"

Ten swords went in front of ten faces.

"Salute!"

The ten swords flashed to one side. Willa answered the salute with her own.

"Permission to join your line Sergeant?" Willa asked.

"Yes of course Your Highness," Nuscomb said.

Willa, effortlessly spun her horse around to face the reviewing stand. She gave the sword salute.

"First Lieutenant Bekenbaum, Second Platoon, Company C, Second Battalion Queens Guard, reporting for duty Your Majesty!" Willa barked out.

Dimitri returned her salute.

"Carry on *Lefteant*," Dimitri said.

He was smiling so Willa knew he was pissing around not pissed off. She smiled back, then removed her helmet and let it hang from the saddle by it's chin strap. An audible gasp went threw the crowd. The left side of her head was shaved bare, showing the big scar there. She had the rest of her hair done in a pony tail that now trailed down her back.

Willa casually took her bow to hand and in fast motion pulled an arrow out of the quiver behind her on her saddle and without looking, shot it into the crowd. It landed in Annes empty chair right beside the now shocked general. It was at the level of where his heart would have been. She quickly drew and shot again and once again. The first one striking between Annes feet, the second between James legs on the chair he was sitting on.

Willa casually placed her bow back in it's case under her left leg.

"Permission to speak Your Majesty!" Willa said.

"Permission granted." Dimitri answered.

Willa walked her horse to where the General was sitting.

"General," Willa began. "I would have killed at least ten of your precious Horse Guard before I even got in range of the blasters you boast about. Five more before I let my axe out to play. And I would not be alone General. I would have those ten with me."

She pointed at her platoon. If anything, they sat taller in their saddles.

"Twenty of us killed over a thousand on Arial," Willa continued. "Twenty of us. We lost one killed and ten wounded. I wear the one who was killed colours with his mother's, my colonels, permission."

Willa walked her horse to once again be in front of her platoon facing the review stand.

"Who are we!" She yelled.

"Magies Eagles!" Her platoon roared.

"I can't fucking hear you! Who are we!"

Now everyone but Margarete in Oaken uniform roared it out.

Magies Eagles, Magies Eagles, Hurrah!

"Janet's Orphans! Janets Orphans!" Willa began to chant in Oaken.

Now it was Janets turn to look at the ground. Only briefly, then she came to attention and saluted.

Willa returned the salute.

"Second platoon! About face! Column of two advance!"

They trotted off the field.

"Well," Dimitri said. "I guess she made her point eh, Your Majesty?"

"To bloody right," George, the Britain's King said. "She was one of the twenty on Arial?"

"So were the both of them," Dimitri said, pointing at William and Hassman.

"But.." George said. "Both of your heirs could have been killed."

"Sometimes shit happens," Dimitri said.

No-one noticed that Anne had disappeared.

"Somebody help me get this fucking armour off," Willa said. "One of you assholes better have some hooch. I'm dying of thirst over here."

Willa couldn't tell who's outstretched hands were offering her a flask. There were ten of them. She grabbed the first one and took a deep pull.

"OH my heart be still," she said "Nectar of the gods. You know how crappy that booze the big shots have is?"

Nuscomb was helping her remove her armour. She had her full uniform, like theirs, under it.

"Thanks Sarge," Willa said. "Was in a rush when I put it on. Was starting to rub in places I don't want to talk about."

"No, thank you Your Highness," Nuscomb said softly.

"What the hell for?" Willa said.

"For the ramparts Your Highness," he answered. "For the ramparts."

Willa saw tears in his eyes. She looked around her. The rookies with looks of awe on their faces, the veterans with tears in their eyes.

"Sorry Your Highness," Akerson blurted out between the tears. "We was trying Your Highness, we was trying hard. We was coming as fast as we could."

Willa hugged Nuscomb first, then Akerson and then all ten of her veterans.

"No. Thank you," she said softly. "We were about done when you guys got there and saved our asses."

"Truth be told Your Highness," Nuscomb said. "Wasn't much left for us to do. They were ready to break, we just helped out a bit Ma-am."

"I never seen anything like it," Akerson said. "You was everywhere, all at once. That big assed hatchet or that big assed knife comes down, wham bam, a man dies. Shit!"

"Just doing my job Akerson." Willa said. "Just like you guys. Ok look. Among us, I am the Lieutenant or LT. Just like normal eh? And I promise to still call you all shit heads."

Every one laughed then.

"Would one of you mind?" Willa asked. "Can one of you look after my horses and my shit? My mom's gonna kick my ass if I don't get back quick."

"And if she don't, the colonel will" Jackson said to more laughter. "I'll do it Your...oops LT."

"Very good corporal Shit Head, carry on," Willa said.

She walked away to laughter in her ears.

"You are a soldier?" Anne said from the shadows. "A front line trooper?"

"No choice on the first one," Willa said. "Everyone on Oaken serves five years.. nor the second come to think of it. We get slotted into whatever position we are qualified for. They just don't give these way you know."

She pointed at her uniform and the eagle in her collar.

"We have to earn them, just like everyone else."

"Did it hurt?" Anne asked, gently stroking the scar on Willas head.

"Nah, looks worse than it was," Willa said. "Head wounds are like that, bleed like crazy."

"It's true then, you were one of the twenty on that rampart on Arial?"Anne asked. "I saw the vid coverage of that."

"Poor you," Willa said. "Not much of a fight. Must have made for a crappy show. The one my brother was in earlier was better. Way better."

"Your troopers, they love you Willa," Anne said.

"Who me?" Willa said. "I'm just a dumb ass rookie right out of the academy. Those guys, especially the sarge, the corporal and the other eight vets, they are the real pros. I'm still learning.

"Hey, try this, now this is well and truly the good stuff."

Willa handed the flask she had in her hand to Anne who took a deep pull and coughed right after.

"Takes some getting used to I'll admit," Willa said. "Still want to come home with this blood thirsty heathen colonial?"

"If you will have me," Anne said. "Bloody heathen colonial with the shit booze and all."

"Willa Greta Bekenbaum, get over here right this second!" Margarete ordered as Willa and Anne walked into the foyer leading to the residences. She had her arms crossed on her chest.

"Ut oh," Willa said under her breath, "Just go with it, say nothing, you'll just piss her off more."

"Yes mommy dear, right away mommy dear," Willa said sweetly batting her eyelashes and looking down at her feet. "I'm ever so sorry for making the general shit his pants mommy dear."

"Oh get your boney ass over here you," Margarete said holding her arms open.

The two hugged. Margarete kissed the scar on her head and turned her loose.

"Anne told us what her horrid Aunt and even worse uncle had said," Margarete continued. "And, how patient you had been all week with them and others of their kind."

"Aw shit mom," Willa said. "It was all good until that damn ass disrespected my platoon and the Queens Guard. Then I kinda lost it."

"Rightly so I might add," Anne said. "Willa has been nothing but courteous and generous with her time all the while you have been with us Your Majesty. What my Aunt and others of her ilk have been saying is all bullshit."

"Willa says you are coming to Oaken with us?" Margarete asked. "Does your father and mother agree?"

"Yes, yes, we agree," George said as he walked in. "You'll be doing us a favour. Get her out from under our feet."

"Love you too daddy," Anne said.

"Do try and not embarrass us Anne?" Mary, her mother said.

"Yes Mommy, whatever you say mommy," Anne said, mimicking what Willa had said and done earlier.

"Talk to your daughter George," Mary said. She turned and walked away.

Unlike when they had arrived, they departed to the spaceport in modern limos. As another round of handshakes, smiles and poses for the vid cameras went on, nobody really noticed the last car arrive. While it was an expensive four door sedan, it was not a limo, thus it was ignored by the news people as carrying no one of importance.

Anne and Willa exited the car to no notice. The security guard from the front seat rushing to the trunk of the vehicle and hauling two medium sized bags from it. He passed them to a waiting transport officer, then hustled back to the car.

"Willa has had a big influence on Anne Dimitri," George said. "Before you people came, she was wild and almost uncontrollable. Parties and night clubs all the time. Different men, sometimes twice in a week. Now, well I have to make sure it is really Anne now. Willa and Anne have been a little tipsy from time to time, but nothing like before.

"You do know our families were once very close and I believe even related?"

"Long ago and far away George," Dimitri said. "All former official treaties and commitments, were rescinded by your ancestors, when mine agreed to the United Nations proposal to be the first settlers in this galaxy.

"While, on paper, our system of government is very similar to yours, there are several differences. The biggest one is that my family operates in the back ground. I have more constitutional authority than you do. But, we seldom exercise it and actually prefer not to use it at all.

"While all your pomp and ceremony are nice, we have no need for those things. I actually feel sorry for you and your family George.

On Oaken, we can freely walk down the streets with no news vid people harassing us"

"Oh my God!" Anne exclaimed as she looked over Willa's 'small' cabin. "This state room is bigger than mother and father's on our yacht. Mine is a quarter of this size!"

"First time we have ever used it," Willa said.

Willa grabbed one of Annes bags and took it to a set of double doors which opened to reveal a walk in closet.

"Put your stuff wherever," Willa said. "I only have my uniforms and weapons."

"But...what of all your clothing?" Anne asked.

"Gave it all to one of your local woman's shelters," Willa said. "I have enough at home to suit my needs."

Unabashedly, Willa began to strip off the clothing she was wearing. In only her under wear, Willa walked to the closet, put the trousers and blouse in a cloths bin and began to dress in one of her everyday work uniforms.

"What?" Willa said seeing Anne avert her eyes as Willa walked back, her shirt still not on. "Shit, in barracks we are co-ed. If you ain't seen a pair of boobs and an ass before, you are in for a shock love."

"Co-ed barracks and you walk around like that?" Anne said.

"We have some simple rules," Willa said. "Girl, or boy, says no, that means no. Person that pushes their luck or worse? Well, if they survive the attempt, it will not be for long."

"But..what about...You know?" Anne asked.

"Boys will be boys, girls will be girls," Willa said. "Girl gets pregnant, out of the regiment and I mean right now. So does the boy responsible. Until the child is born and old enough to be left with a care giver. Then back to the regiment. However long that takes, is how much time they have to do extra to get their five years in."

Willa had been doing up her boot laces while she had been talking. Now she picked up the uniform shirt and put it on. She looked at the look on Annes face.

"You don't do your full five years and you are not a full citizen Anne," Willa said. "You can still live on Oaken, vote, start a business, whatever. But your taxes go to thirty percent from ten. You get no interest free or start up investments from Oaken. You do not share in any profit sharing of Oaken controlled business or investments. You have to pay for all of your education and medical requirements.

"Those who finish their five years, obtain the ten percent tax status and profit sharing, but only half of the profit sharing is payable and only at the end of the year. Once the ten year active reserve portion is over, we receive all the profit sharing, monthly. Plus, any of the hold backs for the last ten years plus interest.

"We also, pay nothing for any schooling requirements in whatever level we wish to partake and are qualified for. We pay nothing for medical care. It's a pretty good deal."

"Oh," Anne said.

"Our doctors and medical facilities are all top notch," Willa said. "Don't forget, all of them are in the army, active or inactive reservists. The medical and educational facilities are all maintained and built by Oaken. In fact, all of the infrastructure is."

"But.." Anne said. "Every one knows you people hate socialism."

"No Anne," Willa said. "We do not hate socialism. We intently dislike authoritarian socialism. Just as we intently dislike authoritarian capitalism. Britannia's culture is both. We, on the other hand, are capitalistic socialists.

"There is little crime or poverty on Oaken Anne. We look after our people. We don't expect our people to look after us. Think about it for a while."

A member of the crew entered the cabin at that point.

"Your Highness's," he said. "We are beginning departure procedures."

Willa led Anne to the sitting room. Three chairs, one by the door, had harness on them. Willa pointed to one and Anne sat.

"I've got this airman," Willa said.

Willa began to do up Annes harness. It had a wide lap belt, two wide shoulder straps and two wide belts coming from the floor between the legs. All attached to a central point on the lap belt. Willa attached everything and pulled them tight.

Anne was about to complain they were to tight, when she saw the airman, then Willa tug much harder on theirs than Willa had done on hers. Willa fished in the pocket of her chair and came out with a plastic wrapped package with she quickly opened and passed to Anne. It was a motion sickness bag.

"I have been sailing all over the oceans of Britannia Willa. I won't need this," Anne said.

"Keep it on your lap," Willa said. "Better safe than sorry eh?"

Anne was just getting comfortable in her chair, when a loud klaxon went off startling her. Right after that, rumbling could be heard and it got louder. Then she was roughly pushed back into her chair by something unseen. The force grew stronger and stronger and just when she thought she would not be able to breath, it was gone. She looked over at Willa and saw Willa's hair splay out all around her. Then it dropped back into place.

Willa hit the release button and her belts came off. She walked over and did the same for Anne.

"If Your Highness's would be patient a little while longer," the Airman said. "Once the all clear is given, you may roam around the deck freely."

"Shouldn't be more than a couple of minutes," Willa said. "You Ok? You look a little green around the gills."

"Oh my God!" Anne said. "You do this a lot?"

"Not really," Willa said. "Just a country bumpkin me. Second trip for me. This was nothing, right Airman."

The Airman chuckled.

"Ya, Greta ain't much of a pilot," he said.

"Well," Willa said. "We couldn't very well walk there. Somebody had to fly it."

The klaxon once again went off.

"Well, come on then," Willa said. "I have to check on my horses."

Anne was looking wide eyed as she went down the passageway that led to the lift at everything she saw. They arrived on the deck required and Willa led Anne to a closed bulk head. Willa put her palm on a pad and a doorway opened. From the horse smell, it was the transports stable area. Willa consulted her wrist unit and started making her way down the aisle ways that connected the horse stalls, finally coming to hers. Both her horses came to her and put their heads on her shoulder. Willa scratched each behind an ear, told them she would check on them later, to relax and behave.

As they left the stable area, Second Platoon was just entering.

"Woo hoo, who's the dish LT?" Akerson said. "Umph!!"

Nuscomb had smacked him with an open palm on the back of his head.

"Way to much woman for you Akerson," Willa said.

Anne sashayed up to Akerson. She ran her hands up and down his forearms, liking her lips as she did.

"My, my," Anne said. "This one would make for a nice afternoon snack."

The three women in Second Platoon started to snicker as Akerson began to back away and blush. Anne sashayed up to one of them and did the same thing.

"Maybe both of you eh?" She said.

Now it was the mens turn to snicker as the woman turned red and tried to back away.

"But," Anne said turning away.

She put her arm around Willa's waist and kissed her cheek.

"I have my own LT."

"Oh stop it!" Willa said as Anne began to stroke her back. "Not in-front of the children!"

They had drawn quite the crowd as other platoons were coming to check on their horses.

"Yes sir, Ma-am," Anne said coming to attention and saluting. She had her chest stuck way out. "Anything for you sir, Ma-am."

The lift door opened then and Willa shoved Anne inside. The hallway was filled with laughing troopers as the lift doors closed behind them.

It opened again on their deck. A male trooper, still in his full uniform was walking away from them.

"Oh my," Anne said. "I might actually enjoy this trip. So much variety of men to choose from. What a nice ass."

The trooper stopped dead in his tracks.

"Ut oh..." Anne whispered. "I think he heard me."

"Ya think so?" Willa said. She laughed. "Take it easy brother. She's just pissing around."

"That's your brother!" Anne whispered. "Shit, shit, shit."

William turned around and walked toward them in his own version of a female sashay. He looked Anne up and down. Anne ducked her head.

"Sorry Your Highness," Anne stammered out. "I apologize for my behaviour Your Highness."

"Nah not my type Willa," William said. "She's a little to flabby and shy for my like. See ya."

"What??" Anne burst out. "Flabby!!!"

Anne took off one of her shoes and threw it at William, hitting him in the back. He stopped and turned around again. Now Anne was actually backing away, trying to hide behind Willa. William stooped, picked up the shoe and looked at it. As he turned, he tossed the shoe back underhanded at them. Willa caught it with ease.

"To big and wide for my feet," William said. "She can have it back."

"Why you!!!" Anne yelled. She grabbed the shoe out of Willa's hand and made to throw it once again. Willa grabbed her wrist to stop her.

"Good job LT," William said. "I might have had to put her across my knee and spank her this time. I think just no desert for diner tonight instead, what?"

"Is he mocking me?" Anne said as William walked away.

"My my," Willa said. "Why, you people can hardly take a joke...what. Tich, tich, you lower classes are no fun, no fun at all."

Anne turned to confront Willa, who had her nose in the air and was examining her finger nails.

"What to do, what to do," Willa said. "The blue or the red for the gala tonight? The blue I think, they will match my gown. Come deary, time for tea what?"

Willa began to walk down the passageway, one foot crossing in front of the other and swaying her feet, with her arms splayed out on each side of her. Anne was flustered. She didn't know what was happening.

"Oh come on pussy," Willa said, stopping and turning around. "Geez, no sense of humour."

Anne was hopping as she caught up, trying to put her shoe back on.

"Oh for shits sake," Willa said and she stopped, only long enough for Anne to put the shoe back on.

They walked into what appeared to be a buffet. The Royals were all seated together. Willa made a bee line right to them. She air kissed each of them in turn. Anne made the same gesture to each. Willa sat down on an empty chair and patted the empty chair beside her.

A server came over.

"The lobster I think," Willa said. "With the chardenai for an appetizer what? The same for my companion."

"I do hope the take off was not to distressful for you dear," Margarete said. "It is always such a dreadful ordeal."

"Oh, she handled it very well mother," Willa said. "Why, you would think she does this kind of thing all the time."

"William," Dimitri said. "What do you think of this years crop of colts. Any potential winners there?"

"There might be a few polo ponies," William said. "But no stake winners. We should look into getting a new head herdsmen. This one clearly has no idea how to do his job."

"Willa," Maragerete said. "We should arrive just in time for the new spring fashion debuts. It will be such a treat for her if you would clear your schedule and take her what?"

"Well mommy, my schedule is offaly full, what with the planning of the annual charity ball and all," Willa said.

Four servers came out of the kitchen. Each was carrying a covered dish. The Royals all took their napkins, jerked them open and spread them across their laps. Anne did the same. A server behind the first four was carrying a tray with a large decanter on it and four wine glasses.

The covers were whisked off the plates to reveal...A large hamburger and french fries. The servers were laughing as they walked away.

"Lobster and champagne," one of them said. "As if."

Anne kept looking at her plate, then the servers, then the plate and finally to the family who were all grinning.

"Gotcha!" Willa said, punching Anne on the arm.

"Oh my goodness!" Willa said as she took her first bite of the hamburger. "Mr. Hamburger, I have missed you so much."

Dimitri poured each of them a glass of what turned out to be a soft drink.

"There are other choices at the buffet if a hamburger does not suit you," Margarete said. "Not much though. Some soup, salad and breads. First meals are always like that. Diner will be a little better. Roast beef tonight I think."

"But no desert for you Anne," William said. "I plan on having some chocolate ice cream. You Willa?"

"Butter scotch I think." Willa said. "Well, that tasted so good, I think I'll go for seconds. Come on Anne. You might find something you like."

"Grab me bun hun?" Margarete asked. She thought for a second then laughed. "A bun hun..."

"Ah Geez mom," William said.

Anne followed Willa to the buffet. She had never been to one before and had to mimic what Willa did. Taking a tray, then a plate and some cutlery. She didn't much feel like another hamburger like Willa, but did take some salad, a bun and a scoop of chocolate ice cream.

As they walked back to their table, Anne saw it was beginning to fill up with uniformed officers and commented to Willa about it.

"Yes," Willa said. "This is the officers mess on board. Enlisted personnel have their own mess. We also have an all ranks club, but it is only open after eighteen hundred. Without the other passengers, we have over a thousand troopers and airmen aboard. Makes it easier for the cooks and us, if we have separate messes."

Willa had brought two buns for her mom and gave them to her as they sat down. William reached over and took Annes ice cream off her plate, putting it on his.

"Naughty, naughty," he said. "No desert for you. Remember?"

Anne glared at him, William laughed.

"Whatever for?" Margarete asked.

"She threw a shoe at me in the passageway," William said.

Dimitri laughed and Anne gave William the finger. Then she stood and ran out of the room.

"Ut oh," Willa said. "I better chase her, she'll get lost."

Margarete followed. They caught up with Anne just as she reached Willa and her, state room, she was banging on the door as it would not open. Willa placed her palm on the pad located by the side of the door, and it slid open. Anne ran inside. Both mother and daughter saw Anne was crying. Anne sat on the closest chair and buried her head in her hands crying.

Willa was instantly crouching beside her and rubbing her back. Margarete came over and squatted down in front of her. Anne looked up and seeing the concern on her face, cried harder. Margarete put her right hand under Annes chin and gently lifted her head to look at her.

"We," Margarete said. "By that, I mean the Plains Clans and especially our family, do not take our selves seriously Anne. Life is to hard and to short. You are not used to that type of behaviour and I apologize for it. We should have gone a little easier on you for the first little while."

"We were just pissing with you Anne," Willa said. "It means we like you, even Will. He would have just ignored you other wise."

"Or been, very, very polite," Margarete added. "What started all this Willy?"

"We were coming back from inspecting my ponies," Willa began. "One of my hotheads made a stupid comment. Anne put him in his place and another, female, trooper. That was fun. We both laughed about it. So did they. We were coming here and ran into Will headed the same way. Anne, not knowing who it was, made a comment about his nice ass."

"Ah yes," Margarete said. "He has his fathers yummy ass."

"Well she said it a little to loud and he heard it," Willa said. "Will, being Will, sashayed over and gave her the once over. That's when Anne saw who it was and did the bow and curtsy and Your Highness routine, apologizing like crazy."

Magarete couldn't help herself and laughed. Willa chuckled.

"So..." Willa continued. "Will says, 'Nah she's not my type. To shy and flabby for me'. So she tossed her shoe at him. Will catches it, looks at it and says, 'Won't fit, to wide for my feet' and he tosses it back."

Margarete was laughing even harder now.

"Then, I started the oh so uppity aristocrat routine with her and you guys were already doing it when we showed up," Willa said.

"Alright I get it now," Margarete said.

She tapped her ear twice.

"Please have Captain Bekenbaum report to me in Lieutenant Bekenbaum's state room at his connivance? Thank you so much."

"Right," Margaete said. "Now I show you how to handle a Will. This is going to be so much fun."

Both mother and daughter were grinning from ear to ear. Anne didn't know what to do, but had stopped crying. A few minutes later, the tone that announced a visitor at the door went off. Margaete put a finger up before Willa could have the door opened. Margarete stood, wiped the smile off her face, placed her feet to shoulder with apart and her hands on her hips. Willa caught on and stood beside and a little behind her, standing the same way, but with her hands tucked into the small of her back. They were blocking sight of Anne.

"Enter," Willa said.

Having gotten his cue on how he had been ordered to report. William marched into the state room, came to attention three paces from Margarete, stomped his right foot into the ground and bowed his head.

"Captain Bekenbaum reporting as ordered Your Majesty!" He said. He kept his head looking over Margarete's head.

"Captain Bekebaum," Margarete began. "You have upset Her Highness' guest. Her self a princess of a powerful and hopefully, new friend. You may very well have not only jeopardized that new relationship, but possibly created an international dispute between Oaken and Britannia. Unacceptable Captain!"

"Your Majesty! No excuses Your Majesty! I will apologize immediately Your Majesty," William said.

Margarete motioned for Willa to move aside. Anne rose from her chair and assumed a regal air as she looked at William.

William, again, bowed his head and kept it down this time.

"I apologize for my behaviour Your Royal Highness." William said. "It was unacceptable behaviour Your Royal Highness. The fault is all mine Your Royal Highness."

"In order to foster better relations between our two peoples, I will accept your apology Captain Bekenbaum," Anne said. "I will however demand that you be punished for it."

"And what would you consider a suitable punishment Your Royal Highness?" Margarete asked.

"I believe, being my escort for tonight's gala will suffice," Anne said. "All of the gala and no desert for him."

Willa snorted, Margarete outright laughed. Anne was standing, both hands on hips and her nose in the air. She was struggling to keep a laugh in. William looked up and shook his head. He started to smile, then caught the look on his mother face and went back to attention, expressionless.

"You never, ever call any woman flabby," Margarete said. "Nor make a comment on the size of her shoes. You're lucky I don't have my wooden spoon handy young man. Especially to one of Willies guests and a royal. I thought I taught my son better manners than that."

"Sorry mom," William said. "I was just pissing around."

"And you young lady," Margarete said to Anne. "Well behaved women never, ever comment on how a mans lower extremities look. Especially your friends twin brother."

"Sorry Your Majesty," Anne said. Her head was now down and her hands by her sides.

"Bloody kids these days," Margarete said. "I have better things to do than baby-sit grown adults. You made her cry Will, unacceptable."

"Oh shit," William said. He walked right up to Anne.

"Sorry Your Royal Highness. I was just making an ill advised joke Ma-am," William said.

"As was I William," Anne said. "I am sorry as well."

Anne stuck out her hand.

"I am Anne, William," she said. "Friends?"

William let his smile come out and hardily shook her hand. Anne thought the sun had completely filled the room with his smile. Her whole body tingled.

"Ok," Margarete said. "My work here is done. And you have work of your own to finish before tonight I think Captain?"

Margarete strode out of the room.

"She's right ," William said. "I have to finish my report on the boarding. See you tonight Anne?"

"Yes of course," Anne said. "And don't be late for our first date heh?"

"First date eh?" William said. "Well, you are a bit to shy for me, but we'll see."

Anne tossed a close pillow at his back as he walked out. She sat on the chair again and looked at the floor.

"What now?" Willa asked. "He was just pissing around."

"It's not that," Anne said. "It was kind of cute in fact. I think I might kind of like your brother Willy."

"Is that all," Willa said. "Good, I thought maybe you had the hots for me."

"Ewe," Anne said. "While I will admit you are good looking and I have been known in the past with a fling or two, I prefer men. And, you are my friend. You won't mind if I chase your brother?"

"Have at it," Willa said. "Make your day. Many have tried, all have failed to get past the third date. I don't know what he's looking for so don't ask, but he hasn't found her yet."

"Shit," Anne said. "I only brought traveling clothing with me. Hardly anything suitable for a gala."

Willa laughed.

"It's just diner with the captain in the main dining room," Willa said. "Traditional first and last, night shit. What you have will be better than most of what the big shot ladies will be wearing. Well, except for Fatima and her daughter that is. They are more like you guys than us. Better keep an eye on Sheena, the daughter. She has the hots for Will and her brother will probably try to get it on with you. He's a player."

William showed up five minutes early. He, like Willa, dressed in expensive tailored business casual. Anne was fashionably late of course. Willa knew she had been pacing the bedroom the whole time. She had been ready a half hour before.

"Wow," was all William said as he saw her.

"Wow right back," Anne said. "You clean up nice. Well, shall we?"

They stopped in front of the formal dining room door and arranged themselves. The girls on either side of William with their arms through his.

"Their Highness's, Prince William, Princess Willa and Her Royal Highness Princess Anne of Britannia." The metradi at the door announced.

The three walked to the table where the captain, Dimitri, Margarete, Greta and Janet were seated. Introductions were made and they sat. Anne quickly proved she could fit in, she was quickly making jokes with the others, mostly at Williams expense.

After diner, which saw William have his desert stolen by Anne, a band started to play. As what happens everywhere. The young people gravitated together and as Willa had predicted, Shamir hit on Anne and Sheena on William. Anne was gracious about it, but Shamir quickly knew she was not interested. Sheena was more persistent, but William knew how to handle young teenaged girls infatuated with him.

Willa caught Anne looking at William more than once and he the same to her.

"Ut oh," Willa said in German to her brother. "Careful big guy. I think your heart is being stolen away."

"As if," he replied in the same language. "Way, way to upper class for the likes of me sis."

"Anne," Willa said in Standard. "You have had a long and tiring day. Perhaps William can escort you back to our state room?"

Once again, Anne took Williams arm and she made her goodbyes to the captain and the table.

"Careful with that one kiddo," Janet said in Oaken to William. "You know what her family is like. Always have some kind of agenda."

"No fear Jan," William said also in Oaken. "I have my eye on her."

"Not your eye Jan is talking about brother," Willa said in Oaken.

To their credit, they waited to laugh until the couple had left the room.

Anne was sitting in the sitting room, a glass of vodka in her hand and looking at the ceiling when Willa arrived some time later. The glass was full.

"How'd it go?" Willa said startling Anne when she walked in.

"We had to wait a few minutes at the door before an airman could come and open it for us," Anne said. "But it was good. Your brother is nice."

"Oh, stupid me." Willa said smoking her forehead with her hand. "I forgot to get you to key the door to you for access."

Anne looked and saw the smile on Willa's face. She tossed a handy pillow at her.

"Ya right," Anne said. "I don't need your help to snare a guy. What were those languages you were speaking?"

"Oaken with the head table," Willa said. "Everyone can speak it here. German with my brother. It's a forgotten, mostly, language from Home World our ancestors spoke. Only the Prairie Clans speak it now."

Anne took a sip of her vodka and looked at the ceiling again. Willa saw her eyes go moist.

"Ah what did my shit head brother do now?" Willa said.

"It's not him," Anne said. "Well a little, but not that way. Your family Willa. You love each other so much and don't care who sees it. My family never does that. My father and younger brother will, in their own way, when we are alone. But never like what you do and never ever my mother."

"Oh my," Willa said. "You poor girl."

She came and squatted down in front of Anne.

Anne hugged her and let the tears flow.

"What am I going to do?" Anne said. "I think I have feelings for your brother. If my family finds out about it, they will push me hard to get him to marry me. For the good of the Monarchy. They won't give a shit about how I feel. Just wait. By the time we reach Oaken an official request for an official visit from my younger brother will be waiting. They were already pestering him about you Willa.

"Shit, shit shit. They will mess everything up between us Willa."

"First," Willa said. "We are not stupid Anne. We may be from the back woods, but we are not stupid. Why do you think Sheena is after William and Shamir after me? A lot of upper class Oaken and other planets people try all the time. Me? Right now, I don't have time. I take my job seriously Anne. I have to, my troopers might die if I don't.

"As far as Will? I told you, go for it. I think he likes you, but who knows with guys? Your brother? Well, he seems nice, but, not really my type Anne. You'll see once we get home. Maybe you'll find another hotty to latch on to."

Chapter Sixteen

The three of them spent nearly every evening in the all ranks club. Anne quickly became popular. With officers and enlisted. She liked to have fun and proved she was intelligent and had an exquisite mind at times. Asking questions on Oaken culture and answering theirs of hers.

The debarkation on landing was another surprise for Anne. There was absolutely no formality at all. They got off the transport and literally walked the short distance to the Palace complex. Their Majesties and the colonel did have a gaggle of aides reporting to them as they walked, but other than that, nothing.

The palace was not as large nor as opulent as Annes home. Her room was tastefully decorated and not that much smaller than her own.

As had been predicted by Anne, an official request for a visit from her younger brother was waiting. The reply sent that while the visit would be welcomed, it was to be understood that William and Willa were serving officers in the Army and had reported for duty to be deployed and would not be able to escort the prince.

"So you do know how to play the game then," Anne said. "How long will you be deployed for Willa?"

Willa shrugged.

"Dunno for sure," Willa said. "It depends on how long you are staying here. I am deployed as your guard escort for the duration of your visit."

Anne laughed.

"You people are just as devious as mine are," Anne said. "And Will?"

"He will be around," Willa said. "Unless something urgent comes up. Then not only he, but all of us, may be gone. Right now we are the only deep Recon Battalion of Eagles. The rest are all light cavalry units."

"Knowing my family," Anne said. "We have at least a month. It will take them that long to set everything up and most likely a full transport of hangers on will be along."

"You have one official function to attend." Willa said. "Can't be helped. Have to meet all the Oaken big shots in the capital. It will be a little closer to what you are used to. Being a big city and all. Lots of clubs and shopping. And media types.

"After that? Up to you. We have enough offers from all over Oaken for a visit from you."

"Let me play it by ear first eh?" Anne said. "We'll see how goes in the capital. But I really want to explore where you live Willa. Big cities are big cities."

"So," Willa said. "Not to worry. We keep a house in the capital and it is only a three hour flight from here to there."

"Oh and here I thought I'd have to go on horse back all the way," Anne said.

"Hey, not fair," Willa said. "We have modern transport you know. It's just easier to walk or ride most of the time here."

Anne laughed and touched Willa's shoulder.

"I was just messing with you," Anne said. "My family made sure I was well briefed on everything Oaken before I left."

Anne was surprised at the quality of the small personal air transporter they travelled in. The seats were soft and comfortable, the ride smooth and quiet. She commented on it to Willa. As her norm, Willa had just shrugged her shoulders and told Anne they were based on a military requirement, upgraded a little for the civilian market and manufactured on Oaken itself. Another of the government profit sharing initiatives a veteran had come up with.

There was a little more fanfare when they landed. Light blue uniformed troopers formed a mounted honour guard. The Emir and his son, the son in the same light blue uniform of the troopers, greeted them and there was a media presence, no where near as big or as intrusive as the media presence Anne was used to.

They were escorted to a well appointed large car and whisked to the house the Royal Family kept in the city. The staff was made up of all older Eagles and Bears veterans. Again, while respectful, it was more like being served by friends than staff. Having the rest of the day to themselves, Willa had them driven to the shopping district. Anne was surprised at the quality of the fabrics and designs on display. Britannia was well known for its fashion designs, but these put her own planets to shame. And this was in the common shopping district. The designs in the different shops had ethnic themes, reflecting on the many different cultures on Oaken.

One of their two body guards was kept busy making arrangements for shipping. The quality of the jewelry was better than Anne had ever seen, except for the most expensive on Britannia. Willa told her they came from Oaken as well.

The next day, all shopped out, Willa took her to experience some of the artistic shops. Again, the quality and the range of goods surprised Anne. As the shops the first day, these all had an ethnic theme. Many using Oaken natural leathers and materials in their production.

That night, Willa took Anne to one of the trendy clubs frequented by people their age. Women and some men, were displaying vibrant and colourful makeup and hair styles. The alcohol was flowing freely and Anne was having a great time. Her raven black hair standing out from all the blonds and brunets. Surprising Willa, Anne kept her alcohol use to a minimum. She always had a drink in her hand, but she rarely took more than one sip from a glass, before setting it down on a table and moving on.

Willa made a comment on it when they got home, early the next morning. Anne borrowed one of Willa's patented shoulder shrugs, smiled and went to bed. Willa was up at eight and eating breakfast. Anne wondered in wearing a dressing gown shortly after.

"Busy day for me today," Willa said. "I have to make an appearance at one of our schools this morning and a hospital this afternoon. Relax until it's time to get ready for the banquet tonight. Mom and dad should show up around four or five."

"No, no,"Anne said. "If it is allowed, I'd like to come along."

She quickly dressed like Willa had, in business casual and they were whisked off to what ended up being a pre-school for children aged five. Anne was an instant hit, almost as fast as Willa herself had been. Willa caught a photographer in the act, shooting through a window and jerked her head at one of the guards and pointed at the window. Then, went back to what she had been doing, playing with a group of children on the floor.

Anne was oblivious. She was deep into the story she was reading to an enraptured circle around her. There was a much bigger media presence when they departed. Some yelling questions at Anne, who just ignored them.

Arriving at the hospital, Anne saw it was an Army hospital for those wounded on duty. One of the places they went to in the hospital was the rehabilitation area. Anne took a special interest in one soldier. He had lost both legs and an arm and was working on a set of parallel bars learning how to walk. Anne rushed over and asked if she could help, the physical therapist nodded and let Anne support the young man as he tried to walk. He was, in her opinion, doing very well and she told him so.

"Not good enough Your Highness," he said. Sweat was running down his face and staining his shirt as he worked. "My buddies are counting on me Ma-am. I can't let them down. I need to get back in the field fast Ma-am."

Anne heard more, many more comments like that from others and some actually apologizing to Willa for letting her down. Some from horribly burned men and women. Those ones tugged at her heart the most. But she never let anyone see it. She was always smiling or making jokes.

Anne had to take break to compose herself, it was starting to take a toll on her. She went to a refreshment station and took a bottle of water, taking deep breaths to calm herself down. As it happened she was not far from Willa.

"Get those assholes away from the fucking windows. Get as much help as you need. Detain the whole fucking bunch. I will have a little chat with them later."

The soldiers she was with saw where she was looking. They made their excuses and left the room. Shortly after, Anne heard a commotion coming from outside the window. Others in the room heard it too. Some looking out. They took off, grabbing what ever was handy.

"What's going on?" Anne asked.

"Oh," Willa said. "The bar must be opening or something. Ok, off we go. Have to get all pretty for the Prime Minister tonight."

There were only two media people present, both across the street, when they left the hospital. Willa let Anne enter the vehicle first, then stuck her head in.

"I'll be right back," Willa said. "Stay put."

She was heading to the rear of the hospital toward where the confrontation had taken place and her walk turned into a march as she went. Anne came out of the car and followed her. Another of a long list of amazing things that day greeted her as she came around the corner.

Their two suited body guards were standing looking over a crowd of over a hundred wounded soldiers, some with table or chair legs in their hands. These were surrounding around twenty media people. Male and female, kneeling on the ground. Many of them bleeding from noses or other areas of the heads, of both genders.

"This is NOT Britannia!" Willa shouted. All the soldiers came to attention. "The photography of private citizens, without their permission is against the law. Photography of a military facility can be charged as espionage! Any form of media coverage of the Royal Family, or their guests is not allowed without prior permission. Questions are never allowed.

"I don't give a shit who you are, who you represent or where you come from. These are our laws, not yours. You are all damned lucky to be alive! My soldiers were very lenient on you. Oh, in case you forget. Everyone on Oaken is a soldier. Everyone. Get these fucks out of my sight!"

Several large van type vehicles roared around the corner and on the grass, sliding to a stop. Troopers armed with not only blasters, but with swords across backs poured out of them. Assisted by the wounded, they roughly hauled the media to the trucks and tossed them inside.

This had been caught by two circling vid drones. Willa looked at them and pointed. One immediately crashed to the ground the other kept circling, but from further away.

"One of ours," a soldier said. Willa nodded her head.

"Tenhut!" Willa yelled. The wounded all formed a line and came to attention.

"On behalf of Oaken, My family, My self and Her Royal Highness Princess Anne, We thank you brothers and sisters."

Willa came to attention and smartly saluted them.

"Aw shit Your Highness, wasn't a problem," Came from the line. "Anytime Ma-am."

"Ya, we was getting bored anyway," came another. "Haven't been in a fight for a while, if you call this a fight."

"Yes thank you," Anne said.

She was standing just behind and to the right of Willa.

"Many a time I have wished to do the same," she continued. "Just not done don't you know."

She had put on her haughty upper-class stance, nose in the air and marbles in her mouth accent for the last. That got a lot of laughs.

"Naughty Willa would not let me run with you after them like I wanted to, then tried to make me sit in the car after," Anne said. She pointed her finger at Willa and shook it like a mother scolding a miss behaving child. "Naughty Willa naughty. Hogging all the fun to yourself."

Willa dropped a deep curtsy.

"Sorry Your Royal Highness won't happen again Your Royal Highness," Willa said.

"See that it doesn't," Anne said her nose in the air. "Now off with you, back to the car."

"Yes Your Royal Highness, right away Your Royal Highness," Willa said.

She started to sashay away and putting her right hand behind her back, gave Anne the finger. She started to run, but to late. She got Annes hand bag in the back.

"You just wait until I get ahold of you Willy!" Anne yelled, running after her.

The troopers, some of them dropping to the ground, started laughing.

"Well that was fun," Anne said. As she came into the car behind Willa. "The last part anyway."

She was looking out the window as they drove away. Looking at nothing.

"You are not really going to send them back in the field are you?" Anne asked quietly.

"Yes," Willa said. "They have to finish their terms Anne. Some, like the soldier you were helping, will be in administration. The rest, if they are capable, back to their units. Or in a support battalion."

"They were apologizing Willa," Anne said. Her shoulders began to shake. "It broke my heart. They all want back so badly."

"Hey," Willa said.

She turned Anne around and hugged her.

"Those of us who serve love," Willa said softly, "Especially those of us in combat arms that have been in combat together. We are all brothers and sisters. We are closer to our teammates than we are with our own families. Your soldiers will be the same Anne. All soldiers are. They fight for all of us Anne. Not just me and my family. All of us. Sometimes we pay a big price for it."

Now Willa turned away and looked out the window.

"A price I am willing to pay to keep a brother or sister alive," she whispered.

The car had barely come to a stop and Willa had flung the door open and was running into the house.

"She, they," the guard who opened the door for Anne said as she left the car. "Take all of our pain Ma-am. When they deploy, the whole family, not just Willa and William, will be in the heaviest fighting Ma-am. They fight to keep us alive. Sacrifice themselves for us Ma-am. We can do no less for them. Your Royal Highness."

At the Prime Ministers reception, Willa was back to her normal self. Later that night, back in her room at the Palace Complex, Anne had trouble sleeping. She had to much to absorb.

"Nice job yesterday sis," William said at breakfast the next morning.

He tossed a tablet at Willa. Royals supervise an attack on British press on Oaken, was in large letters above a picture of Willa, hands on hips looking at the media on their knees in front of her.

"It's even better on the inside," Margarete said. "Fasist dictatorship they call us. Calling for an immediate response from Britannia they are."

"Who gives a fuck what they say on Britannia," Willa said. "The assholes were taking pictures of kids and our wounded. I couldn't give a shit for myself, but that was unacceptable."

"I said as much to the ambassador this morning," Dimitri said. "And reminded the pompous ass on how many of our laws had been broken. That the media gang was lucky they were just expelled from the country and not imprisoned for espionage and the exploitation of minors.

"We have filed law suits against the publications in Britannia and with the Federation."

"Don't bother," Anne said. "They all have armies of lawyers and deep pockets."

"Not as big or as deep as ours Anne," Dimitri said. "The Prime Minister insisted on it. Me? I'm like Willa. Who gives a shit?"

"Oh here we go," Anne said. Her tablet signalled an incoming transmission.

"Hello brother," Anne said. "How are you this morning?"

"What the hell are you up to there," Annes' older brother Charles demanded. "Do you know what kind of havoc your antics have caused the monarchy with this Anne? Do you? You will return home immediately. I am most unhappy Anne, most unhappy indeed."

"Well Charley," Anne said. "Borrowing His Majesties just spoken remarks, I don't give a shit. About what the press thinks or you Charles. You can't order me to do anything and if father orders me home, he will find he has lost his daughter. Now, do us all a favour and fuck off!"

"Fucking asshole," Anne muttered as she tossed the tablet to the corner of the room.

"Your Majesty," a communications officer said coming in the room. "His Majesty King George would like a word when you can free some time sir."

"Getting better by the minute," Dimitri said. "Tell His Majesty sometime this afternoon, I will find time in my schedule for him."

"Ya right," William said. "You are so busy. Doing what, sleeping?"

"Why no, not at all," Dimitri said. "I will be busy escorting Her Majesty to the super market. She always forgets the stuff I want."

"Willy," Margarete said. "A camping trip I think?"

"Ya, makes sense," Willa said. "If Anne agrees that is."

"Oh goody" Anne said. "I told you I wanted to see the country side Willy. When do we leave?"

"Tomorrow morning mom?" Willa said. "That to early for you Anne? We will go shopping for what you need after breakfast."

"The sooner the better," Anne said.

This time when they went shopping, they went to a regular shopping mall in town. To an out doors store. Willa did all the picking of the clothing, just asking Anne her sizes. She waved her communicator over the till to cover the cost of the pile of clothing and made arrangements to have it delivered that afternoon. Then it was off to the food court.

Anne chose an oriental assortment of foods, Willa her normal fries and hamburger. Anne was surprised when the servers at the food kiosks all apologized to her for the actions of the day before. Saying she should not have to put up with all the media harassment.

"A little different than you are used to eh?" Willa said.

"Yes, and no," Anne said. "A lot of the normal people say the same to me back home. When they get the chance that is. So where are we going?"

"No where special," Willa said. "First, my real home. We'll figure it out from there."

It took just over an hour to fly to what looked like a farm on the prairie. It was a little larger than most farms that Anne had seen, but much smaller than the grand estates her family and other aristocrats had on Britannia. It had large barns and outbuildings. The house itself was of a common design, just slightly larger.

"Anne's shit goes in the bedroom on the rear left." Willa said to a farm hand waiting for them.

"Welcome back home Willy," the man said. "Been a while."

"Ya good to be back and away from all the gong show shit at the Palace for a while." Willa said.

She gave the man a hug.

Seeing the amount of luggage in the back of the air vehicle, he tapped his ear and asked for some help.

"Sorry Chuck," Willa said, "Anne didn't have anything and my shit will be to small for me now."

"No big deal Willy," Chuck said. "It's all good. My daughter is just as bad. When she gets time off that is. She'll be here for a day or so. Hasn't been here for almost a year now."

"Oh that's right," Willa said. "Sissy is one of us now. I forgot Chuck, sorry."

"It's ok Willy," Chuck said. "Who notices rookies anyway. I sure as hell don't. Your ponies is out back Willy. I picked a couple of old timers for Her Royal Highness there. Shouldn't be a problem for her."

"I am Anne," she said sticking out her hand. "You needn't do anything special for me. I am a very experienced and accomplished competition rider."

"Not with our type of riding, or horses Anne," Chuck said. He shook Annes hand. "These ain't the pampered toy horses you are used to. Ours work for a living."

"It will be fine Anne," Willa said. "Come on, I'll show you your room and then a tour of the place eh?"

Annes room was large, but a lot smaller than what she was used to. Willa took her to own room. It was smaller than Annes and was loaded and decorated with what a teenager would think was good taste.

"Embarrassing much?" Willa said and laughed. "Haven't been home for a while. Come on."

Willa took Anne on a tour of the farm. She was treated and treated, every one they met as long lost friends. Hugging each man and woman she met. The last stop was at the large stables. They were ready, but had no horses in them.

"They'll be back in come super time," Willa said. "It has to be really shitty or cold outside before they will come in."

They went to an outdoor pen and Willa's four horses came up to her. She scratched each behind the ear. Then, an older large horse barged in and demanded her attention.

"Oh Sammy," Willa said hugging him. "I haven't forgotten you. Have you been a good boy?"

Sammy nodded his head up and down. Then looked down and sideways after Cody had given him a light nip on the flank.

"I thought so," Willa said and laughed. "He is such a smart ass. He was my first real horse Anne."

She hugged him and hard then.

"I was so worried about you Sammy," she said softly. "You were hurt so badly."

Anne could see her tears start to hit the ground. Sammy nudged the scar on Willa's head and whimpered.

"Yes, I am fine Sammy," Anne heard her whisper. "I made them pay Sammy. I made them pay."

'Oh my God,' Anne thought. 'I think that horse is crying.'

Cody put her neck across Sammies back and grumbled.

"Thank you Sammy," Willa whispered. "Thank you for saving my life."

Willa turned and ran back to the house. Sammy trotted to the other end of the pen. He stood with his head low. The other four horses came to him and comforted him.

"They are almost as intelligent as we are," Anne heard behind her. It was a girl Willa's age. The one Anne had made fun of on the transport.

"He took a full blaster shot at close range protecting her," the girl said. "Then killed the asshole that did it. He loves her and she him. She saved him as well. Our horses are family Your Royal Highness, not animals. They grieve along with us when shit happens. One of Charles' horses died right after he did after the ramparts. His heart couldn't take it not being with Charles anymore."

"Anne," she said sticking out her hand.

"Sarah," was the reply. "Or shit head rookie, depending on the circumstances."

She laughed.

"Willa and I grew up and went to school together," Sarah said. "I didn't do basic with her though. They didn't want her to get any special treatment. I was surprised when they told me to report to her platoon. But kept my mouth shut.

"You'll be riding Sammy tomorrow. He's a pretty good guy. You'll be ok. Ya you smart ass, I know you heard me. You be good to Anne here. She's Willies bud. I'll kick your ass if you don't"

Sammy shook his head up and down and to each side in a horse laugh.

"You just wait young man, you'll see." Sarah said. "Smart ass."

"I think they have one of Charles' other horses for you. They are pretty lonely without him."

"Your horses are as bad as you are," Anne said. "I'm sorry for the transport Sarah. I was just messing around."

"Hey, no problem," Sarah said. "I can take a joke. Got my ass harassed for a week after though. No where near as bad as Akerson did."

"Well," Anne said opening her arms. "Like you all say around here. Any bud of Willies is a bud of mine."

"I had better go find Willie before she sends the guards chasing after me," Anne said breaking their hug. "She can be such a control freak hard ass sometimes."

Sarah laughed.

"Don't I know that one." Sarah said. "See ya when I see ya Anne."

"Are you alright Willa," Anne asked when she found her at the kitchen table.

"Ya, it's just hard sometimes," Willa said. "Sammy damn near died. But he still wanted to come with us on the transport. Greta had to sedate him."

Willa flipped an internal switch.

"Ready for tomorrow?" She asked.

Anne shrugged her shoulders.

"I guess we will find out eh?" Anne said.

Chapter Seventeen

Willa struggled not to laugh as Anne came out of her bedroom the next morning. She had styled her hair, had the top two buttons of her denim shirt undone and her lined jean jacket draped like a cape across her shoulders and tied around her neck by the arms. Her wide brimmed hat was canted fashionably to the right. Chin strap done up under her chin. Willa shook her head.

"Ok, time to go," Willa said. "Horses are waiting out side. The rest of your gear is on a pack horse, mine I think."

Walking out side, Anne saw six horses. Two with saddles, one with a pack and paneers on it.

"You behave now Sammy," Willa said. "Anne is my bud. No pissing around."

Willa checked her cinch, about to mount, she had a change of heart and checked Annes as well.

"Ya never know, you being a rookie and all." Willa said. "And Sammy would have gone along with it. Ok, what are you waiting for? Nobody is going to give you hand up around here."

Willa smiled as she saw Anne hop on one foot until she could get up and over. Then she made her stand in the stirrups and adjusted them to suit Anne. Seeing she had a tight hand on both reins, Willa jerked them loose.

"You keep them tight like that and you will confuse him," Willa said. "He will think you want him to back up or stop. We knee or neck rein here. You don't need to saw on the reins to make him do what you want."

Willa effortlessly rose into her saddle, took off her jacket, rolled it up and tied it to the front of her cantle with the leather string found there. Anne saw she had a set of saddle bags and a waterproof jacket wrapped around something round, tied to the rear cantle. Her bow was under her left leg and two encased arrow quivers mounted in easy reach to the rear.

Anne saw the other horses fall into line behind them. Without any urging or halter ropes. The other surprise came as they rounded the corner of the stables headed for the gate. Twenty one troopers, in uniforms and with a full weapons complement were waiting for them.

Janet, in uniform was standing on the ground beside them.

"A whole platoon?" Willa said. "A little over kill don't you think Jan?"

"Another Arial will NOT happen on my watch kid." Janet said. "Thank you for taking Sheila along with you. She is still grieving."

"No problem Jan, least I could do for Charles and you," Willa said.

Willa rode up to the platoon who all came to attention, but the officer. He just grinned.

"OK you bone heads," Willa said. "I am still on leave and don't need your shit. Shit head Captain there will babysit you while Her Royal Highness and I have a great time out in the bush."

"Don't you dare say anything Akerson!" Willa said. "If I don't kick your bony ass all the way around the yard, Her Royal Highness will. You too shit head brother of mine. Come on Anne, we are waisting a beautiful day."

Without any warning, Willa took off at a gallop. Anne right on her heels. She had no choice. Sammy just followed Willa.

"Woo hoo, the hunt's a foot! Bugler sound the charge what?" Anne heard William yell after them. Then she heard the thunder of the eighty horses chasing them.

Anne looked over at Willa. She had her neck along side Busters and grinning from ear to ear. Anne did the same.

"Woo hoo!" Willa yelled back at the chasers. "Catch us if you can shit heads!"

After about five minutes, William caught on and kept the platoon thirty yards behind them. Far enough away to give them privacy but close enough to come to their aide if required. After half an hour, Willa dismounted and began to walk beside Buster. Anne did the same. They had not said a word to each other yet.

"Hope you can ride bare back," Willa said. "We swap horses every half hour."

"Used to all the time when I was a kid," Anne said. "Whenever I could get away with it that is."

"Shit, what a shitty life to live," Willa said. "All that wealth and property and never get to enjoy it. Had you ever seen where we went for our rides?"

"No," Anne said. "Only an hour away from the estate at most and never off the paths."

They walked in silence again. Anne was looking all around her.

"It's so quiet out here," she said.

Anne had placed her hat square on her head now, and like Willa had, put her jacket on the front of her saddle. Willa checked that it was secure.

"It will take few days for you to get used to it," Willa said. "All you city folk are like that, used to all the back ground noise. It's actually kind of noisy right now. Almost ninety horses make a lot of noise."

Willa looked off into the distance and was quiet again.

"See that big hill over there?" Willa asked. "Just on the other side of it was where it happened. It was our last night. We were supposed to meet Will after his graduation and then I was off for basic. Oh well...shit happens. Enough walking eh?"

To her credit, Willa stopped and waited for Anne to struggle her way over Shielas back. Then started off at a slow walk.

"Ready to try a trot?" Willa asked ten minutes later.

Anne took a hand full of Shielas mane and nodded her head. Willa started the trot. Anne tried to do the posting she normally did at the trot and quickly gave up on it after a couple of minutes, Willa took them back to a walk again, but a fast one.

"Feel Shielas back as we go," Willa said. "Try and keep your butt glued to it. It'll come to you."

She brought them to the trot again. After another half hour, Willa got down and they walked again.

"Looks like you're getting the hang of it," Willa said.

"Its starting to make sense," Anne said.

They came to a small stream bordered by some small bushes. Willa took them down stream and let the horses drink.

"Hey!" Willa yelled as the platoon walked up. "What's a girl have to do to get some lunch around here. Her Royal Highness is turning into skeleton!"

"Right this way Your Royal Highness," William said. "Sergeant Nuscomb will see to it for you, Your Highness. Akerson will look after your horses Ma-am."

"Hows she doing?" William asked as Anne walked toward where the sergeant was.

"Alright for a rookie," Willa said. "She's a gamer. She's not complaining, but I think she is getting a little sore."

William nodded his head.

"We'll stop in about an hour or so," William said. "Go easy for the first couple of days. I'll send scouts out to find us a decent spot."

"Thanks Will," Willa said. "You ok with all this?"

"Holiday for us too Willy," William said. "Gets us out of the Palace BS."

"Shit, I feel sorry for her," Willa said. "She was not allowed to be a kid. Even now, every moment of everyday is scheduled. Except when she can sneak off. What a shitty life to have."

"What can you do?" William said. "Different culture sis."

"I think that's why she is wild back home," Willa said. "Her only form of rebellion, even though she is doing damage to her self doing it."

Willa rummaged through her saddle bag and came out with a power bar. She handed another to William. They both squatted down beside the stream looking at the water they did not see.

William stood.

"Nuscomb!" He yelled. "Two troopers to scout for tonights camp spot. Early day today. The LT is out of shape."

"Thanks Will," Willa said. "For Anne that is. I can still ride you into the ground brother. You is just Recon."

"We is Deep Recon!" She yelled. "We can out ride and out fight every outfit in this damn Army!"

"Every day, every night! All day! All night! Recon Recon Recon!" Was yelled back by twenty voices.

"Rub it in why don't you sis," William said. He was smiling though.

"What was all that about?" Anne asked as they started off again.

They stayed at a walk this time.

"Like us," Willa said. "Will is trained for Recon. We have other specialized training though. We like to lord it over the regular recon guys when we can. They do the same to us."

"We'll stop after an hour or so for the night. Your two horses have not been out for a while. As out of shape as they are, they are in better shape than you are. We will go a little longer, and harder each day Anne. By the end of the week, you will be half horse like the rest of us."

They stopped just after an hour later, it was nice spot, sheltered out of the wind by some trees. Anne looked around her. Each trooper automatically doing some chore that needed doing. Willa set up their tent herself. William did the same with his.

Everyone was relaxed around the campfires. Chatting or joking around. Willa saw Anne always looking at William when she could get away with it and sighed. She stood.

"Stay put, I'll be right back," Willa said.

She made her way over to one particular campfire.

"Trooper Shit Head rookie," the trooper heard Willa say. "With me."

She started walking away. Sarah jumped up and ran until she was walking just behind her. Anne kept her eyes on them wondering what Sarah had done wrong. She saw Willa, stop turn around and hug Sarah. Then went back to watching William.

"Sorry Sarah," Willa said. "I forgot you had been posted with us."

"No sweat Willie," Sarah said. "Like my dad always reminds me. Rookies keep their mouths shut and don't do anything to get noticed."

"Have you met Anne yet?" Willa asked. "She's a pretty good shit for a stuffed up city aristocrat. I like her Sarah. She doesn't have any real friends. Be nice eh? She's trying real hard."

"Ya I met her at the corrals right after you and Sammy had your melt downs," Sarah said. "She really cares about you Willa."

"Ya I know," Willa said "I care about her too."

"Not as much as she cares about Will though I think," Sarah said, pointing her chin at where Anne was sitting.

She was not alone and was sharing a joke with somebody. But her eyes always stole to William when she could get away with it.

"Him to I think," Willa said, pointing at William who was doing the same thing Anne was. Looking at her when he could get away with it.

"Guys," Willa said. "Who knows what goes on in their heads?"

"Can't live with 'em," Sarah began.

"Can't live without 'em" they both finished and laughed.

Each day they increased the time travelled by an hour. Also, now, two flankers on each side were deployed each day, as well as two scouts that left an hour earlier than every one else did. Each day, Anne was shown something new. How to look for deer, how to determine which way an animal track was moving, how to start a fire. Simple things like, where to find dry firewood, how to build a fire ring.

William had brought one of their swords along and showed Anne how to sling it across her back. Each day now she joined them in their morning exercise routines. Clumsy at first, she was getting better with experience. She had been given excellent instruction on swordsman ship by experts. But now she was shown real sword fighting, not fencing. That nothing was fair in a real fight. How to use her lighter weight and faster speed to advantage on a larger more powerful opponent.

Although not as competent as the others, Anne was switching horses on the fly now as they did and eating lunch in the saddle. She was given an extra bow and shown how to use it and stow it on her saddle. Corporal Jackson began to teach her how to track a deer and, once she was competent enough with the bow, he started taking her on hunts.

Like the others, Anne found something that needed doing, setting up or taking down camp each day. Sarah showed her how to spot herbs and wild potatoes. Which berries and mushrooms were good, or not and why. With some experimentation, Anne concocted a juicy sauce and every one looked forward to the nights some one in the group had found the right ingredients for her to make it.

Anne and William were sitting together every night now and would go for walks alone. Most days now, William, Willa and Anne were riding together. When she was not out collecting herbs or hunting, Anne was becoming a good hunter now and many days came home with at least a rabbit. She had come back to camp with a brace of partridge one day and while she had been ribbed for the slim pickings for the nights meal, everyone knew how hard it was to kill one of the birds with an arrow.

They had come across a herd of Bison one day and Anne was amazed at how many and how big they were. Even more amazing to her was the fact that this herd was the Bekenbaum herd and that they were still on Bekenbaum land.

Willa's hair had grown back to cover the scar on her head, but she still kept it short on that side. She said it made her look bad ass. Anne was also amazed at how close everyone was. How they joked around all the time, singing on the trails and at the camp fires at night. Often they would dance to the songs. Sometimes, the songs were slow and many looked at the ground or stars or fire while they sang. Their eyes very far away. Especially the veterans. Sometimes in the middle of a conversation, something would trigger a memory for one of them and they would stare off. But never for long.

Anne was able to understand Oaken somewhat now and was getting better as she began to speak it. Soon, most conversations were now in Oaken, not what they called Standard and she called English. She knew that English was a German based language and that many of the words were similar in sound and meaning. Now she was having rudimentary conversations with Willa in German. Sometimes she would get mixed up speaking in her bad German to one of the non German speakers. This caused a lot of joking at her expense, but she knew it was all in good fun.

Anne had been tracking a deer and spotted a new track. An unshod horse, with a man's track beside it. She knew it was a man because of the size. The track was fresh. She followed it and soon dismounted as she could smell wood smoke. Sheila could smell it too and her nostrils flared as she scented the air, her ears flicking around, searching for sounds.

Anne went to a crouch and began to duck walk as she began to hear voices. Then she began to crawl, just like she did when on a hunt. Finally, slithering on her belly, she saw the camp. Three men and five horses and saddles were in a rough camp along a stream below the hill she was watching them from. That meant there were two others around somewhere.

The men and the horses, had seen better days. The men's hair and beards were unkempt and long, their clothing ragged and much patched. The horses skinny and dejected looking. She kept watching, then heard a twig snap behind her. Anne rolled over and saw two men behind her. They rushed her, one grabbing her while the other kicked her bow to the side. The man holding her began to paw her and rip at her shirt.

The other came and held her on the ground trying to pin her arms down. She freed the hunting knife from it's scabbard on her belt. The one trying to rip her shirt off eyes went wide as the blade went first, into his groin, then withdrawn and into his chest under the ribs and into the heart, the final blow, a slash across his throat. As Anne kicked the dying man off her to get at the other trying to pin her to the ground, his head exploded in a mist of red as Shiela's hooves hit him, then her teeth grabbed him by the neck and flung him away, before being stomped on.

Anne quickly grabbed her bow. She saw the three below had seen the commotion on the hill and axes in hand, were charging up the hill toward her. Shiela sprang into motion galloping straight at them, screaming her war cry. Anne had killed two with her bow, before Sheila got there and finished the third. Then Sheila stomped on the other two to make sure they were dead.

The sun was going down when Anne slowly rode into camp. This was not unusual. She often came home slow and empty handed returning from a hunt. Anne rode to the horse line and dismounting, began to unsaddle and groom Shiela. Sarah had been given horse guard duty that day. As she was making her rounds, she looked over at Anne and Sheila. Anne had her arms around Sheila's neck.

"Thank you Shiela," she kept saying softly.

That's when Sarah saw the ripped clothing. The blood stains on the front of the shirt and her arms and Shiela's fore hooves and flanks covered in blood. Sarah sprang into action. Flinging her sword across her back, she grabbed the first horse she came to and jumped bare back on it.

"LT!" Sarah yelled as she kicked the horse into a gallop. "Anne needs you! Now! Stand to! Stand To!"

Instant bedlam erupted as troopers went to horse lines, others grabbing weapons and forming a defensive perimeter. Four charged after Sarah. Willa ran up to Anne and saw her condition. She pulled her away from Shiela and began to check her over.

"Jackson! Check on Shiela! I've got Anne!" She ordered. "Cap! I need your help!"

Willa was having trouble keeping Anne upright as her legs were going numb on her and she was having trouble standing. William took one shoulder and Willa the other and they somewhat walked Anne to their tent. The two remaining female troopers sprinting up with a medical kit and William was banished from the tent as they began to rip Annes clothing off her.

Sarah and the four other troopers rode into camp just before it was to dark to see. Each had a riderless saddled horse behind them. Sarah slid off the horse she had been ridding and the other four took all the horses to the horse lines.

Sarah came to where Anne was sitting, staring glazed eyed at the fire. A Female trooper on each side of her. William and Willa just to the side.

"How's she doing?" Sarah asked quietly.

"Shook up," Willa said. "Blood was not hers, Sheila is ok. More concerned for Anne than herself I think."

"Five dead desperados," Sarah said. "Two with arrows in the heart. One with a bad groin cut, a shot to the heart and his throat cut. Sheila got the other two. I got to go check on my horse."

Sarah saw that Sheila had been cleaned up and tethered to the horse line. She kept looking over at Anne. Sarah untied her from the horse line and Shiela immediately trotted over to Anne, putting her head on Annes shoulder. Then she rubbed her head up and down Annes and nibbled her ear. Anne jumped up and gave Shiela a big hug.

"I'm fine you big goof," Anne said in Oaken. "Now off with you. Go play with Sammy or something."

Sheila grumbled, nodded her head up and down, then butted Anne in the chest and trotted back to the other horses. Anne laughed, sat back down and began looking at the fire again. No one said anything, leaving her to deal with her demons. The veterans knowing what she was going through. The rookies, not knowing what to do, but knowing to keep silent.

Anne took a deep breath and looked up.

"Anybody got any booze left?" She asked quietly.

The trooper beside her was the first to offer. Anne took the bottle and raised it.

"Absent comrades," she said and took a deep pull. "Now I know, I really know what that toast means and why you say it."

Anne stood and turned a circle, looking each trooper in the eye.

"Thank you," she said. "Each and every one of you. Thank you for what you do for me and for all the people, each and every day. Keeping us safe, so we can sleep at night free from fear. Thank you, from the bottom of my heart."

"Ah shit Ma-am," Akerson said. "All in a days work Ma-am."

Akerson stood, came to a rigid attention and saluted. The rest, including William and Willa were not far behind. All standing and saluting a woman of great courage. Anne returned the salute just as smartly and at rigid attention her self. Her arm was shaking and tears were beginning to flow.

"Three cheers for Her Royal Highness, Princess Anne,"Akerson yelled out. "The biggest bad ass on this side of the planet!"

The cheers roared out and Anne was mobbed in a bear hug. Willa began to sing. It was a slow song, the rhythm of a horse at a slow walk. The song she had sung on Britannia. Now Anne could understand the words. It was about a trooper scared out of his mind about to enter battle. One thousand of them against ten thousand enemy. The second verse began and everyone was singing, voices in perfect harmony and the song went faster and faster again. Then the song started again. Troopers, male and female were ringing Anne now. They began to dance. A dance of joy and Anne began her own steps, different from theirs. A dance and song of freedom, of survival. And now she knew and she was free. Truly free for the first time in her life. She and William had sex for the first time that night.

Chapter Eighteen

Despite the event of the previous day, the atmosphere was light the next morning. Willam told Sergeant Nuscomb, they would take the next two days to relax. They had a good camp spot with plenty of firewood and grazing for the horses.

"I see Anne has changed her roommate," Willa said to William as she came to the camp fire, coffee cup in hand.

"Temporarily any way," William said. "Who knows with you women. Man I love her."

"I think the feeling is mutual Will," Willa said. "How is she?"

Willa looked up and saw the look on Wills face. She whacked him on his right arm.

"Not that way asshole," she said.

William shrugged his shoulders.

"Alright I guess," William said. "She held me close all night though, if that means anything."

"Ya ok, " Willa said. "I forgot something in my tent. I'll be right back."

She had seen Anne sneak out of Williams tent and back to the one she shared with Willa.

"All right you floosy," Willa said as she entered the tent. "What are your intentions with my brother? Is this for real, or just a comfort fuck?"

Anne looked at the floor. She had her shirt off to change and the buttons of her pants undone.

"A little of both I think," Anne said. "Well a lot of both actually. God I love him so Willy."

"Ok, good to know," Willa said. "Have you told him? Has he told you?"

"Um...no, to both," Anne said. "I...have problems saying those words to a guy Willa."

Willa sat down beside Anne and put her arm around her.

"I know hun, I know," Willa said softly. "You have been hurt badly in the past. He just told me he loves you Anne. But, clueless man that he is, doesn't know what to do about it. He doesn't know if you are playing with him, or even worse, if you are playing him on behalf of your family."

"Oh God no!" Anne said.

She took Willa by the shoulders and looked her in the eyes.

"I would never ever do that to him, or you, or your family," Anne said. "Or the family I have made here. Never."

"So take a chance Anne, take a chance," Willa said. "I have to report what happened yesterday and all hell is going to break loose. Don't look at me that way. You are my guest, my responsibility and I have to report it to my parents. You know that. I failed you Anne. I am really, really sorry Anne."

Anne took Willa's face in her hands and kissed her on the lips.

"You did not fail me Willa," Anne whispered. "You saved me. You and the others gave me the skill and the desire to survive Willa. With out you and the others, I'd be laying out there dead. Well probably not. I never would have left camp alone.

"Can you do me a favour? Wait until tomorrow to report it? If my parents even care, one more day will not hurt. We can blame it on a comm failure or something right? Yes I know you all have your comm units with you."

"As luck would have it," Willa said. "The Captain has just ordered a two day rest period. I think somebody wore him out last night and he is hoping for more tonight."

Anne smacked her on the shoulder. She stood and quickly changed her pants and put a new shirt on.

"Now," Anne said. "If the Lieutenant could ask the Captain to report to me at his convince. I will inform him of my decision on the report."

"Very well Your Royal Highness," Willa said.

She bowed her head and trotted out of the tent to where William was. She came to attention and rammed her right foot into the ground.

"What's up?" William asked.

"Her Royal Highness has asked that the Captain report to her at his connivance, sir!" Willa said.

William stood, straightened out his uniform and the pair of them marched back to the tent. All eyes in camp were on the pair. No one was talking. Something serious was going on.

"Your Royal Highness?" Willa said.

She was told to enter. She did her report and was told to stay put.

"You may enter Captain," Anne said.

William came in, crashed to halt, came to attention, rammed his right foot into the ground and bowed his head. Then raised it until he was gazing above Annes head.

"The Lieutenant has offered to communicate yesterdays unpleasantness to Head Quarters Captain." Anne said. "I have asked her not to report until tomorrow morning. Will that be an inconvenience Captain Bekenbaum?"

"No Your Royal Highness," William said. "We have good communications capability Ma-am."

"Very well, you are dismissed Captain, Lieutenant, thank you for your time." Anne said. "Now, both of you sit your asses down. We ran out of booze or I'd offer some. I have some questions I would like to ask."

"uh..." Willa said.

"Anne is asking not Her Royal Highness," Anne said.

"Sure if I can," Willa said. William nodded his head.

"I am not sure if you have noticed," Anne began in Oaken. "I have been asking a lot of questions. About your culture, your system of government, how you live. I was briefed on a little of that before I left. Now I know much more. I also have done research on my own.

"Is it true that you will allow outsiders to join your people?"

"Yes," Willa said. "Happens all the time."

"How would one go about doing that?" Anne asked.

"Anyone, or you in particular?" William asked.

"Me," Anne said.

"Um...I'm not sure about that Anne," William said.

"Why?" Anne asked. "I am a person am I not? I am an outsider am I not? I am a commissioned officer in my army and, unlike my siblings, actually completed basic training and served two years, full time, in uniform.

"Again, how do I go about asking to join?"

"You have to find two sponsors to stand up for you Anne," Willa said. "They have to make a formal request on your behalf, in writing. The request has to be reviewed, the sponsors and others interviewed and then put to a vote of your peers first, then the clan you wish to join."

"You would have to renounce your claims on the British monarchy Anne," William said. "Are you sure you want to do that?"

"Like I am going to ascend the throne," Anne said. "Not a chance in hell. I owe the monarchy and my family nothing. All they have ever given me is a life prison sentence.

"Would the both of you sponsor me? I am serious and have given it a lot of thought."

Willa sighed.

"We can't Anne," Willa said. "I want to and I am sure William will want to as well, but we can't. It would be seen as the crown trying to influence the councils decision."

Anne looked at the ground.

"I see," she said.

Willa took her right arm.

"There are twenty out there," Willa said. "That will. You say you have studied us, our culture and that you know us. If you truly do, now is your chance to prove it, not just to us but yourself, if you are worthy of us Anne.

"Bye your leave, Your Royal Highness."

Both the Bekenbaums came to attention, bowed their heads and walked out of the tent. They went to their places by the camp fire, poured themselves a cup of coffee and sat down. William saw the looks of concern on everyones faces and noticed how quiet it was.

"No big deal," William said. "Her Royal Highness asked us to report what happened yesterday, but not until tomorrow. Then asked us a few personal questions. You can relax."

It didn't take long for camp to return to normal camp activity. Anne came out of the tent and walked to the edge of the river bank they were camped next to. She looked into the distance for a while, then turned back to look at the camp.

"It's hard for her," Willa said. "She has a lot of trust issues."

"I would too if I was her," William said. "But, lucky for you I'm not."

Willa squealed as he tackled her off her chair and they were soon wrestling on the ground, to the cheers and encouragement of the troopers.

"Ok sis," William said. "I surrender."

"What?" William said looking around him at all the faces. "Everyone knows it's against regulations for an officer to lay hands on another one."

Willa tackled him from behind and they were at it again.

"Mutiny! Mutiny!" William yelled out.

Willa had him down on his back, her knees on his shoulders and she looked up and stopped smiling.

"What?' William said.

Willa pointed her chin to the horse lines. And they both stood up. Anne was talking with Sarah and Jackson.

Before the mock fight had broken up, Anne had made her decision. She took a deep breath and, first approached Sarah.

"May I have a moment of the troopers time?" She asked.

"What? Who me? Ya sure." Sarah said.

Anne did the same with Jackson. She walked with them to the horse lines. Kept her back to them, took a deep breath to calm herself down and turned.

"Corporal Jackson, Trooper Marshack," she began. "I am asking if the both of you would consider sponsoring me for membership of the Prairie Clans. I am in excellent health, have finished basic and advanced infantry training and am a commissioned officer in the Royal Britannic Horse Dragoons, with two years of active duty. I have led and been responsible for, my own platoon. I believe I have the rudimentary skills to be a valuable member of the Clan."

Jackson looked at Anne, then Sarah who did the same. They both shrugged their shoulders.

"Shit," Jackson said. "All you had to do was ask.

"Hey Cap! Trooper Marshack and my self wanna have a chat boss!" He yelled at the camp fire.

William made the advance to contact signal.

"Get ready sis, here it comes," William said.

Both of them stood to greet the trio. All of them came to attention, all of them gave the hand salute.

"Your Highness's Prince William and Princess Willa!" Jackson belted out.

The rest of the camp were all standing now, watching what was going on.

"The corporal wishes to present a petition to join the Clan Your Highness'!"

"Your Highness," Sarah said. "The trooper wishes to also present a candidate not only for the Clan but the Regiment, Sir! Ma-am!"

"State your cases," William said.

"Your Highness," Jackson began, "the petitioner has proven her value these last weeks sir. I believe she would be a great asset to the clan Your Highness!"

"The candidate has completed basic and advanced infantry training Your Highness," Sarah said. "She is a commissioned officer and has spent two years of active duty commanding her own platoon of the Royal Britannic Horse Dragoons sir. She has proven her skills as a tracker and a hunter of both animal and men sir! It is my belief she would not only be a worthy candidate, but a valued asset sir!"

"Candidate Windsor!" William said. "Do you approve of this application and are you aware of the duties and responsibilities of a member of Prairie Clan? And do you agree to them?"

"The candidate is aware and approves Your Highness!" Anne said.

William stood looking at the trio for a moment then lifted his eyes to look at the in formation line of troopers behind them. Every one present knew the seriousness of the moment.

"What say you brothers and sisters?" William asked.

"Fuck ya!" Akerson said for all of them. "What took you so long Anne?"

William and Willa walked away as Anne was mobbed by the platoon.

Anne chased them down a half hour later. They were not hiding, just sitting on the river bank.

"God that was hard," she said planting her self down on the other side of William. "One of the hardest things I have ever done."

"I know love, I know," William said softly.

Annes eyes went wide, her heart started to race.

"Did you just call me love?" She said.

"Did I? Omph," William said as Willa smoked his shoulder. "Piss off Willa."

"No," Anne said. "Willa stays right where she is. Did you just call me love?"

"Yes god damn it! I called you love, happy?" William said.

"Not yet," Anne said. "I love you William. Not brother and sister love. I love you William."

Now it was Williams turn to look across the water.

"And I love you, with all my heart and all my soul," he said softly.

He turned and looked at her, saw the love in her eyes. He put his hands on her face.

"Will you marry me Anne?"

"Are you sure William," Anne said. "I come with a lot of baggage."

"Yes I am sure dummy," William said. "Are all you women that daft Willa?"

"Nah," Willa said. "Just the stuck up British ones. I'd have tied you down and dragged you kicking and screaming to the priest."

"Piss off Willa," Anne said.

"Yes. Yes I will marry you William."

"Right," William said.

He stood and reached his hand down to help her up.

"Come on then, we have something to do," he said, taking her arm and dragging her with him.

Anne looked back at Willa expecting to see her shrug. What she got was Willa smiling from ear to ear and running ahead of them.

"Stand to! Stand to!" Willa yelled as she ran to the camp. "Captain has something to announce!"

The platoon crashed into line and were properly formed up when William and Anne came into camp. William put Anne in front of him and placed both of his hands on her shoulders.

"This is Annabelle, Victoria, Windsor, my wife," he said loudly. "What is done to her is done to me, so say I in front of God and all of you here!"

"What?' Anne said, spinning around to look at him. He was serious.

"You say you have studied us," William said. "Then you know what those words mean."

She looked deep into his eyes and put both her hands on his shoulders.

"I am Annabelle, Victoria, House of Windsor, this is my husband, William House of Bekenbaum. What is done to he and his, is done to me. So say I in front of God and all here."

Then she looked over her shoulder.

"And shut the hell up Akersion," she said. "I'll kiss him when I'm good and ready."

And she did.

"Aw, get a room already," Sarah yelled.

"Always a smart ass in the crowd!" Anne yelled out.

"You ready for this? William asked the next morning.

He had his tablet on his lap. Anne took it from him.

"Me first," she said.

William watched as she quickly tapped out her message to the palace.

"*I, Her Royal Highness, Princess Annabelle, Victoria of the house Windsor, hereby renounce all claims to the Crown of Britannia and her royal rights as a member of the Royal family.*

"Former Princess Annabelle, announces her marriage to His Highness, Prince William of Oaken."

"Your turn," she said handing the tablet to William.

The evening two days ago, William typed. *The former Princess Anne of Britannia, repulsed an attack on her person while hunting. The result was five dead, no wounded, enemy. No casualties on our side. The former Princess was responsible for three of the deaths personally, one at close hand to hand contact. The other two enemy dead were made by her loyal personal mount Shiela.*

Former Princess Anne, has renounced all her claims and affiliations with Britannia. Annabelle Victoria, Windsor, with the required two sponsors, has applied for membership in Prairie Clan. This application was endorsed by Second Platoon, Company C, Second Battalion, Queens Guard, Lieutenant Bekenbaum and the writer.

He hit send and began another.

Mom, dad. In the evening two days ago, Anne was out hunting. She tracked down some unusual sign and in the process of scouting the location, was discovered and attacked by five desperadoes.

She killed two with arrow shots to the heart at a hundred yards and one in close combat with her knife. Shiela, her horse, killed the other two. Neither Anne nor, Shiela were injured.

This morning, Anne asked for and was sponsored for membership in Prairie Clan. The application was approved by all of the platoon. Willa and I also approve.

We are also asking that she be a candidate for Eagle training. Her skills are better than most of my rookies already. She has completed basic and advanced infantry training, was commissioned as an officer and commanded her own platoon for two years full time. You can verify all that yourselves.

Yesterday, I asked Anne to marry me, she accepted and we were married. This morning, she renounced anything at all to do with the British. That's all in my official report.

Unofficially, we ran out of booze two days ago and it's kinda hard to celebrate a marriage without any booze eh?

Will

He hit send. Anne had not seen that message. She was pacing around the tent.

Less than a minute later his tablet beeped.

Help is on the way. Stay put. Mom.

"Come on," William said. "No sense fretting about it in here. It's a nice day out."

They went out and sat by the fire. Anne would sit for a while, then stand and walk away to the river or the horse lines then come back and sit again. When she was sitting, her feet were always tapping the ground and she was biting her lip.

Finally William had enough. He pulled her to sit on his lap, wrapped his arms around her and kissed her.

"It's all good love," he said. "And if it Ain't?"

"We is the biggest, baddest assed Recon troop on Oaken and every bloody day is a great day to die!" He yelled out.

"Recon! Recon! Recon! Hurrah!" Was yelled back.

"Told ya," William said.

Anne kissed him.

Just at that moment, two air transports came in at high speed and low altitude and shut down after landing. The doors of the first one opened and Margarete ran out of it and toward the fire pit. Dimitri followed at his normal sedate pace.

Margarete skidded to a stop, bent down and hugged the seated couple. She kissed Anne on the lips and smoked her son on the shoulder.

"You could have at least waited until you got home," she said. "Men!"

"If you shit heads think I'm gonna unload all this booze by my self, you got another thing coming!" Janet yelled, coming out of the transport behind Greta.

Anne pushed William's arms off of her and rapidly stood and curtsied.

"Your Majesties," she said. "Your Grace."

"Oh shut up you," Dimitri said. "Come, give your father-law a hug eh?"

"You are ok?" Dimitri asked Anne. "First kills suck."

"I'm getting over it," Anne said. "I have a lot of help. Not just William and Willa Your Majesty. The whole platoon sir."

Dimitri sighed.

"I am Dimitri Anne, not Your Majesty, not out here, not with my family and you are my family now." Dimitri said.

"Shit," Akerson yelled."That's a shit load of booze ya brought boss. You trying to drown us?"

"Nope," Dimitri said. "Captain, form your troops up. You too lieutenant, your leave was over yesterday. You stay put candidate."

The platoon, joined by the aircrews formed a line. Dimitri motioned Anne to follow and approached them. He put her in front of him and placed his hands on her shoulders.

"I am Dimitri, house of Bekenbaum, this is my daughter Annabelle, Victoria. What is done to she is done to me, So say I in front of God and all of you."

"So say we all!" Was yelled back.

Anne turned around and said her words to Dimitri.

"Welcome to Prairie Clan daughter!" Dimitri said. "Wait! Wait!"

The line of troopers was making to rush.

"Candidate Bekenbaum! Attention!" Dimitri ordered. "That's you love," he whispered to Anne.

Anne came to attention.

Greta came forward and placed a black beret on her head. Janet a battalion crest on the beret. The last was Margarete with the eagle for the collar.

"Welcome to the regiment trooper Bekenbaum," Margarete said. She stepped back.

"By order of King Dimitri of Oaken. Trooper Bekenbaum is promoted to second lieutenant Bekenbaum," Marargete said.

"You ain't done yet kid," Janet said.

She had a bottle of clear fire in her hand.

"No drink, no beret," Janet said. "You want it or not?"

Anne grabbed the bottle out of Janet's hand spun the top off it to hit the dirt and drained it.

"Now," Dimitri said. "Before you guys get to crazy, I need your officers for a few minutes. But other wise, carry on."

"I won't bore you with the details on how this happened so quickly Anne, William or Willa can fill you in later. They know how I operate," Dimitri began.

"General," he said referring to Margarete.

"It has been decided to expand your company to full company size William," Margarete said. "To that end, a fourth platoon has been added to your company. Second Lieutenant Windsor will be the commander of fourth platoon. Why Second Lieutenant Windsor? There already is a Lieutenant Bekenbaum in Company C for one thing. Less confusion. Give the rookie LT a gang of wet behind the ears rookies is the second. They don't know who you are, yet."

"You only have eighteen troopers at this very moment," Janet said. "We pulled them out of the academy two months early. Not a big deal, what they will learn out here in the field will be better training than the academy any way. Next, you will be loosing two of your troopers Willa. Anne requires some experienced NCO's. Anybody but Nuscomb, we have plans for him."

Willa looked over at Anne and raised her eyebrows.

"I can choose?" Anne asked. "Jackson and Marshack."

"Ok," Janet said. "Willie, go bring the two poor boneheads over here before they get to pissed. Bring Nuscomb with you."

Sarah was well on her way, the other two were just getting a buzz on.

"Corporal Jackson, you are now promoted to sergeant. Trooper Marshak, you are promoted to corporal. You will be section leaders of Second Lieutenant Windsors fourth platoon. Platoon Sergeant Nuscomb, you are promoted to Master Sergeant and will over see the training of the fourth platoon along with Lieutenant Bekenbaum. You will be receiving your two replacement troops shortly. Questions?"

"If the Second Lieutenant may?" Anne asked. "When can we expect the new troopers to arrive Ma-am?"

"They are standing beside the second transport," Janet said. "Your horses should be arriving tomorrow afternoon along with first and second platoon. Anne, you will have two new horses as well. Sheila has obviously chosen to serve with you and will. You can keep Sammy for now. He is getting a little to old for this crap now and he knows it. Once we get back home, you can pick his replacement. Good?"

Seeing no more questions forth coming Janet started walking toward the rookies motioning the others to join her. As they approached, somebody yelled out flag officer approaching and the twenty rookies quickly formed their lines.

Janet started walking up and down their lines looking them over. She came back to the centre and put them at ease.

"I am the Colonel of Second Battalion," she began. "Now pay attention there will be an exam after. Behind me are, Captain Bekenbaum, commander of Company C, Lieutenant Bekenbaum of second platoon, Second Lieutenant Windsor, your platoon commander, Master Sergeant Nuscomb, your training supervisor, Sergeant Jackson and Corporal Marshack, your section commanders.

"I will leave you to it Second Lieutenant. Oh wait. Pick your two replacement rookies Nuscomb. It won't matter who, they are all bone heads at this point."

Nuscomb chose two of the rookies, seemingly at random and he, they and the three officers walked away toward the growing party.

Trailed by her two new NCO's, Anne went down the line of oh so young and clueless troopers. Remembering her early days.

"For now," Anne said. "We have no orders. As the least senior platoon, we can expect every shit detail they can find to give us. Your horses will arrive and be issued, sometime tomorrow afternoon. Be prepared for that.

"Recommendations on a camp area Sergeant?"

"Yes Ma_am, got it all in hand Ma-am," Jackson said.

He discreetly tapped Marshack on the back of her leg with the toe of his boot. She was beginning to sway slightly and a smile had started.

"Get your gear and form up!" Jackson ordered. "All under control Ma-am."

"Very well," Anne said. "Report to me when all is in order Sergeant. Inform the troopers they have the rest of the day after their camp is set up Sergeant."

Anne turned and walked toward where the rest of the other officers were located.

"Jackson is getting them all squared away," Anne said, grabbing another mug and filling it from a handy vodka bottle.

William pointed his mug to where Willa was lining up her platoon, all slightly more than a little tipsy now.

"Watch this," William said.

"Jackson and Marshack have been reassigned," Willa said. "These two green as grass, wet behind the ears rookies are their replacements."

A series of groans came from the lines.

"Just what we fucking needed, two more rookies," Akerson said. "We just got the last ones to where they are half assed competent LT."

"Oh, it gets better Akerson," Willa said. "You are promoted to corporal and take over Jackson's section. Carry on people."

"Good move Willy," Janet said when Willa came back to where the officers were congregated."

"Learned that from pop," Willa said. "Always promote the smart asses Jan. You should know, you're the smartest assed person in the army."

Janet looked at Willa and away and back again.

"You little shit, did you just trash me?" Janet burst out as she exploded from her chair. Soon the two of them were wrestling like teenaged girls on the ground. Giggling away.

"Kids these days," Dimitri said to Greta. "We were never like that Grets."

"Nah," Greta slurred. "We was all prime and proper. Yes sir, no sir, two bags full sir."

"Ya right," Margarete said, as she bounced two stones off their foreheads. Then she was struggling as both brother and sister attacked her and began to tickle her.

The five stopped and lay on their backs, arms out stretched laughing. Maragete looked over at Anne sitting on Williams lap, her arms around him and his around her.

"Aw... will you look at that," Maragete said sweetly. "Young love."

She sprang up, grabbed a handy bucket of water and Anne squealed as Margarete splashed them with it.

"Water fight!" Margarete yelled.

"Will you look at that," one of the rookies said. "Arn't the generals and the colonel part of the original one hundred."

"Yes," a more than slightly tipsy Sarah said as she was making her way to the horse lines.

She stopped and thought about it for a second. She sat down with a thump beside the rookies camp fire.

"The Queen and the colonel was green as grass rookies like you guys," Sarah said. "The first ten. I won't bore you with that story, we all know it.

"The Captain and his sister the lieutenant, were on the ramparts at Arial. Half the guys, including corp..oops Sergeant Jackson relieved them.

"The King and Grand Duchess are the original Eagles. They started it all. Somebody pass me a bottle eh?"

She took a deep pull of the one handed to her. She pointed the bottle at Anne.

"Our Lieutenant?" Sarah continued. "Just three days ago she was out hunting alone and was ambushed by five desperados. She killed them all. Well her horse got two. She shot two right in the heart as they was rushing her, with her bow, then slit the throat of the third, or was it the other way around? Don't matter. I saw the results with my own eyes. Bloody man had almost been gutted by a knife thrust to his balls, then she got him in the heart and sliced his damn head almost fucking right off.

"Me? I'm just a dumb ass rookie like you guys. I dunno why I was promoted. I only been outta the academy for less than a year. Goota go before I piss myself."

"Don't let her kid you," Jackson said as Sarah staggered off to the nearest bushes. "She's tougher, a lot tougher than most of us. She was the first one that was helping our lieutenant when she came back. Then she tossed her sword over her shoulder, grabbed the nearest horse and charged out to make sure there were no more bad guys around.

"Before the rest of us could even get our shit together. Look, you guys are all good, or you would not be here. But First and second platoon are coming to join us. Half of First platoon was on the ramparts. Most of second was in the relief column like I was.

"The King, Queen, Grand Duchess, the colonel and the rest of the one hundred smashed a hole so big and wide in the enemy lines you could fly a transport through it for the rest of us.

"This is why we are Eagles, this is why we are C Company. Deep Recon. This is what you are now part of. See ya. Enjoy the night, 'cause in the morning your asses are mine."

"Who are we?" Jackson yelled as he walked back to his Mates.

"Magies Eagles!"

"Who are we?"

"Janets Orphans!"

"Recon! Recon! Recon! Hurrah!"

The rookies looked on, eyes wide as the words were yelled out and fists were punched in the air, including the officers.

Chapter Nineteen

F ourth platoon was roused out of bed as the sun was coming up to yells of stand to, stand to you lazy asses. They arrived and formed their lines in various stages of undress. But all had their weapon with them ready to fight.

Anne made her way down the line inspecting them.

"If the children are going to drink like adults at night, they will damn well be ready to work like adults the next damn morning Sergeant!' Anne said. "What a disgusting mess that is front of me Sergeant!"

She marched up to one trooper and went nose to nose with her.

"For shits sake trooper!" Anne yelled. "You've got a nice set of boobs and all, but I don't need them in my face! At least make sure you have a shirt on next time you form up!"

"Fuck me Sergeant! Sort this shit out!"

Anne moved away a few yards and made a point of turning her back and examining her nails, to stop them from seeing her smile.

"You got five minutes to get your shit together!" Jackson yelled. "Move it!"

"Stupid asses," Jackson said. "Reporting in their underwear."

He couldn't help the snigger.

"About time you showed up Corporal!" Anne yelled as Sarah ran up. "You in the habit of reporting late for duty Corporal! Did I make a mistake promoting you Corporal?"

The rookies poured out of their tents and formed up to see Sarah doing pushups with Annes foot on her back.

"Join your stupid ass rookies Corporal!" Anne yelled. "Next time you are late, I will kick your ass so hard you won't sit down for a month!"

"Dumb Asses, drop and give me twenty!" Anne said as Sarah reached the line. "Corporal, you keep count."

"Are you mumbling Corporal?" Anne yelled. "I can't hear you corporal!"

Sarah began to yell the count.

"I think you screwed up my count Corporal! Start again!"

Third platoon was lined up in front of their tents watching and laughing. Anne gave them the finger, which only made them laugh harder. Then Akerson suddenly turned on his two rookies.

"What you laughing at dumb asses!" He yelled. "Drop and give me twenty!"

"Ma-am," Sarah said. "The troopers have finished their punishment Ma-am."

Anne and Jackson turned and looked at the line of troopers.

"Fourth Platoons duty for the day is to collect the firewood for the camp," Anne said. "The sooner you get that done to the Captains satisfaction, the sooner you can eat. In the future, when I arrive in the morning, I will expect my coffee hot and waiting for me.

"Deploy your troopers Sergeant and report back to me when that is done."

Anne walked away toward the officers camp.

"Recon troopers never go anywhere or do anything, without their weapons," she heard Jackson say. "Recon troopers never operate alone, always in pairs. Get at it, the lieutenant is in a bitchy mood today."

Anne was waiting for him at the edge of the officers camp.

"Deployed Ma-am," Jackson said.

"Thank god for that," Anne said. "Some hair of the dog I think eh?"

Both of them walked up to the lounging officers, following Annes lead, they both came to attention and Anne saluted.

"Fourth Platoon all present, accounted for and deployed Your Majesty!" She yelled.

"For future reference, we do not salute when deployed in the field under arms Lieutenant," Dimitri said.

"I understand Your Majesty," Anne said. "The Lieutenant is not under arms Sir!"

"What?" Dimitri said.

"The Lieutenant has not been issued any weapons Sir!" She said.

"What the hell Will?" Dimitri said.

"Well..it's like this.." William began.

"I don't give a shit," Dimitri said. "I know she has a bow, get her a bloody sword. Shit on a stick Will!"

He looked over at the still at attention Anne and Jackson.

"Sit down already," Dimitri said. "I can tell you never served in the field Anne. Everybody is low key in the field. Had breakfast yet?"

"Only was allowed to serve in garrison sir," Anne said. She saw the frown on Dimitri's face.

"And no, the sergeant and I have not had our breakfast yet Dimitri," she said. "The dumb asses were to hung over. I don't think that will happen again."

"Ya, seeing your corporal doing pushups with the LTs foot on her back will do that," Jackson said. "Another dumb ass."

"But we love all our dumb asses equally Mags," Anne said.

"But of course Anne," Margarete agreed. "We must always love our dumb asses equally. I did. Right Willy?"

"Depended on the day mom," Willa said. "Some times dumb ass Willa got more love than dumb ass William and vice versa, depending on what kind of havoc we had created on any different day."

Janet snorted her coffee out her nose,

"What the fuck do I know?" Janet said. "I treat everybody like shit, equally of course."

"On a different note," Dimitri said. "We seem to be having a little issue with our comms right now. The satellite in this district must be malfunctioning or something. I do know that when we left the Palace, the com shack was catching fire from all the messages coming in.

"Officially, Company C is deployed training for a super secret mission in an undisclosed location for an undisclosed period of time and are to operate comms dark. Second Lieutenant Windsor is now platoon four commander and as such is also deployed.

"That should buy us a month."

"Ever the expert master bender of the rules my husband," Margarete said.

"Well I did wright the rule book you know," Dimitri said.

"I'll keep them off your back for as long as I can Anne," Dimitri said. "But at some point you'er going to have to face the music.

"In the mean time, use this as an opportunity to train yourself and your rookies up. There will be no better opportunity Anne. This whole company was hand picked and are the best of the best. We are expecting all of our future leaders from this company Anne. Not just for this battalion but for all the future Eagles."

Third Platoon was positioned in an L shaped ambush around the rookies camp. Anne had done an amazing job getting the rookies up to speed. Willa was Willa though. They had the rookies. This was going to be fun, the rookies had no idea what was coming. So far, all fourth platoon had been experiencing was attacks on them while they were on the move. They were getting very proficient at discovering those before they happened.

Third platoon had crept into position two hours before dawn. They would attack at daybreak, very soon now. Willa was about to give the order to attack, but stopped. Four air cars were approaching the rookies camp. Willa decided to await developments. This might add some more fun to the day.

"We hit the new guys," Willa said to Akerson. "Nuscomb can handle the rookies."

Willa jumped to her feet and screamed her war cry, the rest of her section right behind her. They charged the people coming out of the air cars. With a roar, Nuscombs section attacked the rookies camp. Then everything went to hell in a basket.

Arrows started sprouting in the ground in front of the attackers. Lots of arrows. Then the roars and high pitched female screams began from behind the attackers as a section each made their attacks from the rear.

"You fuckers is all, dead, dead ,dead!" Anne screamed.

Willa looked behind her. Ten troopers covered in dirt and branches were standing behind her section, bows in hand and arrows knocked, two more in the mouths.

"Ya you got us," Willa said.

She tapped her ear.

"Third platoon stand down," she said.

Anne did the same.

"Who are those guys?" Anne asked pointing at the air cars. "Ah shit. Never mind."

Soldiers, complete with blasters at the ready, in British uniforms came out of the vehicles. Several of the high ranking officers, in the typical over done British high ranking dress uniforms.

"I guess the jig is up sis," Willa said.

A Captain flanked by two armed guards approached the watching troopers. The captain didn't look to happy. He stopped in front of the troopers, who of course just stood there. Willa shrugged her shoulders.

"What can we do for you Captain?" Willa said.

"His Royal Highness demands to see Her Royal Highness, Princess Anne!" The Captain said.

"Hey yahoos!" Willa yelled. "We got a Her Royal Highness Princess Anne that some how snuck in around here someplace?"

Those around her all looked around and shrugged their shoulders.

"Don't look like it Captain," Willa said.

The Captain appeared to be becoming frustrated.

"Your people at your headquarters assured us Her Royal Highness was at this location!" The Captain said.

"Hey!" Willa yelled. "Any of you boneheads at that camp see any Her Royal Highness Princess Anne over there!"

"Got a bunch of pussy princesses here from third platoon LT," Jackson yelled back. "No Her Royal Highness though!"

"Well, there you have it Captain," Willa said. "No Her Royal Highness Princess Anne hanging around here."

"You do not salute superior officers in your army Leftenant?" The Captain was definitely not happy now.

"Oh," Willa said. "I'm sorry, let me introduce myself Captain. First Lieutenant Bekenbaum, Princess Willa of Oaken."

To his credit, the Captain and his men, came to attention and the Captain saluted. Willa waved her hand in the general direction of her forehead in response.

"And no captain," Willa said. "We do not salute when we are in the field and serving under arms. I command third platoon, this is Second Lieutenant Windsor. She commands fourth platoon."

"With Her Highness's permission," the Captain said. "I will report this to my superiors Ma-am."

"Whatever makes your day Captain," Willa said. "I have to buy the dumb shit rookie LT a beer now for her killing me."

"Got you good too," Anne said in Oaken.

"How long do you want to play this game?" Willa asked in the same language.

"Not to long," Anne said. "Looks like my brother is headed over here now."

Charles, Annes older brother and heir to the throne, was marching forward in his ornate Colonels uniform, surrounded by four armed troopers.

"What are you bloody people playing at!" Charles demanded. "I was told I could see my sister here!"

"Don't mind Charles Willie," Anne said. "He has always been a little dumb, didn't think he was blind though."

"You know these stuffed up flag officer pencil pushers sis," Willa said. "Can't see past their noses most times."

Charles did a double take at the two women. He nodded his head at Willa.

"Your Highness," he said.

Willa nodded back.

"Anne, you WILL, come with me right this instant," he demanded. "And you WILL be transported back to Britannia immediately!"

"Couple of issues with that order Colonel," Willa said. "The dumb ass second Luie is a member of the Oaken Army. At the moment, her platoon is not serving alongside a British unit, therefore is not compelled to comply with any orders given by a British commander. She is also deployed on active duty under arms. As such, she will need permission from her company commander, who will have to apply for permission from his colonel, in order for her to leave her post. Lastly, she will have to apply to the General of the Queens Guard, through the proper channels off course, to be allowed a special leave in order to leave the planet.

"Our hands are tied Colonel. I am sure something can be arranged in time. Just not right now."

"Not only that," Anne said. "I would have to obtain permission from my husband."

"You are a member of the Royal family, second in line from the throne and a British officer," Charles said. "I can bloody well order you to do any bloody thing I want. Including using force to make you comply. Your marriage was never approved by the Monarchy as required, thus is null and void!"

Anne walked up, nose to nose with her brother.

"I renounced all claims to the throne, the monarchy, my titles and commissions and my citizen ship brother," she said.

She pointed around her.

"As far as forcing me to do anything," she said. "Your puny body guard and yourself will look like pin cushions if you so much as lay a hand on me. Not to mention what I will do with the knife I have at your balls."

Charles looked down as he felt a prick in his groin and saw the huge knife in Annes hand there.

"Now, *brother*, why don't you be a good little paper pushing pussy and fuck off before you loose something you might need and our little brother inherits the throne instead of you," Anne said.

"Guess she ain't going with you then," Willa said. "Good day to you Your Royal Highness. Hey, one of you boneheads get our ponies over here. Be fucked if I walk back to camp!"

Charles was left standing there, with his mouth open as troopers began to disperse.

The command to return to barracks was received in Willa's ear piece before her horses arrived.

"Yo, fourth platoon!" Willa yelled. "Grab all your shit. You might as well travel with us back to our camp. We've all just been recalled to Barracks!"

Before the British had finished loading into their vehicles, Charles having a temper tantrum outside. They were treated by the sight of forty mounted troopers, fully armed and sixty spare horses leave the area at the trot.

Late that night, third and fourth platoons were back at the Palace complex. After grooming their horses, Anne grabbed her gear and walked up to Willa.

"I don't even know where I am to barrack Willy," she said. "Never been here before."

"Follow me my lost puppy sister," Willa said.

Willa and Anne, duffle bag of clothing in one hand, of weapons in the other, walked down the main street of the barracks, just like a few hundred other troopers were doing. She led her to a small house, in a street of other small houses. Willa knocked on the door and walked away.

"What?" Anne said. "This where I stay? Where are you going?"

"To my own barrack sis," Willa said.

The door opened. Anne dropped her bags and was instantly wrapping her arms around William.

They had been in the field so long, everyone had lost track of what day it was. It turned out to be Friday. C Company had been in the field for a month, 3rd platoon for almost 2. Not sure what to do, Anne arrived at her assigned cubical in the companies office and asked the corporal behind the desk.

The corporal smiled and shook his head at the poor lost rookie LT. He spun his chair around took a binder from the book shelf behind him and tossed it on the desk in front of Anne.

"Good place to start Ma-am," the corporal said. "Normally, you check your platoon first thing in the morning. Issue orders or whatever, then come back here, morning meetings are around ten, the Cap is pretty flexible. Then whatever paper pushing you have to do. After lunch, training with your platoon or whatever. Right now, you have to write up your report for last month and the encounter with the British yesterday. I would do the latter first Ma-am, shit has kinda hit the fan about it. Don't worry about your horses or equipment LT. A member of your platoon will handle that for you Ma-am. You have the last cubical on the right Ma-am."

Anne thanked the man, picked up the instruction manual and headed to where her cubical was. Two lieutenants were at the coffee counter. Willa was banging away at her computer terminal. Anne found her small cubical space, dumped her beret and binder on the desk and was undecided what to do next.

"Be me," Walker, the second platoon commander said leaning against Anns cubical wall. "I'd grab a coffee first. Oh look, I did so. Just use your retina to turn the comp on."

Walker had an insulated tall coffee cup in his hand. He waved at her with it, then entered his own cramped cubical. Anne made her way to the coffee station and saw only take out, small cups there. She poured one full, took a sip, made a face and walked back to her cubical. She looked at her computer and it immediately began it's boot up sequence. She saw she already had an email and opened it. It was from the corporal informing all the Lieutenants of a meeting with the Captain at ten fifteen. Anne looked at the time, swore, found the app that she could write her reports on and was banging away writing them. She was finished and had retrieved the reports from the company printer with three minutes to spare.

Willa was already there and patted the chair next to her. She handed Anne a cup of coffee after she had sat down.

"I brewed this batch," Willa said. "Walker couldn't brew a decent pot of coffee if his life depended on it. Drop your report on the pile there."

Anne stood, added her report to the stack already there and was making to sit, when William breezed in and she had to stand with the others. Then wait until William sat. Like everyone else, William had an insulated coffee cup with him.

He quickly scanned the reports and tossed the pile to the side.

"Right," William began. "Boss is happy with the training. Nice job at the end Windsor. Caught third platoon napping. That hardly ever happens. Willa must have been hung over or something."

Willa gave a raspberry sound, the other two lieutenants laughed.

"You have done a credible job getting your rookies in shape Windsor, the boss is happy," William continued. "Starting Monday, every body has next week off. Unless something really important needs doing, let your bone heads take off after lunch. Alright, everybody but Windsor take off. I'm a busy guy and have a hot date tonight. Close the door behind you."

After the door had closed, William slid his tablet over to Anne. It was open to a news article. The article described the encounter with her brother, saying only that an unpleasant encounter had occurred between a British officer who had interrupted an important training mission and two platoons of the Queens Guard.

Anne paged down and saw a much more graphic and explicit article below. It was British.

PRINCE CHARLES ASSAULTED BY OAKEN TROOPS TRYING TO RESCUE PRINCESS ANNE FROM UNJUST FACIST REGIEM.

The headline took up the top two thirds of the front page. The other third showed an archive photo of Charles in combat uniform.

The two page article in the next two pages basically said Anne had been unjustly detained on Oaken and forced to marry Oaken's crown prince against her will. It demanded Parliament act immediately, up to and including, declaring war on Oaken, to effect Anne's release. An immediate apology and reparations.

"I am so sorry Will," Anne said. "What do you want me to do? I can issue an immediate repudiation of those facts. But I don't think the Brits will care. They will just say I was forced to make it."

"Above our pay grade Anne," William said. "Britannia is almost bankrupt Anne. War will push it over the edge. We have a tradition of compromise Anne. They are counting on that. I can assure you that our diplomats are aware of all the facts and are working hard at a resolution. It won't be us starting a war Anne. We will finish it though."

Anne nodded her head and looked out the window. She rubbed at the tears starting to form in her eyes. William came to her and squatting down, forced her to look at him.

"It isn't your fault Anne," he said softly. "You are just a pawn in a much bigger game."

"I know Will," Anne whispered. "I have been my whole life."

William hugged her.

"Mom wants us for diner Sunday," he said. "You ok with that?"

Anne nodded her head.

"Good," William said. "I'll let her know. Now get the hell out of here I have a ton of shit to do. I've got a hot date tonight."

"Oh you do do you?" Anne said. "Does the poor girl know what she is getting herself into?"

William shrugged his shoulders.

"She's kinda standoffish," he said. "But I think I'm winning her over. OC tonight?"

"Yes you big meany," Anne said.

She stood, hugged and kissed him, then flaunted out the door.

Anne finished her inspection of her platoon and their bunkhouse. She joined Jackson and Sarah by the door.

"For some reason," Anne began. "The colonel has decided to reward you bone heads for the work you did last month. Why, I have no idea. The colonel also said good job. Half an hour after I walk out that door, if I see any of you anywhere near this barracks or the base, I'll have you cleaning every toilet in every company barracks for the rest of the week. Dismissed."

She turned and accompanied by Jackson and Sarah left the building.

"That includes you two," Anne said. "Go home or what ever and relax. God knows you both need it. Thank you for all the help guys."

"No problem LT," Jackson said. "Way ahead of you. NCO jungle drums Ma-am. I probably knew about it before you did."

Anne smiled and shook her head. Same in every army she thought.

"And LT?" Jackson said. "Was you that did the good job Ma-am. I just followed your orders and answered your questions Ma-am."

He and Sarah came to a rigid attention and saluted Anne. Confused by that, she returned it.

"By your leave Ma-am," Jackson said and both he and Sarah took off headed for their NCO barracks.

"Hey sis," Willa said coming beside Anne as she walked to the house she shared with Will. "Whatcha doin' for the rest of our free afternoon? Wanna go to the mall?"

"I'll have to stop at the palace to pick up some cloths first," Anne said.

'Nah," Willa said. "Your fine the way you are. I'm going like this. Come on, my car is just over there."

Willas car turned out to be a seen better days used suv.

"Hey," Willa said. "Be nice. It's all I can afford."

"What do you mean?" Anne said. "Your parents are loaded."

"Why, yes they are," Willa said.

She started up the vehicle and backed out of the parking stall.

"I have to make it on my own Anne," Willa said. "I don't get paid much more than you do. At least you and Will can share resources. I don't have that option."

There were a lot of uniformed people at the mall, most showing Queens Own shoulder patches. They were doing the same as Anne and Willa. Shopping.

Anne took a fast look at her bank statement and swore. She only had one months salary in it.

"So much for the latest designer fashions," Anne said.

Willa gave her a sideway squeeze.

"At least we don't have to pay rent and buy work clothing," Willa said. "You and Will have a kitchen and can cook your own meals. I don't have that option. No kitchen in the junior officers quarters. Mess bills at the OC aren't to bad, but it's cheaper at the All Ranks Club."

"Oh," Anne said. "I guess that's why all the junior officers hang out there."

"Got that right," Willa said. "Rookie."

"Yak it up Willy," Anne said.

Anne purchased some jeans a few blouses and a couple of skirts from a box discount store. Willa bought her one of those insulated coffee mugs every one else had. Then they drove back to the housing area of the base. They parted ways, each headed to their own residences.

"I have just enough money left in my account to buy my handsome husband diner and a beer at the All Ranks tonight," Anne said later on to Will laying on their bed. She kissed his naked chest.

"Pay day is every Friday Anne," William said. "Not to worry. Two week holdback. That's why you didn't have a lot in the bank. Only two weeks worth."

"Oh, ok," Anne said. "Not to bad then."

"Sorry Anne," William said. "Family rules. We have to make it on our own."

"Willa told me earlier," Anne said. "I didn't marry you because I thought you had money Will. And I hope you didn't marry me for that reason. I am flat assed broke."

"What? You're broke?" Will said in mock astonishment. "That's it, where's my damn lawyers when I need them?"

A brief wrestling match broke out on the bed that rapidly turned into something else.

They had a good time at the club that night. The atmosphere was light and fun. They sat with their company group at first. Then other tables. Will had a lot of friends in the battalion, both officer and enlisted. Willa was seldom at any one table for long, rotating around the room. Equally at home at officer and enlisted tables.

"I need some air," Willa said to Anne. "Care to join me?"

"You're having fun," Willa said.

"Yes," Anne said. "You and Will have so many friends. Real friends, not hangers on. I'm not used to that."

"We have our fair share of suck ups too Anne," Willa said. "But they don't hang out here. Go to the OC, different story. You Ok? Has to be hard, all that Brit media BS."

Anne looked away and Willa saw a tear run down a cheek. She quickly hugged Anne.

"If I had known this would cause such a fuss," Anne whispered. "Maybe even a war, I would never had married Will and gone home to my shitty life."

"Hey!" Willa said pushing Anne to arms length. "Look at me. This is not your fault. It's just a bunch of greedy people trying to make money off you. This will all blow over Anne. Some other dummy is going to do something that grabs the media attention and this will all go away."

"I hope so," Anne said.

"Come on Anne, I still owe you a beer for letting you beat me the other day," Willa said.

"Oh you let me beat you then?" Anne said.

They were bickering away in good natured fun as they walked back into the club. Anne wasn't just learning her job. She was also learning how to flip her internal switch like Willa and the others did all the time.

"Well," Margarete said Sunday before diner. "At least some one knows how to dress for a family diner. And I don't mean you Will."

She hugged her son dressed in his normal business casual. Then hugged Anne dressed in blue jeans and cotton blouse. She and Dimitri were dressed in casual jeans themselves.

"Only chance I get to wear this stuff," Will said. "Cost me loads of cash. My wife will kill me when she sees the bank balance."

"She will not," Anne said kissing him on the cheek as they sat down. "She might cut him off though. For about five minutes."

Margarete and Dimitri laughed.

Willa breezed in dressed like they, in jeans and a polo shirt.

The meal was fun and light and all to soon over. Especially when a comms officer arrived and spoke into Dimitri's ear. Dimitri hit a button on his chair. A panel opened, revealing a large screen. A British functionary was caught off guard and put a stern look on his face.

"His Majesty King George of Britannia demands an immediate audience with Your Majesty." The functionary said.

"Sure, why not," Dimitri said. "Just having diner with the family. Nothing serious."

The picture switched to show George and Mary in official garb standing.

"What can I do for Your Majesty?" Dimitri said.

"WE demand you immediately release Princess Anne from custody to return home!" George said.

"My my," Dimitri said."WE demand eh? Well, WE will consult with Anne as soon as we can and see if she wants to go home Your Majesty. Hey Anne, you want to go home?"

"Not in this bloody life time," George heard his daughter say. "Who the hell would want to go back to that shit show?"

George took a step back, blinking rapidly. Mary put her hands to cover her mouth her eyes wide.

"Anne?' George asked "Is that you?" Dimitri looked over at Anne and raised his eyebrows.

"Depends if I am talking to their Majesties the King and Queen of Britannia or my parents," Anne said.

"Annie, please," Mary said. "Talk to me. Are you alright?"

Anne nodded her head. Dimitri hit a switch and the picture the king and queen saw switched to show the whole family at a small family sized table. Glasses of beer in front of them.

"High daddy, mommy," Anne said. "How are you?"

"Oh my God, we were so worried!" George said. "The media..."

"Ya ya, the media," Anne said. "Who gives a shit about the media? All you had to do was contact me on my personal account daddy and ask."

"Oh," George said. "I can do that?"

Anne shook her head and smiled.

"Yes daddy, you can do that," Anne said.

"You are happy Annie?" her mother asked.

Anne could tell her mother was genuinely concerned.

"Yes mommy I am happy," Anne said. "I found a man stupid enough to fall in love with me that I love with all my heart mommy."

Mary took a tissue from her hand bag and dabbed at her eyes.

"He also has all the right parts in the right places and knows how to use them," Anne said.

"Annie!!" Her mother said.

Margarete and Willa began to laugh their heads off.

"Must get that from his dad," Margarete said between chortles.

"We finished with all the Your Majesty and WE shit now George?' Dimitri asked.

George nodded his head, pulled a chair around and helped Mary sit on it. He put his hands behind his back and began to pace. He stoped and faced the monitor.

"I am quite cross with how Charles was treated Dimitri," George said. "He was only asking if Anne would schedule some time to come home. The officer should be reprimanded for their behaviour Dimitri and to make an apology."

"I most certainly will not!" Anne said. "Charles threatened me and my team mates with armed violence daddy. He's damn lucky I was in a good mood that day, or James would be your new heir."

"What?" George said. "Surely not!"

"If Anne agrees," Maragerete said. "I can show you audio and video of the encounter taken from Willa's uniform camera."

Anne nodded her head. Margarete touched her tablet and the screen split to show the whole encounter.

"He was just supposed to see how you were doing!" Mary said. "Damn that boy! Get off your ass and do something George!"

"What can I do?" George said, he plumped himself down on a nearby chair and looked at the floor. "Parliament is demanding a full mobilization and declaration of war."

"Fuck!" Dimitri said, shocking both the King and the Queen. "We don't need this shit! We saw this coming, long before you did. So did Anne, that's why she renounced everything. A complete and I mean complete report, including video and text of Anne composing her resignation and renunciation announcement. William proposing to her, the wedding, her requesting permission to join Prairie Clan, the acceptance of it and her induction as a member. Her induction into our Army, her being awarded her Eagle and commission. All of it, was sent to the Federation a month ago.

"Our Prime minster and diplomats have been struggling to get a trade agreement completed and been stymied by your people at every turn George. Your people have been rude and insulting, demanding concessions that are excessive and inappropriate given the trade goods you want from us in exchange for the ones you are offering.

"You will get no backing form the Federation George, none at all."

Nothing was said for a long while.

"If your Parliament is stupid enough to declare war on us George, God help you, because no one else will. The Federation will cut all trade with you. We attacked Arial with only two battalions of our personal troops George. You declare war on Oaken? We fully mobilize George. Our navy is twice the size of yours. We have three million active duty troops and about ten million or so Active reservists. Double that for inactive reservists."

Another silence broke out and George began to pace again.

"If I may Dimitri?" Anne asked. Dimitri nodded his head.

"Daddy," she began. "You know I never wanted the crown. I also know that you, mommy and everyone else knows that Charles is a power hungry disaster waiting to happen. He has manipulated all this to make you look weak and he the hero saving the national pride. Denounce him for what he is. Renounce him as your heir. Make James the heir. He deserves it, you know it. The people love James. They hate Charles.

"Daddy, the people of Oaken hate war. But they love their planet and way of life. They fought hard to gain their freedom from Home World. They freed the whole Federation from Home World and the Federation loves them for it.

"The people of Oaken love their monarchy daddy. They will sacrifice everything including their lives for them. So will I daddy."

She said nothing for a second, then took a deep breath.

"You know I have served in our Armed Forces Daddy," she said. "I can tell you without a shadow of doubt, my barely trained just out of training academy rookies will kick the shit out my old unit. If my fourth platoon attack my whole former company, they would kill them all daddy. No doubt of it. You served on the line daddy. You know our men are not well armed or trained."

"What to do, what to do," George kept saying pacing and pacing.

"Release the video daddy," Anne said. "Schedule a full live press conference and show the people what their Crown Prince really is. Just tell your handlers to schedule a live broadcast concerning developments with Oaken daddy, nothing else. Then spring the video on them. Let the people and the parliament work for you daddy. Petition the House to remove all titles from Charles and give them to James."

Mary stood and embraced George.

"Yes George," she said. "We have to. Not for us, for the people. Many of our people will die in a war with Oaken George. Please?"

George nodded his head.

"Yes," he said. "I must. For the people. Thank you Anne, Dimitri. Can you help us Dimitri? Talk to your parliament?"

"Hey," Dimitri said. "I don't have to talk with them George. None of us want war George. We will fight, no doubt about it. But we won't start it George. I will issue an alert status George, but not a mobilization."

"Yes, yes," George said. "Only prudent on your part. We are in agreement then? Stop war from happening?"

"No problem form us George," Dimitri said.

"I must go now," George said.

The screen went black.

"Think it will work?" Dimitri asked Anne.

"It should," Anne said. "Parliament and the people have no love for my brother. He'll be lucky to survive. The people will go nuts. They kind of like me you see."

"Oh they love you and you know it," Margarete said.

She came out of her chair and hugged Anne.

"And so do we," she said.

Back home cuddled with William, Annes personal tablet announced an incoming message. It was her mother. Anne pulled the covers up to cover her bare chest and answered it.

"Hi mom," Anne said. "Say high Will."

"Hello Mrs Windsor," William said.

"Anne! For God's sake!" Mary said. "He does have nice abs though. Anyway. I am happy you are happy. But, I really don't want to be a grandmother yet."

She laughed.

"Not good for my image," Mary said. "Your father has scheduled a live nation wide broadcast after diner tomorrow. Every one is all abuzz about it. Charles is making appearances on every media outlet he can, beating the war drums. He's in for a shock what?"

"No babies for a while mom," Anne said. "Have to finish my mandatory term first."

"Oh poppy cock," Mary said. "Margarete didn't. Will and Willy were born during the war if I recall."

"Different story," Anne said. "Plus, I may not end up not liking my new boy toy and want a different one. You know me."

"Ya right," William said. "Maybe I'll find a cute blond cheerleader type myself."

"Now now children," Mary said shaking her finger at them. "Play nice eh? You will come home from time to time? I do miss you you know."

"I have to finish my first year of service before I am allowed off planet mom. Just like with our army." Anne said. "But yes I would like that."

"Good, I want to meet my new son-in-law in person." Mary said. "Good night Annie. I love you daughter."

"I love you too mom," Anne said.

She saw her mom's eyes tearing up before the screen cut out. Anne snuggled up to William and held him close.

"I knew she loved me," Anne whispered. "I knew it."

Two weeks after the British kings national broadcast, parliament stripped the Crown Prince of all his titles and awarded them all to James. Charles was disinherited by his family and was running for his life from an enraged planet.

War was avoided and active and progressive trade relations were occurring between Oaken and Britannia.

Marageret and Dimitri returned to their real life as farmers.

And the kids?

Well they were young you know. Doing what young people everywhere did. Living their lives.

Don't miss out!

Visit the website below and you can sign up to receive emails whenever R.P. Wollbaum publishes a new book. There's no charge and no obligation.

https://books2read.com/r/B-A-DWJC-DMUEG

BOOKS 2 READ

Connecting independent readers to independent writers.

Also by R.P. Wollbaum

Baren und Adler
Baren und Adler

Bears and Eagles
Bears and Eagles
Eagles Claw
Eagle's Talon
As Eagles Swarm
Bears Maul
Desert Eagle
Eagle's Nest
Bears Maul and Eagles Claw

Oaken
Rebellion
Retribution

Wind Riders

Oaken
Wind Riders Zebra
White Ghost
Wind Riders Mitchel

Standalone
Cal's Quest Part 1
Joss Lynn

Watch for more at www.bearsandeagles.com.

About the Author

R.P. Wollbaum lives in the shadow of the Rocky Mountains in Southern Alberta Canada.

When not busy composing a new novel, he can be found exploring North America in 'Da Buss'.

Read more at www.bearsandeagles.com.

www.ingramcontent.com/pod-product-compliance
Lightning Source LLC
Chambersburg PA
CBHW031342020726
47499CB00005B/1369

*9 7 8 1 9 8 9 2 1 0 2 2 2 *